SOMEbody STEALING
ASHLEE ROSE

Ashlee Rose
Copyright © 2021 Ashlee Rose

Special Edition

The author has asserted their moral right under the Copyright, Designs and Patents Act, 1988, to be identified as the author of this work.

All rights reserved. No part of this publication may be reproduced, copied, stored in a retrieval system, or transmitted, in any form by or by any means, without the prior written consent of the copyright holder, nor be otherwise circulated in any form of binding or cover other than that in which it is published and without a similar condition being imposed on the subsequent purchaser.

This is a work of fiction. Names, characters, businesses, places, events and incidents are either the products of the authors imagination or used in a fictitious manner. Any resemblance to actual persons, living or dead, or actual events is purely coincidental.

Cover Model: Andrew England
Photographer: James Rupara

Cover Designer: Irish Ink Services
Editor: Liji Editing
Proof Reading: Lea Joan

Dedication

MUM, OUT OF ALL THE BOOKS I HAVE WRITTEN, DON'T READ THIS ONE

OTHER BOOKS BY
Ashlee Rose

***Entwined in You Series*:**

Something New
Something to Lose
Something Everlasting
Before Her
Without Her
Forever Her

***Standalones*:**

Unwanted
Promise Me
Savage Love
Tortured Hero

***Duet*:**

Love Always, Peyton
Forever Always, Knight

Novellas:

Welcome to Rosemont

All available on Amazon Kindle Unlimited
Only suitable for 18+ due to nature of the books.

Prologue

I see her. I have always seen her. I hide in the shadows, but I play in plain sight. She doesn't know who I am, or that I even exist.

But I am here, watching, waiting.

I will wait as long as I need to.

I won't give up.

Something so precious needs to be kept, to be loved, to be owned. She is rare, like a red diamond. You would burn the world to cinders just to touch her. Just to get your hands on her delicate skin, your mouth on her pink, bow lips.

She was something worth stealing.

And that's just what I am going to do.

She just doesn't know it yet.

CHAPTER One

SAGE

Achievement unlocked: Eat entire 15" pizza to yourself.

Groaning, I sat on the floor, counting my bag out. The night was slow, but for some reason it always was on a Thursday. A hundred pounds. That's all I'd earned. Sure, a hundred is nothing to turn your nose up at, but it wasn't a lot. Secret Promises was one of the most prestigious clubs in the heart of London. It wasn't a sleazy strip club; it was an upmarket gentleman's club with some added extras. You can read that any way you want.

I needed this gig more than any of the other girls would know.

This place is like my dirty little secret, and only Wes knows I work here. This isn't where I thought I would work, but I don't have a choice. I need the money.

"You okay, Vixen?" Bruce called as he sat at the large

ornate mirror that was surrounded with bulbs, checking out his make-up before he went out to finish his set off as Secret Promises' drag queen, Betty Mae.

Bruce was like a father to me; he was always there for me when I needed him.

"Yeah, Bruce, I'm fine." I smiled at him sweetly, my face warming with a glow as he re-set his bright pink wig.

"You don't look fine, honey." He spun in his chair, his black, thin pencilled on eyebrows sat high on his forehead.

I rubbed my temples, dropping my head quickly and sighing.

"Just a slow night." I nodded slowly and rubbed my lips into a thin line.

"Baby face, you know you're one of the best there is. It's been slow *all* night." He rolled his eyes. "Even the Anodonis Gods only sold half their normal show."

"Glad it's not just me then," I grumbled, stuffing the notes back into my money bag.

Clutching it as I stood, my fishnets were ripped, the balls of my feet throbbing from the ridiculous heels I wear on a nightly basis.

I couldn't wait to slip into my chunky docs and head home.

"Why don't you wait around, angel? I'll give you a lift," I heard Roman's voice echo around the changing room.

"Bite me." I groaned, rolling my eyes. Bruce sniggered as he stood, his hands clamping the tops of my arms before kissing me on the forehead. "Get home safely, kiddo. I'll see you tomorrow. Give that beautiful mum of yours a kiss for me."

"Will do." I smiled up at him as he let me go, slapping Roman's arse as he walked past.

"Sure you don't want that lift?" He stepped closer to me, his hand hovering over my hip.

"I am very sure." I spun on my heel, giving him my best smile before storming past him and walking out to my locker. Grabbing my tatty leather bag, I threw it over my shoulder before slamming the locker door shut.

Roman was there, his eyes raking up and down my body.

Don't get me wrong, he was a good-looking lad, but just a man-whore. He slept with anything. As long as it breathed, he was game.

I snarled, shaking my head from side to side.

Devlin walked towards me, smirking. He has a warm smile. I loved Dev.

"Hey, Vix, hope Ro isn't being too much of a sleaze." He nudged into me.

"Not too bad." I smirked, my head snapping over my shoulder as I looked him up and down in disgust; it was evident on my face. No point hiding it.

I was outspoken and fiery. I never bit my tongue.

"Good." Dev groaned, wrapping his arm around my shoulders as he walked me to the back entrance. "Get home safe, Vix, we will see you tomorrow. Late shift, isn't it?" he asked, pushing the door open for me.

"Yeah, eight 'til five in the morning." Even thinking about it was exhausting.

"Well, I have a few mates coming down tomorrow for a couple of drinks. I'll get them front row seats for your set." He winked.

"Please don't." I blushed.

"You're the best though." He nibbled his bottom lip, his eyes widening as he looked me up and down.

"Night, Dev." Sighing, I pushed into the cold and wrapped my leather jacket around my body, heading towards the taxi rank. Our gentleman's club was in the heart of Mayfair. You only got the best of the best in Mayfair. Only on a Thursday and Friday were the guys there, and that was for a few hours for ladies' night. They hadn't been there as long as me, but the owner, Jax, wanted to branch out slightly. The guys were put on a three-month trial. I hoped they stayed. I liked them. The girls weren't bad. Some I didn't talk to, others I did. But my cards were close to my chest. I didn't open up.

No one knew what went on in my life and why I took this job.

We lived in the east end; I didn't want to get on the

underground. Not tonight. I was too tired. Hailing a cab, I climbed in, gave my address, then put my earphones in and blasted my music.

It was gone three by the time I got home.

We lived in a two-bed terrace on a main road. It wasn't ideal, but it was home.

Locking the door behind me quietly, I walked through into the kitchen to see my dinner sitting under a plastic lid. My stomach groaned. Pie and boiled potatoes. I didn't even heat it up. I stood, leaning over the brown work top and shovelled it into my mouth. The gravy was congealed and thick, but I didn't care. I was starving.

Once finished, I washed the plate up and boiled the kettle. I needed a coffee. I had to be up in four hours, but I needed a little pick me up. I couldn't go straight to bed.

Sitting in the dark and quiet lounge, I sipped on my coffee, my mind going over tomorrow's playlist. I needed to switch it up a bit. Plus, I had three stage sets, and then it was wandering around the club to see if anyone wanted a dance.

I hated doing it.

But it's where the money was.

I placed my cup in the sink and dragged my tired arse up to bed. Peeling off my fishnets, I chucked them in the bin. My high-waisted shorts were next to go. I folded them up and placed them on my bedside unit. I had on a white crop top which I peeled off my skin and threw on the floor for the wash.

I didn't even have the energy to put my pyjamas on. I fell onto the bed wearing my thong and my bra, my eyes shutting as soon as my head hit the pillow.

I grumbled as my alarm shrieked in my ear. How the fuck was it time to get up already?! Hitting my hand on my phone, I tugged it towards me, my eyes barely open which was making everything blurry.

Six a.m.

Groaning, I dropped my phone onto my lumpy duvet and pushed my face into my pillow.

I was so over this shit.

We're broke as fuck.

Reluctantly pulling myself from my bed, I grabbed my shorts and a black tee before storming into the box bathroom for a shower. The hot water had run out, which meant we were running low on electric. I internally cursed as I wrapped the stiff towel around my curvy body. Wiping the steam from the little mirror, I looked at myself for a minute.

My eyes were red and bloodshot, and they stung from the tiredness. I was already pale skinned, but it looked almost translucent, the black in my tattoos sitting brighter against my skin somehow. My mum hated every single one of them. But each one had meaning, from the ballet slippers to the little girl standing with her back to the world and holding her teddy bear.

Most of my arms were covered. I didn't have full sleeves, but I had tattoos inked into my skin with small gaps between. I had a love heart on my right index finger, and a feathered arrow on the other. The last two I had sat just under my boobs. Two big roses, all outlined in black, joined together by their entwined stems. They were for me and Mum.

We were always linked, always together…no matter what happened.

Sighing heavily, I dropped the towel and got myself dressed.

I had large boobs, my waist was small, but my bum, hips and legs were thick. The perfect hourglass figure.

I hung the damp towel up and opened the small window to let some ventilation in. Padding across the narrow hallway and back into my bedroom, I fixed my face, eye lining my emerald-green eyes and finishing off with a flick of mascara. I always went for a nude, matte lipstick. My lips were plump but all natural.

Brushing my jet-black hair through, I then pulled it into a high ponytail. My hair was long, I never really cut it, maybe just a trim here and there. It sat just under my ribs. I got bored easily, so I currently had light pink ends to my hair.

Pulling my lips into a tight smile, I stood and made my way downstairs.

SOMETHING WORTH STEALING

My stomach grumbled, but I wouldn't have time for breakfast. I needed to get to work.

Walking into the stuffy lounge, my mum was sitting looking absent while watching the tele.

"Morning, Mum," I chirped, walking past her and pulling back the curtains. "It's a lovely day, why don't you walk down to the coffee shop with me?" I smiled as I stopped in front of her, placing a kiss on her cheek.

"Not today, Sage. Maybe tomorrow?" Her voice lifted as she finished her sentence.

"Okay." I rubbed my lips together.

It was the same every morning. I always asked. She always said no.

My mum was consumed by anxiety and depression. She is better than she was, but it's taken time to get there. She has tried to take her own life a couple of times, but luckily, I have always been here to stop her.

The pain pangs in my chest. The thought of me one day, not being able to save her flashes through my mind and fills my heart with a searing pain.

My father left when I was three, he told my mum he didn't love me or her anymore. He upped and left and never looked back. My mum always said he was her greatest love; she has never quite gotten over him.

I didn't get it personally. How could you pin all of that love and emotion on one person?

How could they mean that much to you that you

would want to sacrifice your own life and leave your daughter behind in doing so? I watch as the pain cripples her.

She hasn't been able to work, and she hasn't in years. I just about passed Uni and graduated, but I have student loan debts coming out my ears. I need to keep us afloat until Mum is better and can work again.

But until then, it's all on me.

CHAPTER Two

You would think serving coffee all day would make me hate it, but I'm still a lovesick fool.

Walking the familiar streets of London, the cold air was nipping at my skin. Spring was my favourite time of year. The flowers ready to bloom, the birds singing, and the sun shining behind the broken clouds.

The air felt clean. I know that's not the case in London, but it did. It was like a fresh start, a do-over to the crappy year.

This year has got to be better than the last.

It has to be.

I need it to be.

I can't keep up with the jobs. I want to be doing a job I love. Dancing around poles and serving grouchy people and bored housewives coffee wasn't what it was about.

I tolerated it for Mum's sake. Not mine. Needing to make ends meet, it worked. But I was hoping and praying that this year would be different.

I wasn't a girly girl. Sure, on the outside, people saw a face full of make-up and cute clothes. But on the inside, I always wanted to get my hands dirty and dive in. I studied mechanics at university. I don't know why, but something appealed to me. No one would hire me because of being a female. We lived in a sexist world. I mean, why would a man want a woman working on his car?

I struggled to get work experience and got my degree by the skin of my teeth. I had to beg, borrow and steal to get a couple of days work so I could complete my exam. One of the guys at the gentleman's club managed to sort it out, but of course it came with a hefty price that I vowed I would never pay again.

My purity.

But needs must.

And that was a must.

Sighing deeply as I pushed the heaving door to The Coffee Run, I was already over my shift.

"Hey, girl," Wesley called as he held his hand up, making sure all the cups were stacked and sitting perfectly.

"Hey, Wes. You okay?" I asked as I hung my denim jacket in the storeroom.

"I'm okay, peach. Are you?" He eyed me as he popped his head around the storeroom door.

"I am. I am just tired." I couldn't help the yawn that left me. Covering my mouth, I shook my head.

"That's what bed is for, doll. Sleeping." He winked, skipping back behind the bar.

"Ha, you're funny." A fake smile crept on my face before I pushed my lips into a flat line, my face falling as I pinned my eyes to him.

"Have a coffee, help pick you up a bit. You've got a six-hour shift, you need something," he said as he busied himself at the coffee machine. I didn't reply, I just hummed in agreement. I wrapped my apron around my waist and tied it at my back while I waited.

No words were spoken as he handed me the small cup of espresso.

"Three shots, baby girl, enjoy that and wake that grouchy soul of yours." Wesley smiled, kissing the side of my head as he walked past. I watched him as he pulled all the chairs from the table tops and tucked them under the tables.

He was right.

I needed this.

I was off Sunday night, and I planned on scrubbing every man's touch off of me before I fell into my bed and slept for a solid twelve hours.

Putting the espresso cup in the industrial dishwasher, I nipped into the storeroom to get the cakes and sandwiches from the fridge that were delivered last night, so I could put them out.

Looking at the time, it had just gone eight. Me and

Wes were on our own until eleven, but it was fine. We worked well together.

"Ready, peach?" he asked as he strolled towards the door, his fingers grabbing the door sign as he went to flip it.

"Ready." I smiled, standing behind the till.

"Let's do this." He nodded, flipping the sign before he walked towards me and stood by the coffee machine.

The hours started to blur; the coffee shop was rammed. It always was on a Friday for some reason. You got used to the regulars, some were kind, others were complete arseholes.

"Ten o'clock, ten o'clock." Wes slipped behind me, his hands on my hips as he reached across and grabbed a cup.

My eyes darted up from the till as I looked up.

"Mr tall, dark, tatted and hot as fuck is here again," he whispered as he filled the cup.

I blushed, ignoring him.

Something about him intrigued me. I don't know what though, I couldn't quite put my finger on it.

"Welcome to The Coffee Run, do you want your usual?" I asked him as he stood in front of me, his deep brown eyes running up and down my top half.

He had one side of his nose pierced, and not one piece of his on-show skin was bare. He was covered in tattoos. His brown hair was styled back and to the side. It was long on top and shaved around the sides. I couldn't help but wonder what it would be like to push my fingers through it and grab it. His plump lips were a beautiful pink and parted as his tongue darted out, wetting his bottom lip.

I felt myself falling into a Mr tall, dark, tatted and hot as fuck haze.

"Peach," Wes barked in my ear, pulling me from my thoughts. I shook my head.

"I'm sorry," I whispered, dropping my head as I focused on the till.

Shit.

"Not a problem." He laughed, rubbing his chin with his large tattooed hand. "And yes, my usual please."

"Not a problem," I mimicked, hitting the keys and putting in the price. "One Cortado to go, please," I called out to Wesley, putting the receipt on the side, passing it over to him.

"That'll be three-pound-eighty," I said with a smile.

He held his phone out and hovered it over the card machine.

"I'll see you tomorrow, *peach*." He smirked before winking and walking over to where Wes was making his coffee.

I couldn't pull my eyes away from him. He was wearing a fitted white shirt with the top three buttons open. It was tucked into a pair of tailored trousers, showing off his physique.

"I'll have an iced latte, please." A woman's high-pitched voice sliced through me, pulling my gaze to her.

"Sure. Is that to eat in or take away?" I forced a smile onto my face.

CHAPTER Three

Thank you pole dancing for burning off the entire pizza I just ate

It had just gone three p.m. by the time I was out of The Coffee Run. Kissing Wes on the cheek, I hung my apron up and headed for home.

I needed to sleep. Even if it was only for an hour. I just needed to recharge. I had a late night at work tonight, and I still hadn't sorted my playlist.

The club could sort a playlist, but I liked to put my own spin on my routines. But all I could think about now was my bed. It was calling me.

My legs felt heavy, but my steps fastened. I felt as if someone was watching me, following me. Pulling my frayed wired earphone out of my ear, I stilled, looking over my shoulder.

No one was there.

My eyes wandered across the street, but I saw nothing. Furrowing my brow, I pushed my earphone back in and kept my head down for the remainder of my walk. I just wanted to get home.

Dumping my bag on the floor, I kicked my shoes off at the door before darting up the stairs.

Fumbling with my phone, I set an alarm for an hours time.

That's all I needed.

An hour.

My phone buzzed. How the fuck was my sleep over already? I needed more. I craved more. Always more. I hit snooze... just five more minutes.

I groaned, rolling over. It took a moment for my eyes to adjust. My stomach fell, and my heart pumped and thrashed against my chest.

"No, no, no, no..." I scrambled over my bed, looking for my phone. My eyes widened as I looked at the bright screen.

It was six thirty.

"Fuck, shit!" I called out, pushing off the bed then stubbing my toe on my bedframe. I wanted to scream, but I didn't. Placing my fist at my lips, I bit down on my fingers. I was so annoyed with myself. What the fuck?

I threw my phone on my bed and opened my battered laptop. I needed to get the songs transferred to my playlist. Plugging it in, I started moving them across.

My skin tingled at some of the song choices, but I

needed something different.

Once happy with my choices, I skimmed through them on my phone one last time.

> *Pour Some Sugar On Me – Def Leppard*
> *Dangerous Woman – Ariana Grande*
> *Me & You - Cassie*
> *Carousel – Melanie Marinez*
> *You Don't Own Me – SAYGRACE*
> *Habits – Tov Lo*
> *Take Me To Church – Sofia Kalberg*
> *Brain – BANKS*
> *I Feel Like I'm Drowning – Two Feet*
> *Naughty Girl – Beyoncé*
> *I'm A Slave 4 U – Britney Spears*

That was enough. Bass can sort me out with some more once I'm at the club. I was doubting my routines. Fuck, I was doubting everything.

I shouldn't have taken that nap.

Moving to my bedside unit and grabbing a handful of my evening clothes, I shoved them in my rucksack and reached for my phone.

Running down the stairs, I found my mum in her usual spot, sitting in front of the tele.

"I'll be back later, Mum. Late shift at the bar," I muttered before kissing her on the cheek.

She nodded.

"Love you."

"Love you more," she replied.

Slamming the door behind me, I was already on my phone to book a taxi. I couldn't be late. I wanted nothing more than to leave this job behind, but I couldn't. Not yet. I needed to save some money. Once I had enough saved, I could get us out of this shit that we were wrapped up in. It wasn't my mum's fault, fuck, it wasn't mine. But it was only me that could do this, that could help us. And I would do anything in my power to do that.

Rushing through the door, my eyes were wide as I saw my boss Jax standing there.

"I am so sorry! Traffic was a mare." It wasn't a lie, but it wasn't the complete truth.

"Vix, you've got ten minutes to get your fucking arse on that stage." A playful smile spread across his lips.

"I know, I know." I wrapped my arm around his neck and kissed him on the cheek.

"Phone?" he called as I brushed past him and towards the dressing room. Halting, I turned and threw the phone towards him.

"Thanks, baby girl! Now, go get dressed," he said, his eyes flicking down to my phone as he searched for my songs.

I hated that I always felt like I was being watched,

but whenever I looked over my shoulder, there was no one there.

Shaking my head softly from side to side, I ignored my subconscious. She was playing games with me.

Pushing into the changing room, I saw Bruce sitting on the sofa, a cigarette hanging out of his mouth as he sat looking through his phone.

"Cutting it fine, little Vix." He smirked.

"I know! Honestly, I fell asleep. I am exhausted." I groaned, flopping down on the seat in front of the lit mirror as I pulled my make-up bag out.

"Oh, Vix, you're burning the candle at both ends." He shook his head, tsking as he did.

"I know, Bruce, I know. But I can't not…" I trailed off as my head dropped. This wasn't the time for a pity party. My stomach groaned. I was starving. We couldn't get a lot for the money I earned last night, I had to leave some cash aside to pay some money off one of our bills. We had about thirty pounds to our name for food until my day job money came in. That didn't leave us a lot.

I felt Bruce's big hands on my shoulders, giving them a squeeze. "Let me do your hair." He smiled as he reached for my brush, detangling the knots.

I flicked my lashes with thick mascara and lined my eyes in black eyeliner. My green eyes popped against the black.

Covering my lips in a bright red lipstick, I wanted to

go overkill.

Bruce back-combed from the root, lifting it with volume. I hated having my hair down, but Jax always insisted. He said it made it a lot sexier. I don't see it; I feel like I am more of a sweaty mess, but what do I know? I am a twenty-three-year-old broke girl who is desperate for money.

"Thanks, Bruce." I smiled at him, pushing off the chair. My stomach tightened like a coil, the nerves crashing through me. I knew I was good; I knew I could do it. It just made me anxious.

"No worries, go smash it!" He winked, kissing the top of my head.

Striding towards my locker, I grabbed my platformed heels. I always wore clear; I just think they looked better with any colour outfit. I padded back to where Bruce sat and grabbed my bag. Slipping into the changing area, I pulled the ivory curtain back as I peeled my clothes off of me. Grabbing my black knickers that had three lines on the side that showed my pale skin, I pulled them up. Next was my bra, I hated just wearing a bra but needs must.

I inhaled deeply, puffing my cheeks out as I looked at myself in the mirror.

Pulling back the curtain, Bruce smiled, his eyes trailing up and down my body. "You're going to kill it, Vix." He scoffed. "Gina said she wanted to make you some outfits, would you like that?" he asked as he stood. I loved Gina, she was like a second mum to me, and Bruce was like the father I never had. I loved them as if they were my own flesh and blood.

"Oh wow, really?" I smiled.

"Really, she loves it. And to be honest, she would probably prefer making your outfits instead of keep making her big brute of a husband drag queen outfits." He laughed loudly. "She is coming in later, so I will get her to come and see you."

"Thank you, Bruce," I said genuinely, and my green eyes glistened.

"Not a problem, now go, before Jax spanks your arse."

I nodded quickly before slipping into my killer heels and running for the stage.

I took a deep breath as Shanay walked off the stage, smiling.

"Good luck, Sage. I'll see you in a bit." She gripped my shoulder as she walked past.

"Thanks," I muttered. I liked Shay, she was a nice girl and always had my back if I needed her to.

"Did you like our little spitfire Shanay?" I heard Jax's voice booming over the sound system. I heard the crowd cheer. "Well, we're not done yet. Ready for her first set of the night, please welcome Vixen to the stage," he called out.

I heard the hooting and cheering as I stepped out onto the stage, the bright white light shining down on me.

Standing next to the pole, my right hand gripped the cool metal.

My eyes searched the crowd, a few familiar faces popping up in the heaving club. Then they rested on *him*.

Him who has no name apart from dark and stormy.

He was always at the club whenever I was. Could it be a coincidence? Maybe, but truthfully, I didn't think so.

I felt the cool sweat blanket over me as his brown eyes raked up and down my body.

Shake it off.

Shake it off, Sage.

With *Slave 4 U* pounding through the speakers, I didn't have a moment more to think about it as I walked around the pole first, my hand tightening as I got ready to move into my first spin. I gracefully moved, both of my knees gripping the pole as I begun to turn, kicking my right leg out straight before wrapping it around the pole and leaning out as my body swung quickly. My body slid down the pole, my eyes pinned to his as I body rolled the top half of my body up, slowly. My left hand grabbed the pole behind me as I lifted my legs up and split them open, spinning slowly. I liked this song; it wasn't too fast, but it was an easy routine. As I started to slow, I split my legs open and slipped down onto the floor, arching my back as my hair fell and brushed against my spine. Tucking my right leg under me, I spun on my bum, closing my legs and bringing my knees together. Grabbing the pole, I rolled my body up, out stepping and kicking my leg out as I did and doing one more spin on the pole as soon as the song ended.

I smiled, my eyes flicking to him again before I focused on Jax who put his thumb up.

The rest of the set went smoothly. One down, two to go. I already felt dead on my feet. Once I was finished, I kicked my shoes off and sat in the room where Bruce was getting himself ready for his first set. My mouth dropped open when I saw a beautiful brown bag on the dressing table.

"Bruce," I breathed out, my eyes moving to him.

"You're welcome, eat." He smiled as he dotted a black beauty spot to the side of his top lip.

"Thank you," I muttered, my eyes glassing over. I was so hungry my stomach hurt. Grabbing the bag off the side and falling onto the plush, large sofa next to Shanay who was scrolling through her phone. I opened the bag and saw two cheeseburgers and chips.

My stomach groaned as I took the burger out of its foil, admiring it. There was lettuce, tomatoes, gherkins, mayo and ketchup. It looked amazing. I took a big bite, moaning in appreciation.

Fuck.

"Do you and the burger want some privacy?" Shanay laughed as she pulled her eyes from her phone.

"Fuck off," I said through a mouthful of burger.

She cackled before her eyes fell back to her phone.

I didn't give a shit; I was enjoying this burger too much. I was too hungry to care what I looked like.

My second set was done, and I was beat. Jax had agreed to drop my set to fifteen minutes if I done another hour on the floor.

I didn't argue. Walking the floor with the odd sleazeball groping me was a lot better than three sets on the pole. It didn't matter how much I did pole work, I always ended up with blisters on the top of my palm.

Getting changed out of my outfit and into white sequin hotpants and a matching bra, I slipped my feet back into my heels. I winced as the burn coursed through my feet, but I started walking. I had to keep going, I needed the money and Fridays were one of my better nights to work. They were like gold dust, all the dancers wanted them, so you had to be committed.

The music was pumping through the club as I began my walk with Shanay.

"I need some money tonight." I groaned in her ear as we scoped the tables, looking for a bite.

"You'll get some, you might just have to work a little harder for it, if you know what I mean?" She winked, nudging into me.

I knew exactly what she meant. Private dances, men's hands touching me. I shuddered at the thought of it. But I just needed to think of the money.

It's all about the money.

"But if you didn't want to do it, I know something that you might want to do..." she mumbled as we stopped at a huge bachelor party as they slipped notes into our hotpants.

I smiled wide, my eyes on the table before we started walking.

"What do you mean?" I shot a glare at her as we stalked over to the next table.

"Hey, angel, how about a bit of one-on-one time." This red headed male stood from the table, losing his footing as he stumbled into me.

"Woah, easy." I smirked, pushing him back down into his friend's arms, his friend giving me an apologetic look.

"Give me a lap dance, whore," he growled as he pushed off of his friend and tried to grab me.

"Hey, Gabe, calm the fuck down, man." His friend reached for him as Gabe's hands touched my body. "You'll get us kicked out."

"I want to pay for a fucking dance," he growled.

His eyes bulged, the veins popping in his neck as he got more and more annoyed.

Then it was him. The guy who watched me every time I worked. My mysterious man. I felt his presence long before I saw him.

"Don't fucking touch her," Dark and stormy growled behind me.

I froze, I didn't want to look round.

Shanay's hand was gripped around my arm, her head turning to face him.

"Or what? She isn't your property. And it's her job. If I want a fucking dance, I'll get a dance," the drunk Gabe bellowed.

"Over my dead body." The dark and brooding stranger snarled behind me, his tattooed arm shooting forward and grabbing the drunk around the throat. "Get her out of here," he boomed at Shanay.

Shanay just nodded, tugging on my arm as she pulled me away and into the dressing room.

"Who the fuck was that?" she asked, her eyes moving to the door before they were back on me again as they looked me up and down.

"He comes into the coffee shop every morning, and he has been here the last few weeks I have. I don't even know his name," I stammered out, my own head turning to look at the doorway.

"Oh wow, maybe he has the hots for you?" She

winked.

"Stop it, no way. Just a coincidence."

"Mmhmm." She rolled her eyes, her hand moving to her skinny hip.

"Anyway, moving on…" I smiled, taking a seat on the sofa for a moment. "You said I might want to do something to make more money…" My voice trailed off as Shanay sat next to me, grabbing a water out of the mini fridge and unscrewing the lid.

"A sugar daddy."

I spat my water out of my mouth, my eyes widening.

"A what!?" I half laughed, the shock apparent in my voice.

"A sugar daddy," she repeated, smiling at me.

"No fucking way." I shook my head, screwing the lid back onto my bottle.

"Why not? I do it, and I do this just for fun." She wiggled her eyebrows. "Honestly, Sage, think about it. It would rid you of yours and your mum's money problems, giving you a little security."

I pondered over her words for a moment. "And do you have to sleep with them?"

"Some you do, some just want the company and like treating you to nice things." She shrugged her shoulders nonchalantly.

"Do you?"

"That's a secret I won't tell…" She winked. "But if you

want to do it, I can get a number off of my guy for a friend of his and you can go from there. Obviously, you meet them and chat for a while, see if you get the same vibes. But just make your limits set from the get-go. That way, you both know where you stand."

I went to reply when Jax rolled through the door.

"What the fuck happened out there?" he asked, panicked, his eyes scanning over our bodies. "Any of you hurt?"

"No, we're fine, Jax." Me and Shanay smiled at him.

"Fuck... good." He let out his held breath. "It's been dealt with, and the guy has been barred. He won't be back." His head dropped. "I'm sorry, girls, I should have had eyes on you." He walked slowly towards us and flopped down on the sofa between me and Shanay.

"Hey, Jax, it's fine. We're okay. It's not your fault. Just some idiot who can't handle his drink." I rubbed my hand up his arm.

"We're heading back out there now, just needed five," I admitted, taking a mouthful of water.

"I get it." He smiled at me, then turned to face Shanay. Standing slowly, he started walking to the door. "I'll see you out there." Then he was gone.

Maybe I'll meet her guy's friend, even if it's for a couple of months. I can give this up and focus on what I actually want to do, not what I *have* to do.

"Ready to go back out there?" Shanay's voice ripped

me from my thoughts, and she was standing in front of me, holding her hand out.

"Ready." I smiled, taking her hand. "Oh, and Shanay, set it up." I smiled, my heart jackhammering in my chest. Was I really going to do this?

I woke with a jolt in the morning. I was so ready for a day off, I felt like all my days were rolling into one. I loved being busy, but some days I just felt like I was burning the candle at both ends.

I was exhausted.

Rubbing some lip balm into my chapped lips, I reached for my bag and headed downstairs to my mum. She was sitting in the lounge like usual. Her tired, bloodshot eyes pinned to the television.

"Mum, I'm off to the coffee shop," I called out, her head turning and giving me a weak smile.

"I love you." My voice cracked. I couldn't really remember my mum before this. She was a shell of the woman she once was.

In the pictures I have seen, she was always a doting and loving mother, but for as long as I can remember, it's been like this. Me being left to my own devices, as such. It was fine, I was used to it.

Me, myself, and I.

Closing the warped and swollen wooden door, it took

a couple of yanks for it to shut properly. I looked at my phone, I had half an hour before I started. I liked it when I didn't have to rush, I could take my sweet as fuck time and walk. Most of the time, I imagined how different my life could be, but I always came back down with a thud when reality bit me in the arse.

Literally.

Reaching for my bottled water, I grabbed it and brought it to my lips.

In my daydream, my body crashed into another hard body, my water spilling out of my mouth and bottle and running down my white tee.

Brilliant, must have not got the memo for wet tee competition.

Lifting my eyes from my wet top, they found the culprit.

Oh, of course, it was him.

The guy from the coffee shop. Mr tall, dark, handsome and covered in tatts.

He was dreamy.

But he also seemed like trouble. Trouble I couldn't wait to have a little taste of.

"I am so sorry," I whispered, stepping back before my eyes fell to my top. Brilliant. White tee, pink bra. *Nice colour choice, Sage.*

I internally groaned at myself.

"Don't apologise, I get a little teaser of what I have

waited so long to see." He winked, his tongue darting out and licking his lips.

"You're a creep."

"A creep you find hot, no?" His voice crashed over me, my skin turning pink at his words.

He wasn't lying.

But was I going to tell him?

Nope.

"You wish." I scoffed, reaching into my bag for something to dry myself. Damn it, I didn't have anything. I sighed, my head snapping up as Mr tall and dark handed me a handkerchief out of his tailored suit pocket.

He dripped in money. His suit probably cost more than our mortgage every month.

"Thank you," I muttered, taking it from his large hand and rubbing it over my top. It didn't do anything, but it made me feel better in a way. I went to hand it back to him, but he held his hand up, shaking his head from side to side.

"You need it more than I do, I think." He smirked; his eyes pinned to my chest.

I smiled awkwardly, nodding my head curtly as I put it into my bag.

"I better get going." My voice was hushed.

"You better, don't want to be late for your shift…" He ran his thumb over his bottom lip, his eyes raking up and down my body, and for some unknown reason, I am turned on by this.

I shouldn't be.

But I am.

"No," I breathed, my legs finally listening to my brain as they began moving forward. I didn't look back; I kept my head down and walked ahead.

Five minutes into my walk, I felt someone's eyes on my back. But this time, I didn't feel uneasy because I knew who it was.

Giving in to the temptation, I slowed my steps and looked over my shoulder to see if my intuition was right.

And it was.

"Do you really have to follow me?" Hands on hips, I stilled, turning around to look at him.

"It seems I do; I haven't had my coffee yet so I may as well follow you and get it from my favourite server." He shrugged his shoulders in a nonchalant way.

"Brilliant," I breathed under my breath, turning on my heel and walking. "Stalker."

"Maybe I am." He smirked, his eyes on me but I refused to look at him.

We walked in silence to the coffee shop.

Please be still my racing heart.

CHAPTER Four

Dear life, can I suggest you use lube next time?

The next couple of weeks flew round, the club was busy, and I was earning good tips. I always tried to stay away from the one-on-one dances, but sometimes, needs must. I was desperate for the money, I needed to keep us afloat. I just felt we were always treading water, and as soon as I stopped, I would drown.

The washing machine packed in, so the money I had started to save went on that. We weren't even living to our means; we were so far out of that. The mortgage was due this week, that's all I cared about. Fuck the food, fuck the electric, I could cope. Just about. But the house payment, we needed a roof over our heads. I couldn't do that to Mum, she wouldn't survive. She was my reason for existence, and I had to do everything in my power to look after her. Always. She was my number one, my priority, and she always would be.

I had a rare day off from The Coffee Run today, and I didn't have a shift at the club either, which was welcomed.

Laying on my bed, my stomach grumbled. I hadn't eaten much today; we had a few slices of bread, and some left over chicken that I cooked last night. I would rather Mum ate than me. She would always protest and push for me to eat, but I could eat at the club if needed.

Maybe going for this sugar daddy thing was a bad idea, I hadn't heard anything from Shay's guy's friend. I was all excited the day after, but after a week and no call or message, I started to lose hope. Was I desperate? Yes. Did I care? No.

I just wanted something a little better for me and my mum, and if it meant I would have to be some old guy's girlfriend, that was fine by me.

Sighing, I rolled on my side and opened up YouTube. We only had one television and that was downstairs, so I used to watch make-up tutorials on my phone. We couldn't afford the little luxuries like Netflix or Sky.

I felt tired, but it was still early afternoon. The last few days had caught up with me. I was due to meet Shanay later on at The Coffee Run, which I was looking forward to, plus I could use the staff discount.

My phone vibrated, making me jump. Looking, I saw Shanay's name. I hope she wasn't cancelling. Unlocking, I read her message, my heart dropping.

SOMETHING WORTH STEALING

Keep your phone close. You'll be getting a message soon. S x

Oh shit.

I tapped a quick reply then put my phone next to me. I didn't want to miss it. Did this mean that whoever it was wanted to meet me? He wouldn't message if he didn't want something, right?

For the next hour, I kept checking my phone. Nothing.

Maybe he wasn't going to message after all?

Flopping my hand down next to me, I pulled myself from my bed and padded towards the shower. Turning it on, I left it for a minute or two to warm up before stepping under it. The hot water didn't last long, it ran out just as I was washing my hair. After braving it and washing the shampoo and conditioner off with freezing cold water, I stepped out and wrapped myself in a towel.

Dragging my tired arse back to my bedroom, I got myself ready for bed, pulling my hair into a high ponytail while it was still wet. I would regret it in the morning, but right now, I didn't give a flying fuck.

I fell onto my lumpy mattress. The springs squeaking as I did as I grabbed my phone to lose myself in YouTube for an hour, when I noticed a message from an unknown number.

Fuck, this was it.

I closed my eyes for a moment and inhaled deeply as I unlocked my phone.

`Hi, Sage, it's Rhaegar. I got your number from Vance. When would you be free to meet?`

Rhaegar? What a name.

I opened the calendar on my phone and looked for my next evening off.

`Hi, Rhaegar, I can do Wednesday at about four? Where would you want to meet?`

I sent it before I could hesitate and change it. I felt nervous, but I had no reason to be nervous. It was just a chat. Just to set the terms. It was fine.

He replied almost instantly.

`Are you free tonight, Sage? Send me your address, I will pick you up at six.`

Oh fuck. I didn't want him coming here.

`I am, but we can do next Wednesday if`

that works better for you? And honestly, I can walk and meet you wherever you want, it's fine.

My heart raced.

No, Sage. I will come and get you. Tonight. See you at six.

Fuck it.

I ignored his message and tapped Shanay's number. Ring, ring, ring.

"Please pick up, please, please," I cried out to my empty room. No answer. Damn it.

I tried again.

"Sage?" she answered abruptly.

"Shay! He wants to meet tonight! What the fuck..." My hand moved to my still wet hair, gripping it tightly.

"And? What is the problem? Go get yourself dolled up and ready, babe! Go and have fun."

"I'm nervous."

"Don't be nervous, Rhaegs is amazing." I heard her giggle and a man's voice in the background, who I was assuming was Vance. "Honestly, Sage, go and enjoy your evening. Call me when you get home."

She cut me off.

I closed my eyes and inhaled deeply. Pulling my

phone out I text him my address and throw my phone on the bed.

It's fine.

I had this.

Of course I had this. I was Sage James.

Now I just had to sort out my outfit.

Shit.

I stood for a moment; my hand pressed to my head as I looked into my room. What the fuck was I going to wear?

Opening my poor excuse of a wardrobe, my eyes scanned the rail. I grabbed a skinny black pair of jeans and a black cropped top. Slipping them on, I had to do a jiggle to get them past my wide hips. I stood back and looked in my full-length mirror. This would do. The jeans sat up by my waist, clinging to my curves.

I pulled a disgusted look, my brows pulling as I looked at my hair. There was no hope.

I dropped my head back before snapping it forward and scraping it into a high ponytail. Even if I straightened it there was no saving it. My hair was thick, and if I didn't blow dry it while it was wet, then it was game over.

Rubbing some product into the palm of my hands, I smoothed the flyaway hairs down. I rubbed a small amount over the pink ends of my hair and gave myself a small smile. Not too bad. Now I needed to sort my face.

SOMETHING WORTH STEALING

Once happy with the way I looked, I stood and grabbed my tatty black bag and threw it over my shoulder. I text Rhaegar to let him know that I was ready, and I would meet him outside. My heart was jackhammering in my chest. I was so nervous. What if I didn't like him? Oh God, did I really want to be doing this? What if he kidnapped me and I was never to be seen again? Shit. I was going to turn on my location app, just in case. Shay had my details, and so did my mum. I made a mental note to text Shay and tell her that if I send a poo emoji, locate me on 'find my mates.'

Walking into the lounge, I gave my mum a kiss on the cheek. "Mum, I am just heading out for a couple of hours, okay? If you need me, call me." I smiled at her as I stepped back.

"Okay, darling, have fun. You look lovely by the way." She smiled back at me.

My heart warmed a little inside, swarming me with love.

"Thanks, Mum," I muttered as I walked down the narrow hallway and grabbed my chunky soled Dr Martens. They were a little worse for wear now, but I loved them so much. I saved for months to be able to afford these, I would never throw them out.

Pulling them on and doing the laces, I inhaled deeply, my phone buzzing in my hand.

Outside, angel. Rhaegs.

I could hear the blood pumping in my ears, and my heart thrashed against my rib cage. It was going to be fine. Shay wouldn't set me up with someone she didn't trust. Plus, it was her sugar daddy's friend. And a bigger plus, I needed the money.

Tugging the wooden front door that had swelled, I heard it drag along the lino floor and winced. I closed it behind me and walked down the steps slowly as my eyes dragged up and down the street. I couldn't see him.

I stood in the middle of the pavement; my brow furrowed as I nibbled on my bottom lip. My eyes dropped to my phone. Ping!

Look to the left.

I did just that, my jaw dropping as I saw a white Rolls Royce Phantom roll towards me. Holy fucking shit. It was a three hundred grand car in the middle of a not very nice street. We didn't live in a nice area, and I was worried that someone would come along and steal the wheels from under it.

What I would do to pop the hood on that just to see what that baby was hiding.

I fumbled with my phone, dropping it in my bag as I

watched the car stop at the kerb in front of me.

The window rolled down in the back of the car, the blackout window disappearing and showing a handsome older man.

"Sage?" His voice was smooth, the raspiness apparent as my name slipped off his tongue easily.

"That's me," I squeaked. I felt so self-conscious all of a sudden.

"You coming to join me? Or are you just going to stand there?" He smirked, his brown eyes glistening. His skin was glowing, a glorious sun-kissed look to him. His greying thick hair was pushed away from his face, showing just how handsome he was. I watched as his smile grew, his perfect teeth appearing. His dark brown eyes seeked me out.

I couldn't believe how handsome he was.

He reminded me of someone, I just didn't know who. He was the definition of a silver fox.

"I'm getting in." I smiled, opening the door, inhaling deeply as I took my seat next to him. He was wearing a fitted white shirt with the three top buttons open, that made his eyes pop against his skin. His shirt was tucked into dark denim jeans. He finished his outfit off with white trainers. They had red soles; I think they were Louboutin's. But how was I to know? I wasn't privileged when it came to designer wear.

"Come a little closer, I don't bite." He winked.

"Unless you asked me to…"

My breath caught. Filthy thoughts began to flood my brain. Where would he bite me? How hard? Would he fuck me while biting me? What was wrong with me? He seemed to have some sort of control over me, and I flushed at his words. I nibbled on my bottom lip to try and stop the crimson blush that crept across my face.

"Hungry?" he asked.

"Famished." It was the truth. I was starving.

"Good, let's go eat and get to know each other a little better." His hand moved over to my thigh, squeezing it tight. I felt the buzz course through me, and my heart raced in my chest at his touch.

I smiled at him, bowing my head slightly as I did, my eyes focusing on where his large hand was still resting on my thigh as it slowly slipped between my legs.

"You really are beautiful, Sage. I mean, I knew you were going to be beautiful… But…" He pulled his bottom lip in-between his teeth and let it out slowly, and fuck if that didn't do something to me. I would be lying if I said it didn't affect me.

My cheeks flushed; I felt my skin burning. I couldn't remember the last time I had a nice compliment. It felt nice to be wanted by someone, and not just because I was half naked and sliding up and down the pole.

"You're very beautiful too, in a masculine sort of way…" My eyes widened at the fact that I called him beautiful.

"Thank you, that's nice to hear." He leaned across and kissed me on the cheek, and butterflies swarmed in my stomach.

"You're welcome." I fidgeted in my seat, not through uncomfortableness, no. I was more than comfortable. I wasn't sure why I felt so nervous about meeting him. I knew Shay wouldn't set me up with someone that wasn't kind.

The car slowed outside a restaurant called Sexy Fish. The light green exterior caught my eye, followed by the red canopy that wrapped around the corner restaurant that sat on Berkley Square.

I had never been into this part of London before, and I was in awe. I suddenly felt very self-conscious and underdressed as I watched the slick and sleek women that walked into it, their scrawny hands clung to their partner's arms.

"You look perfect, don't worry about the stuck-up snobs," he whispered as he let go of my leg and shuffled closer to me as his driver opened my door.

I inhaled deeply; my breath shaky as I stepped out. His words made me feel better, but I still felt well out of my depth.

Rhaegs slid out of the car, nodding at his driver before he tucked a loose bit of his shirt back into his jeans.

"Ready, kitten?" He smiled at me as he laced his

hand through mine. His nickname for me turned me on.

"Ready." I nodded. I wasn't ready at all. I was so unprepared for this. I thought we would go to a little coffee shop and talk over cheap and shitty caffeine. But no, he brought me to an upmarket restaurant where they wouldn't let trash like me come in normally. They only let me in because I was with him, of course.

If this was going to be my life from now on, I needed to get used to the well-dressed whores dripping in Chanel, looking down their noses at me.

CHAPTER five

Dear lady flow, don't play me like that. You know we haven't had the D.

I clung to Rhaegs hand like a lost little schoolgirl who was out of her depth. But that was just it. I *was* completely out of my depth.

I felt uncomfortable. My eyes shot around the room as I took in the extravagant interior. It was something else and truly something special. It was brightly decorated in burnt oranges and reds, but the lights were low and dim, giving it the sort of intimate feel you would expect from a little romantic restaurant.

I felt Rhaegar's hand leave mine as he pulled my chair out for me. I was fully aware of people's eyes on me, looking up and down my outfit. I was well out of place. But Rhaegs made me feel better. I thanked him as I sat down in the burnt orange chair, him pushing me in towards the table.

He walked around the square table and sat opposite

me, his eyes glistening with glee as his beautiful smile crept onto his face.

"You okay?" he asked, his hand moving over the table and grabbing mine. He rubbed his thumb across the back of my knuckles.

"I am," I lied. Of course I wasn't okay. I was anxious and my insides were wrecked with nerves. But I had to put on the pretence. Now I know how Julia Roberts felt in *Pretty Woman* when she was judged by the women in the shop.

"Good. What would you like to drink?" he asked.

My trembling fingers picked up the menu as my eyes scanned the list of drinks, swallowing hard, my throat tightening at the prices. God, I hoped he was paying. Of course I would offer, but what the fuck would I do if he wanted me to go halves? How embarrassing would it be for my card to decline... I had no money, barely two pennies to rub together.

I felt my heart rate escalate, my palms sweaty as I dropped the menu and rubbed my hands down my jeans.

"Order anything you want, Sage, this is on me. I don't expect a penny from you." He winked as he gestured for the waiter to come over by holding his hand up and summoning him.

The waiter bowed his head and stepped closer to the table.

"What can I get you, Mr Rutherford?" he asked, as if

he knew him well, his hands resting behind his back.

"Do you mind if I order for us both?" Rhaegs eyes fell from the waiter and to me for a moment. My breath hitched, and I shook my head from side to side.

"Can we have a bottle of the Dom Perignon, and my usual surf and turf, but for two, please." He smiled at the waiter, taking my menu with his and handing it back to him.

"Certainly, sir, I'll be back with you in a moment." He bowed his head and walked into the hustle and bustle of the restaurant and towards the bar.

"I assume that Champagne is okay?" One of Rhaegs brows pinged in the air as he rested his elbows on the table, moving closer to me.

I nodded. My throat was tight and my mouth dry. I couldn't even speak. I only scanned the menu and saw how expensive things were, so I dreaded to think how much he was going to be spending.

Almost instantly, the waiter was back with our Champagne, popping the cork and pouring us both a glass then putting the bottle in its chiller at the side of the table.

"Will that be all, Mr Rutherford?" he asked as he stepped back from the table once more.

"Yes." His eyes were pinned to me the whole time, the waiter getting ready to walk away. "Actually, can we have two pornstar martinis and a bottle of water for the table, please."

He nodded, staying mute before he disappeared.

"Tell me about you, Sage. I want to know everything about you." He licked his upper lip, his eyes falling dark as his stare penetrated me.

"There isn't much to tell honestly…" I heard my voice crack. What the fuck was wrong with me? I was never like this, especially around a guy. I think he intimidated me, but not in a bad way. "I'm just little old, Sage." I choked out a laugh, pushing my hand forward and wrapping my fingers around the stem of the glass as I brought it to my lips and took a well needed mouthful. The champagne was delicious. It was light and bubbly and swam down my throat like silk, but not before my taste buds exploded with its rich taste.

"Nice?"

I nodded, my tongue darting out and sweeping across my wet lips.

"You were saying you're just *little old Sage*." He repeated my words. "Well, you're definitely not old." He smirked, this time bringing his own glass up to his mouth as he took a mouthful.

I laughed softly, my fingers still gripping onto my glass tightly. I was worried I was going to snap the glass.

"Okay, so I'm not old." Another laugh bubbled out me. The bubbles were going to my head already and I had only had a couple of mouthfuls. The joys of not eating. "I'm twenty-three, live with my mum, I am the sole earner; I work two jobs..." *Shit,* did I tell him I was a pole dancer?

My eyes widened as the panic shook through me.

I ignored my intuition.

"So yeah, that's basically it. I am full of debt, trying to keep my head above water and a roof over mine and my mother's head." My eyes fell to my lap, nodding to myself. I felt the sting in my eyes, the burn in my throat as a lump lodged itself there, but I wouldn't give in.

"Sage, look at me." His voice was low, soft but stern.

I obeyed.

"You won't ever have to worry about that life again, do you understand me?" His eyes flickered with something, but I didn't know what. Was it pity?

"Rhaegar, you don't have to say that... I've done just fine working..." He pushed his finger to his lips, shushing and silencing me.

"It's not up for discussion, Sage. From this moment, you're mine. I knew from the moment I laid eyes on you that you were mine. This dinner was just to make sure you had some food in your stomach. I know a lot more about you than you think." He smiled. "Once dinner is finished, we will go back to mine to talk about my requirements and *needs.*" The last words drawled off of his lips, making the hairs on the back of my neck stand and my skin prickle in goosebumps.

We were interrupted when the waiter placed two

pornstars down on the table, with two shots of prosecco.

"Drink up." He smiled as he pushed the cocktail towards me. It smelled delicious. The passion fruit and vanilla tones swam through my nostrils, making my mouth salivate and my taste buds explode.

I took the cocktail, bringing it to my lips.

He shook his head, his eyes moving to the shot glass of bubbles. I retracted my hand quickly, grabbing the shot glass and bringing it to my lips, mirroring his moves before we both knocked it back then washed it down with the cocktail. It really did taste as good as it smelt.

We lost ourselves over easy chatter, mostly about my university degree and luckily not about my jobs or how poor we actually were. Dinner was delicious, my belly bloated and slightly popping out as it stretched from the amazing food that I had just devoured. We had prawns, shrimp, lobster thermidor, king crab, steak, lobster tails and ribs. Honestly, everything was out of this world. I had never tasted food so delicious. Even thinking about it made my mouth water.

Rhaegs was a true gent, paying for our dinner and drinks. I did offer to pay, even though I couldn't afford it, but I had to offer.

His arm wrapped around my waist as he walked me towards his car that sat kerbside, waiting for us.

"Thank you, George," he greeted him, pushing me

forward to get in the car first, him slipping in behind me.

As soon as the door closed, his eyes found mine. They danced as they trailed all over my body, the heat swarming me. His large hand moved to my face, cupping my cheek as I leaned my face into it. A small smile slipped across my lips as I lost myself in his beautiful brown eyes. He truly was beautiful. I don't think I have ever seen a man so handsome. He really was a delicious treat on my eyes.

"Thank you for this evening." I licked my lips, trying to break the trance he had me under. I felt like I couldn't breathe. He had a hold on me, and I couldn't explain it. As if I was grounded and anchored to the ground, but in a good way.

"You're most welcome, but the evening has not even begun yet." The delicious growl in his throat awakened something dormant in me, something that hasn't been relit in months.

I whimpered as he dropped his hand from my face, his large hand securing itself in-between my thighs once more, giving my skin a gentle squeeze every now and again. The ride from the restaurant to his place seemed relatively short, but it could have been because my mind was elsewhere and thinking of all the dirty scenarios between me and Rhaegar. We pulled into an underground car park; my heart rate spiked but in the best way. He was like a shot of adrenaline, coursing through my veins. The feeling was like ecstasy. I was desperate, almost craving for his touch to be on me. I have never wanted to be kissed by someone so much in my life. I found myself pulling my bottom lip between my lips, my mind drifting to a place of pure bliss.

"Sage, don't bite that bottom lip, baby," he groaned in my ear, his hand gripping the skin on my thigh through my jeans.

Letting it go quickly, I cleared my throat, shuffling in my seat slightly. Pulling into a car parking space, he opened the door before his driver had a chance. He wrapped his fingers around my wrist and pulled me out the car with him. I giggled like a child as he wrapped his arm around my back and pulled me closer to him, his neck craning down as he placed a kiss on the top of my head. I was short. Five foot four, and he was easily six foot three. He towered over me. But I loved that. I loved that I was so small in comparison to him.

"Come on, kitten, let's get you inside," he whispered, his lips pressing against the shell of my ear, a shiver ripping through me, my core alight with desire. What the fuck was wrong with me? I was walking around with a constant lady boner.

I stayed close to him as he guided me through two double, glass panelled doors. He greeted the doorman and ushered me through as we walked across the high gloss cream marble floor tiles, my eyes wandering around the beautifully decorated room. The ceilings were high with thick white coving hugging it. The chandeliers were gold and huge, the lights glowing brightly.

Pressing the button to call the elevator, we stood, his fingers digging into the skin of my waist. I felt the electricity hum through both of us, as if we were in tune. It was a delectable feeling.

He dragged me into the elevator, pressing the button for the penthouse. He dropped his hand from my waist, and I instantly missed the connection, the feel of his fingers on the small bare piece of skin that was on show between my crop top and jeans waist band.

As soon as the door shut, he turned to face me, both of his large hands cupping my face as he pushed me against the mirrored elevator wall. I didn't care that the gold, solid handrail that ran around the large, square lift was pushing into my back. I welcomed it. Anything to hide the desperate whines leaving my lips as Rhaegar pushed his lips to mine. An explosion erupted in my stomach, and my heart thrashed in my chest at his touch. My hands wrapped around his white shirt, pulling him closer to me if at all possible. His kiss was hard, but his tongue was soft and gentle as it stroked across mine, awakening all of my senses. Our teeth grazed, our lips locked, and I was in eternal bliss, if only for a moment. The doors pinging open distracted Rhaegar as he stepped away, grabbing my hand and pulling me out onto the floor. I was dazed, my chest heaving, my cheeks flushed, my lips burning in the most delicious way.

I needed so much more.

I had just had my first hit of him, and I wanted so much fucking more.

Stopping in front of a large oak door, he pulled out a card from his back pocket and slipped it through the card reader on the door slowly, his eyes on mine as he did. I didn't fucking know if he was or whether it was just my horny as fuck subconscious teasing me. All I could think about were his lips, his tongue and my aching pussy.

I shook my head, trying to bring me down from this erotic cloud I was drifting on.

"After you." His husky voice broke through me. I dipped my head down as I walked past him and into the lavish open-plan penthouse.

"Holy fuck," I breathed, my eyes widening at the beautiful surroundings in front of me. "Wow."

"I'm glad you like it." He beamed, standing behind me, his fingers trailing across the base of my neck and slowly dipping towards my collar bone.

I nodded; I didn't have any words. The room was screaming at how expensive it was, the walls dripping in glorious art that most likely cost more than the watch he was sporting. The bright colours radiated, the chrome accessories dotted around the rooms, mirroring certain points of the penthouse.

"Come," he whispered in my ear, his lips pressing against it before he took my lobe into his mouth and sucked it.

My insides squirmed, and I am adamant I just come on the spot.

I coughed, walking forward and down the three shallow steps that took us into the large lounge space. There were three black, leather sofas. One facing a huge television that sat over a fire, and two opposite each other. They were all nestled around a large, square, glass topped coffee table that sat on four chrome legs. I turned my head to the left to see a large eight-seater table, it was the same as the coffee table, but around this table were clear plastic chairs.

"Big old table for just you," I teased as I stood in-between the lounge and the dining room.

"Who said it was just me?" His brows pinged up high on his forehead, the skin around his brown eyes creasing slightly as he smiled.

I rubbed my plump lips into a thin line.

"Go sit down, make yourself at home. I'll grab us a drink." He strolled towards me, placing a kiss on my temple and walking past me as he disappeared into a room off of the dining room, which I assumed was the kitchen. I walked slowly over to the sofas, flopping down. I exhaled deeply, I felt like I hadn't been able to breathe while he was close to me. But now he was away from me, the breaths flowed easily out of my lungs. My eyes searched the room for any warning signs, anything that could make this scenario so wrong. But there was nothing. But then again, he could hide what he liked. I don't know him, just like he doesn't know me.

I wasn't left with my thoughts for long when he walked back into the room, his shoes now gone as he padded across the white high gloss tiles. I frowned, kicking my boots off.

"You didn't need to take your shoes off." He smiled warmly at me as he handed me an orange drink in a short, crystal cut tumbler.

"Manners and all... I should have done it as soon as I walked in," I admitted, feeling silly all of a sudden. "What is this drink?" I asked as I looked at the liquid sitting over a sphere of ice. There was a curled orange peel sitting over the ice and a cocktail cherry sitting on a stick, resting on the rim of the glass.

"It's called an Old Fashioned. It's delicious." His voice burned through me. How could someone's voice be such a turn on?

I watched as he took the cocktail stick and wrapped his tongue around the cherry, before slipping it slowly into his mouth.

Holy fucking fuck.

I swallowed hard; my mouth dry as my eyes stayed

pinned to his.

"Try it," he ordered as he brought the rim of his glass to his lips and took a mouthful. My eyes moved from his before they fell to the glass. Inhaling deeply, I brought my own glass to my lips and let the amber liquid wet my lips, the liquid slipping down my throat. It was warm, bitter, but it also had a kick of sweet that stayed on my tongue for a moment.

"It's good." I nodded, taking another mouthful. "It's really good," I said, greedily licking my lips.

"I'm glad you like it." His eyes filled with desire.

The room fell silent for a moment, and I felt a small pinch of awkwardness fill me, but I was unsure why.

"I had a contract drawn up, more for your sake than mine." He leans forward and places his glass down on a coaster that is sat on the glass top table. "Just a few things that we need to discuss, how our *arrangement* will work per se."

I felt my grip on the glass tighten. All of a sudden this was feeling more real, more like a business transaction than a dinner and date like it did only half an hour ago.

The queasiness swam in my stomach, but I was unsure whether it was the mix of drinks or the realisation of just what I was getting myself into. Rhaegs stood from the chair and disappeared without a word, my eyes followed him as he wandered down the hallway.

I sat back on the sofa, I couldn't calm my heart from

thrashing around in my chest, and it was battering against my ribcage as if it was trying to get out. Was this a sign? Was this a warning? Should I leave? I could get my shoes now and make a run for it. Fuck, I wouldn't know how to get home, but I could walk. The only issue with that was he knew where I lived. Idiot. *Shit, Sage, you should have never agreed for him to pick you up from your house.* My skin prickled in fear and anticipation, but I didn't have any reason to be afraid around him. It was more the fact that this was all getting a little too real. I liked it when it was a date.

Knocking back my drink and wincing, my eyes closed as the burn ruptured in the back of my throat.

I coughed slightly, spluttering some of the drink over myself when I saw Rhaegar walk back towards me, clinging onto a wad of paper.

"Sage, are you okay?" he asked, the look of concern all over his face as he rushed to my side.

"I am fine." I nodded, swallowing hard. "My drink went down the wrong hole." I smirked, trying to lighten the mood.

I watched as his face pulled into a frown, and this time he sat next to me, his hand gripping onto my knee.

He placed the file of paper down on the table, then placed two pens on top of it.

"Don't look so worried, there is nothing bad in here. Nothing will change between us, and like I said, this is more for you than me."

I nodded but remained silent.

"Okay, so as I said earlier, I know a lot more about you than you think. Your beautiful friend Shay has filled me in. I know where you work, and I am still happy for you to do that if that's what you want. But I need you to know that you won't *need* to work. You'll be kept, and so will your mother. But I understand the drive in some women. Even if you work only temporarily, until you find your feet and see if this is what you still want." His eyes softened as he looked at me, and it took me a moment, but I finally lifted my head and looked at him. Our gazes met, our souls crashing together as the ache in my heart grew.

"How about we start on a three-month term? See how we both feel, and then, if it isn't working, we can either go through the contract and terms to tweak it slightly, or if you're still not happy then you are free to leave." His lips pressed into a thin line, and I don't know why but the thought of saying goodbye to him made my stomach twist into knots. It was an unbearable thought, but I hardly knew him.

"Okay," I finally breathed out. "That could work."

His face lit up, his eyes devouring me.

"Let's go through this contract then, shall we?" His hand moved towards me, grabbing my chin and pulling my lips to his.

CHAPTER
Six

Life is over. Run out of batteries for BOB.

He broke away from me, the fire instantly put out in my lower stomach. There was no point kidding myself. I was so fucking turned on. Shuffling forward to the edge of the sofa, he started flicking through the pages of the contract. I copied, shuffling myself forward.

"Okay, so… first things first…" He stopped, his eyes finding mine as he turned his head towards me. "Once this is signed, you're mine. No little coffee dates with anyone but me." His voice was low, threatening almost. But I knew he wasn't meaning to come across that way.

I nodded. "But what about my job? I have to dance to be able to earn money…" I stopped, pressing my lips into a thin line when I realised the words that had just left my lips.

"That's your job, it's different. But I will be there every night that you work so I can watch you." His eyes darkened as they trailed up and down my body. I blushed under his gaze.

"Like I said before, I haven't got a problem with you still working and earning your own money, but you don't need to work anymore if you don't want to." A smile crossed his lips before his attention averted back to the contract.

"You will stay here Friday to Sunday, weekdays you will spend at home with your mum." He nodded at his own command. "I will buy your clothes, shoes, bags, food and pay the mortgage on your house."

I was speechless. He licked the pad of his index finger as he turned the page. "Moving forward with our relationship, if that's what we are calling it..." he winked. "If we were to have sex, condoms are to be worn at all times. I don't care if you are on the pill, on the shot or barren, a condom will always be worn." His brows pinched; the playful smile that was on his face only seconds ago had vanished.

"Understood." I nodded.

"Good... moving on." He swept his tongue across his bottom lip. "I will eat your pussy when I want, that is a term I won't move on. Your pussy is mine, and if I want to eat it five times a day or in the middle of a street then I will." I clenched my pussy tight, pushing my legs together to try and dull the burning ache that was present.

"I want us to be together as much as possible, so I will be dropping in and out where I can. I would like to meet your mother; I feel it is only right that I get to meet the woman that birthed you." He smirked, his eyes down on his paper full of check boxes.

"Okay," I finally managed to breathe out.

"Are you okay?" he asked as he sat back. I could hear the caution in his voice. I managed a nod. "I am just a little overwhelmed," I admitted.

"I get that, but I promise you, I will never make you do anything that would make you feel uncomfortable. Fuck, if you don't want to sleep with me, you don't have to. But the pussy eating? I'm sorry, that is something that has to stay." I saw the devilish smoulder that replaced his concern, and I was hot. I felt hot, clammy and sweaty. I needed a cold shower, I needed to cool off.

"Okay," I managed again. I don't even think my brain was registering what he was saying.

"I want us to share a bed, I don't want you sleeping without me."

I nodded. "That's okay, I would rather sleep next to you too." I gave him a small smile.

"Good." He nodded curtly.

"Is there anything you want to add?" he asked.

I sat and thought for a moment. I felt foolish asking this, but I had to.

"Can I give you oral back?" I asked, the familiar blush that I have become all too accustomed with making a return, colouring my cheeks a deep red.

"No." He shook his head from side to side softly. "I don't need or want it in return. It's a control thing, so no, no oral back. This is all about you, me taking my time and spending my money on you. I want to make you feel like the queen you deserve to be. All of this is for you, kitten." He dropped his pen, his hands finding my face as he cupped it and crashed his lips to mine. I heard a growl in his throat. I don't know what come over me, but I pushed my body into him, climbing into his lap as my legs dropped either side of his. I felt his bulge pushing underneath me, my hips rocking forward just to feel the friction from him.

"Not tonight, kitten, but I promise, when you're ready, I am going to fill your tight little cunt and fuck you until you're begging me to stop," he whispered against my lips as he pulled his lips from mine.

I whimpered, my chest heaving fast as his eyes fell to my breasts.

"I think it's time I take you home..." His voice was low and drawled out as his eyes flicked back up to mine.

I nodded. My breath caught at the back of my throat before I nibbled on my bottom lip. It took me a second to climb off of him.

Shuffling forward to press myself off of the sofa, his fingers wrapped around my wrist and pulled me back down, his lips hovering over mine as he pecked them softly.

"Don't forget to sign the contract…" he whispered. My skin covered in goosebumps at the feel of his breath over my lips. Like a drug, he intoxicated me in that moment. Even if I wanted to, I couldn't stop myself from falling, from becoming completely and utterly addicted to him.

My fingers moved to grab the pen, and I signed on the dotted line, not even reading what was printed on the page.

"Good girl, you're mine now, kitten," he growled.

I stood on the pavement outside my house, watching him pull into the distance. Even when he was out of sight, I still stood there. I was just trying to wrap my head around the last couple of hours. Dinner, drinks, kisses…hot as fuck kisses and contracts. I felt myself pale slightly. Had I really just signed myself away to someone I didn't even know? I was so caught up in the lust, the moment…the panty wetting moments that I didn't even pay attention to what I was signing. Sure, I knew the terms, but did I really know what I had just gotten myself into?

I rolled my eyes, turning on my heel but stilling. My skin smothered in goosebumps. Was I getting paranoid?

Turning slowly, I looked up and down the road, my eyes laying on a figure that was shadowed under a dimly lit streetlight.

Were my eyes playing games on me?

Shaking away the thoughts and ignoring the fear that coursed through me, I stormed towards the front door. I took a moment to catch my breath, letting my heart calm. The fear was drumming through me. Once I had calmed a little, I locked the door.

It had just gone eleven. My mum was already sound asleep, and moving slowly, I reached for a glass and ran the kitchen tap for a moment and filled my glass with water. I dragged my tired feet up to my room, shutting my bedroom door with my foot. I was exhausted and sexually frustrated. Strolling towards the window, I stood at the side and peeked through the curtain, my eyes staring at the streetlight where I thought I saw someone. No one was there. I was letting dark and stormy get into my head, I was letting an obsession start. Sighing in relief, I pulled the curtains shut and flopped down onto my bed. Reaching over, I placed my glass on the bedside unit and fell back onto my duvet. I just needed a minute. One little minute to let the last few hours replay over in my head. I felt my phone vibrate in my bag next to me. I groaned; it was an effort even lifting my arm to move it. Pulling my phone out, I saw Rhaegs name on my screen, and furrowing my brow, I unlocked my phone.

What.

The.

Fuck.

He sent me a fucking dick pic?

After my eyes had adjusted to what was on my screen, I saw the message underneath.

This is what you do to me, kitten. Soon, angel. Soon. But for now, I am going to imagine what it would feel like to be deep inside of you. Sweet dreams, Sage.

R x

He was something else, and by this picture, so was his dick. It must be the angle. The light. Like, holy fuck. I had never, and I mean never, seen anything like it. It was like the ultimate dick of all the dicks.

King dick.

I felt my pussy pulse as I stared at my phone a little longer. I couldn't take it. Rolling on my front, I reached across into my drawer and pulled out my vibrator. Rolling back over, I dropped my phone beside me and shuffled out of my jeans. Fuck, it felt good to be out of them. Grabbing my vibrator and slipping it inside my lace, black knickers, I switched it on. The vibrations pulsed and massaged my clit. My spare hand reached for my phone as I clicked reply on Rhaegar's message and opened the camera. I snapped a picture and sent it back before I could decide against my pre-orgasmic haze that I was currently swimming in.

I felt my pussy clench, the delicious build bubbling inside of me. My eyes watched as I saw Rhaegs typing.

`Do you know how hard it is to stop myself coming over there? If I was there, I would have my tongue flicking and sucking over your clit while I fucked you with my fingers. Imagine that, kitten, imagine you're about to cum over my soaked fingers.`

My legs began to tremble at the dirty scenarios that were playing out in my head, when suddenly, the vibrator cut out.

"No, no, no, no," I moaned out, the tingling spreading all over me as my pussy ached and throbbed. I pressed the button continuously; it wasn't even flashing to indicate it needed charging.

My phone pinged again; I was more than frustrated now.

`Have you come, angel?`

I sighed.

`No, vibrator died.`

Dropping my phone on the bed, my eyes pinned to the ceiling. My phone pinged again, but I ignored it. After a moment or two, it started ringing. It was Rhaegar.

I answered it and immediately saw his face on the screen.

"Don't pout, angel, finger yourself while I watch." He groaned as he moved the camera away, his spare hand wrapped around his cock, moving up and down his thick, long dick. It definitely wasn't the angle, or the light for that matter.

I skimmed my fingers across the bare skin of my stomach, slipping them into my knickers.

"That's it, kitten." His voice was tight, his hand still pumping up and down himself.

My fingers glided softly and rubbed over my clit as a moan escaped my lips.

"Oh, you sound so good when you moan," he whispered over the phone. "I can't wait to hear what you sound like when my cock slips into your tight, wet pussy for the first time."

And that's all it took.

His filthy mouth pushing me over the edge as I came fast and hard, Rhaegs following behind me.

I instantly cut the phone off, I felt so embarrassed. My phone pinged, my eyes moved to the screen, the messages between me and Rhaegar still open.

> **`Ordered you a new vibrator. It'll be with you tomorrow. Sleep tight, sweet dreams. X`**

Fuck.

-
UNKNOWN

Does she see me watching her? Does she feel my eyes on her at every second I get? To say I was obsessed was an understatement. And now, after two years of walking ten steps behind, she is with the old guy. She was mine. Okay, so she didn't know it yet, but she is. She has been mine from the moment I laid eyes on her, and I wasn't about to give up. Fuck, I would never give up. I don't like the fact that he thinks he can steal what's mine.

I don't think so.
It doesn't work like that.
She belongs to me.
Not him.
Bide my time.
That's all I had to do.
Bide my time.

I'll continue hiding in the shadows, watching from a far.

Stalker? Maybe.

Obsessed? Absolutely.

And I would shout it from the fucking roof tops.

I watched as she looked around her curtain, and that was my cue to step back and fall back into the darkness.

I wasn't quite ready to give up my identity yet.

But it won't be long.

I won't stay a secret much longer.

I am going to make my presence known, and when it's time… I am going to come in like a fucking wrecking ball.

CHAPTER
Seven

Panic over. In unrelated news, my TV control now doesn't work.

My alarm screamed at me, hitting the snooze button for an extra five minutes. My eyes felt like they had grit inside them, I slept well but for some reason it was like I had barely closed my eyes.

Finally giving in, I rolled over and turned my phone alarm off. I wasn't working at The Coffee Run until later on this morning, which meant I could laze for a couple of hours. I had washing to do, and I wanted to give the house a quick blitz round before I left Mum for the day. I wouldn't see her until tomorrow morning, due to the way my shifts have worked out. As soon as I am finished at the coffee shop, it is straight onto the club. I didn't mind days like this, it made the hours slip by quickly, and the money was normally good on a long shift. I felt the stir of uneasiness swarm my tummy. Rhaegs would be there tonight. And after our little sexting chat last night, I was feeling embarrassed. Not that I should, it's normal, he had his cock out, I was sorting myself out... it's human nature. Right?

I shook the thoughts quickly from my mind, the blush on my cheeks lingering a little longer than I would have liked.

Once showered and dressed, I went about my morning, mentally ticking off my chore list as I did them. The house didn't take too long to clean, but where I was always busy with my jobs, it fell behind.

So many times, I have wanted to shake my mum and pull her from her depressive state, to rid the anxiety that is consuming her more and more every day. But how could I? She was so deep underwater, my fingers barely holding onto her. One small nudge and her fingers could slip through mine before she sinks into the unknown.

Flicking the kettle on, I made me and Mum a cup of tea. We sat in light chatter. Rhaegs' name sat on the tip of my tongue, I wanted nothing more than to tell her about him. But I couldn't. She would judge. I needed to keep him my dirty little secret for a while, only I needed to know about him.

My sugar daddy.

The guy who owns me.

I washed our cups up and left them on the draining board as I took myself back upstairs to top up my make-up and grab my bag for work tonight. Reaching for my phone, I smiled when I saw Rhaegs' name.

Morning, kitten, how are we feeling today?

I nibbled my bottom lip.

I'm okay, just getting ready to leave for work. You?

The three dots appeared on my screen instantly.

I am more than okay; I can't wait to see you at work tonight. Mine. All mine. All those greedy, dirty men will be looking at my property, and fuck if that doesn't turn me on.

My eyes widened slightly at his words, three dots appearing again.

Has your parcel arrived yet?

I tapped a response.

No, not yet. See you tonight x

I pushed my phone in my back pocket before I could fall into the temptation of replying, my mind swirling of thoughts of Rhaegar being there tonight. What if he kicked off if another man touched me? Surely, he wouldn't? It's my job, of course he wouldn't. He knows what I do, plus Shay definitely would have told him.

Unless she lies to her guy.

Sighing, I grabbed my bag and threw it over my shoulder as I headed for the door.

I shouted bye to Mum, pulling the door open when I was greeted by a young delivery driver.

"Sage James?" he asked as he looked at his tablet.

"Yup, that's me." I smiled at him as he handed me a long, narrow box.

I swallowed hard.

I knew exactly what this was.

"Thank you," I muttered, kicking the door shut before running back up the stairs and stashing the box under my pillow. I was intrigued, but I didn't have time. I was going to be late for work and I didn't want to piss my boss off.

Slamming the front door behind me, I slipped my old earphones into the bottom of my phone and pushed them into my ears, my head dipped low, my eyes on my phone when I walked into a hard body.

"Shit." My eyes darted up to see Rhaegar.

"I didn't mean to startle you, kitten," he whispered, his thumb brushing across my bottom lip as his eyes lit with desire.

"You didn't, sorry, it was my fault," I admitted, pulling my earphones from my ear and wrapping the frayed cable around my phone.

"Don't apologise, you have nothing to apologise for." The back of his hand skimmed along my jaw, running down the side of my body and linking his fingers through mine.

"I thought I would accompany you to work." He beamed as we started walking towards the car.

"You really don't have to." I blushed, tucking a loose bit of my black hair behind my ear.

"Oh, I know. But I want to."

Rubbing my lips together, I didn't answer. Just followed as he led me to his car.

His driver was there, tipping his head down as he greeted me and opened the door.

Rhaegar let me in first, then slipped in beside me.

He watched as his driver shut the door before his eyes were on mine. "I saw that your parcel was delivered, did you like it?" He winked, his teeth pulling on his bottom lip. My insides burned, I don't know what it was about this silver fox, but I just couldn't get enough of him.

"I didn't get a chance to open it." I breathed, looking at my watch "I was running late…" My voice trailed off.

"What time do you start?"

"Eleven."

"You'll be there at ten-fifty-nine." He smirked, placing his hand in-between my legs, squeezing my inner thigh softly.

Pulling up to the kerb, I slid closer to the passenger door when Rhaegs stopped me, his hand cupping my cheek, his lips slanting over mine as he kissed me softly, tentatively.

Not like last night.

His kiss bruised my lips but in the best way.

"Have a good day, kitten. I'll see you tonight." He broke away, his eyes dropping to my lips as a smile danced across his lips.

"See you tonight," I just about managed; the air being completely stolen from my lungs.

Darting out the car, I ran across the street, not even looking at the cars that were hurling towards me.

Pushing the door of the shop, I held my hand up to my boss, apologising for my lateness. Sure, it was a couple of minutes. But my boss was a bit of a dick when he wanted to be.

I watched as he shook his head from side to side in disappointment before walking into the back office.

Throwing my bags in the back, I wrapped my apron around my front as Cynthia huffed, barging past me as she slipped into the back room for her break.

"Jeez, what the fuck is her problem?" I snarled, my eyes finding Wes.

"Morning, peach, and fuck knows. Her tampon is probably up the wrong hole." He scoffed before snorting a laugh.

I laughed with him, pushing my hair away from my face as I tightened my ponytail.

I loved Wes; he was like a brother. I had known him since I started at The Coffee Run. We were both fresh out of school and looking for weekend work. He is the yin to my yang. The Bill to my Ben. The stars to my moon.

If he wasn't gay, I would have snapped him up years ago. He was beautifully handsome, his red hair sat curly on the top of his head, his pale skin was covered in freckles, and his ice blue eyes were simply hypnotizing.

But he was truly the best friend I could ever wish for.

My shift was over quickly, it was busy which always made the hours slip past that little faster, plus I had Wes. And everything was always better with Wes.

Hanging my apron up, me and Wes walked out the staff room door, arm in arm. It had just gone five.

"What time are you working till tonight?" Wes asked as he slipped his phone out his back pocket, his fingers scrolling.

"Five," I whined. "I am so fucking tired," I admitted,

the exhaustion clear in my voice.

"Why not give it up?" Wes eyeballed me as he lifted his eyes from his phone.

"Pay's good." I shrugged my shoulders.

I saw his perfectly shaped brow lift in his forehead.

"Mmhmm, is that right?"

I nodded.

"Wes, I feel like I'm going mad," I admitted, walking back out on the floor as I stood at the serving hatch, Wes resting his elbow on the counter.

"Why?" He furrowed his brow.

"Well, for starters, for the past couple of weeks, I keep feeling like I am being followed, then last night I was sure I saw someone standing opposite my house under a streetlight." I rubbed my forehead before letting my arm fall. "But once I was back in my room, I looked out the window and no one was there."

"Prob tiredness, hun, you're working like a horse, burning the candle at both ends as such," Wes suggested.

He was probably right.

"I suppose it could be." I nodded, my eyes focusing on Wes's wide ones as he cocked his head to the side.

I slowly turned my head to see what he was telling me to look at.

It was dark and stormy, his eyes on his coffee cup as he smirked. His smile made me blush, it made me feel something like I had never felt before. My heart thrashed against my rib cage.

Ignoring the feeling of my blood pumping around my body at the sight of him, I turned to face Wes again.

"Anyway, moving on…" He wiggled his shoulders up and down. "Who was the hot bit of hunk that dropped you off outside work this morning?"

Fuck.

"Just someone from the club."

"Oh yeah?" He stepped closer to me, his eyes narrowing on mine.

"Yeah," I breathed.

"I smell bullshit."

"That's on you, boo." I flicked my hair over my shoulder. "Gotta run."

And I did. I scampered away as fast as I could. I wasn't quite ready to share my dirty little secret with the world.

Stepping into the club, my skin burned, and my heart raced. The thought that he was going to be here terrified me. I didn't even know if he had been here before. My eyes scanned the dimly lit room, but I couldn't see him.

My beautiful silver fox.

Was he actually mine though?

We were in a contract at the end of the day. A business transaction.

He paid me to be his companion and to eat my pussy.

I didn't even have to have sex with him if I didn't want to.

"Hey, beaut," Shanay said as she wrapped her arms around me.

"Hey, love." I tightened my arms around her. I loved Shanay, she made me feel welcome when I first started at the club. Don't get me wrong, the rest of the girls were lovely, but we just said 'hey' and 'bye.' Our friendship didn't go past these four purple coated walls.

"Well, there she is, my Vix," Bruce bellowed as I walked into the dressed room, swooping me up and spinning me round.

"Hi, Bruce." I smiled lovingly at him.

"Gina gave me your outfits she made, they're over by the dressing room." He nodded his head back, my eyes moving from his as I looked behind him and saw the dress bag hanging up.

I squealed, running over there and rushing to open the zip. My eyes widened as I saw the diamond covered hot pants and matching bra. She had also made me a sheer cover up with long sleeves that were cuffed with lace at the wrists and covered in the matching diamonds.

I loved diamonds.

My mum always said I was like a magpie as a child, anything shiny and I had to have it.

Way to my heart? Diamonds.

Diamonds are a girl's best friend after all. But diamonds are never going to be sitting upon my fingers or around my neck. What is it they say? Champagne taste with beer money pockets.

That's me.

CHAPTER
Eight

Life hack. If you walk around with your tits out, everyone will ignore the huge spot on your forehead.

I finished my first set. Rhaegs was sitting up front, his eyes pinned to my every move. I made a point of getting a little closer to him as he slipped a couple of notes into my panties. He made me melt. I didn't know if it was just a physical, sexual attraction or if we had something between us. I have never felt the way I do around him with another man. When I am near him, I feel like I am in a magnetic force field. I can't stay away from him. The current that runs through my blood, a full force rush that consumes me. My skin tingles, an electric spark that courses through my veins. Every fibre in my body wanted him, every nerve ending in my body burned.

It was desire.

Full sexual chemistry building through us.

But was it just sexual tension? Could I really fall in

love with a man thirty years older than me? More to the point, could a man thirty years my senior fall in love with me?

I couldn't see myself with him, but then I could.

Battling with my inner thoughts, I slumped down on the chair in the dressing room, touching up my make-up when Bruce squeezed my shoulders.

"Hey, baby girl. That was some set." He wiggled his shoulders up and down as he pouted at me in the mirror.

I blushed.

"You put on quite a show. Somebody out there of interest to you?"

My cheeks deepened in crimson.

"Aha, I knew it. You can't hide anything from Daddy Bruce." He winked at me as he squeezed my shoulders again.

I couldn't even respond. My eyes just followed as he shook his hips, walking back to his dressing table, laughing.

Topping my lipstick up with a matte red that pops against my almost translucent skin. Drinking water through a straw, I stand and sashay over to my locker, opening it as I checked my phone. I couldn't help the furrow in my brow when I had no messages from Rhaegar.

Shrugging it off, I let out an exasperated sigh and shut my locker, jumping when Rhaegs' dark brown eyes found me.

"Hey, kitten," he purred, his voice so low it hummed through me, the goosebumps smothering over my skin.

"Hey." I smiled at him, my arms crossing across my chest as I tried the best I could to cover my heaving chest. His eyes fell to where my arms were, stepping towards me.

"I must say, my dick was hard while I was watching you up there, putting on that little show," he whispered, the smell of bourbon lacing his tongue, his breath on my face.

"Tell me, kitten… Was it for me?" His fingers brushed some hair from my face, tucking it behind my ear, his thumb rubbing across my bottom lip.

My eyes burned into his.

He knew the show wasn't for him. Did I put a little extra into my performance? One hundred percent.

I jumped in my skin when I heard Jax call out my name. My head snapped to the side to see him running towards me.

"Vixen, you're on. Go, go," he called out. I ducked out of Rhaegar's hypnotic stare and hurdled towards Jax.

"Come on, baby girl, head back in the game. Don't get distracted." He winked, his eyes moving from me to Rhaegs who was staring at me, I could feel his eyes burning a hole in my back.

Slapping my arse as I started to walk again, Jax let out a soft chuckle as I disappeared down the corridor and towards the stage.

Damn Rhaegar.

Shaking the brown eyed, grey-haired God from my mind, I stood at side stage as Shay finished her set. She was phenomenal. She used to dance as a kid, ballet and contemporary. She owned the stage like the queen she should be. I hoped she went back to her dream one day, because as much as I am grateful that she works here... she was too damn good for this place.

A sweaty Shay bounced towards me, grabbing my hands and air kissing me. "Your man is out there, front stage and centre waiting for you, little Vix. Go out there and show him what you got." She nudged me, licking her top lip seductively and slowly as she waltzed down the long corridor and towards the dressing room.

My name was announced. I closed my eyes and inhaled deeply. I strutted onto the stage, my eyes on the pole and not taking them off for a second.

My skin prickled, a cold shiver ran across me.

Because his eyes were on me. Not Rhaegar's.

No.

My dark eyed, dark haired, mystery man. He's everywhere.

Don't look at him. Don't look at him.

I wanted to seek him out, challenge and stare him down. But I also wanted to thank him for the other night, saving me like he did when that jackass got a little too handsy. I haven't wanted to bring it up the other times I've seen him because it was outside the club and felt it was too awkward since he's seen me half naked on a stage.

Gripping onto the pole, I walked around, looking into the crowd but ignoring Rhaegar's penetrative gaze.

My leg locked around the pole as I spun slowly, my feet touching the ground before dropping to the floor and pushing my legs open. The crowd cheered as I continued my show, *Give Me More – Britney Spears,* blasting through the PA system.

My fingers glided between my breasts, continuing into the hem of my diamond covered hotpants. Falling forward, my palms slammed onto the stage, and I seductively crawled to the edge of the stage, sitting on my legs, spreading them open. Just as a man's hand reached for me, I pushed myself back, spinning away then laying on my back. My head turned to the side as I stared at Rhaegar, trying desperately to avoid the pull I felt to look at my dark and stormy stranger that was lurking in the crowd.

Arching my back off the cool stage floor, my hands skimmed over my curves as I imitated pleasuring myself between my legs.

The heat burned on my cheeks at my blush.

The cat calling echoed around the large room, the hounding from the men spurring me on.

Rolling on my front, I pushed my arse in the air

before body rolling myself up. Standing on shaky legs, I sashayed my hips as I strutted towards the pole. My skyscraper heels clicked across the stage, my long black hair whishing across my bare back. My fingers wrapped around the cool pole as I stepped wide, and standing close to the pole, I lifted my legs off the floor, tipping back slowly, wrapping my ankles around to hold myself in position. I hated going upside down, the blood rushed to my head. I slid down the pole slowly, my hands touching the floor, my top half away from the pole, my legs still firmly wrapped as I slid down seductively. My thick black hair fell around my face. My legs slowly dropped, the top of my feet gracefully falling to the floor. As soon as they touched the stage, my body lay flush for a second. Slowly rolling, my right leg swung around the pole as I rolled completely on my back. My back arched, the pole between my legs. My head fell to the side as my eyes connected with a hazy eyed Rhaegs. It didn't take long before they found dark and stormy's, who was standing not too far from Rhaegar. The air was snatched from my lungs as his eyes devoured me.

Slowly sitting up, I snapped back into pole dancer mode.

I scissor kicked my legs out from the pole, lying next to it, my fingers fastening around the bottom of the slick steel pole again.

Lifting my bum slightly off the floor, my legs

wrapped gently around the pole. I arched my back, my head tipped back as I took the crowd in.

My heart thumped in my chest.

I couldn't help the smile that graced my lips.

Unhooking my legs, I spun over onto all fours before standing up, my fingers finding their place as I hooked my leg closest to the pole and spun around, making both my feet touch behind the pole as I spun elegantly until both of my knees touched the floor.

Dropping my head forward, my skin covered in a sheen of sweat, I stood on trembling legs. I felt like I had been on the stage for ages. I was done.

I was exhausted.

My muscles ached. I needed an ice bath. Or a massage.

I hadn't done a pole work-out like that in months.

My head fell to the side as I saw Jax on the side-line, mouth dropped open, eyes bulging out of his head. I couldn't help the laugh that fell from my lips.

Standing on trembling legs, I threw my hips from side to side as I exited the stage.

"Oh my fuck, Sage!" Jax exclaimed as I strutted towards him. I nibbled on my bottom lip, the blush creeping on my cheeks.

"I'm sorry, but where the fuck did that energy come from? Shit… and what a song to end it to. The guys were *loving* you. I have three up close and personals booked already."

My heart jackhammered, stopping me in my tracks.

"Really?" I felt the small bit of anxiety crawl into my chest, expanding and tightening.

"Yup, tell me your limits, baby girl, I don't want you feeling uncomfortable." His hands gripped my shoulders, stopping me from turning away so I had to turn to look at him.

"Vix, talk to me."

I blinked a few times, my heart thumping in my chest. I was reciting Rhaegar's words in my head, letting them play over and over.

"No sex." I shook my head from side to side.

"Got it, no sex. Anything else?"

I hated that I even had to set these boundaries. Sure, this was an upmarket gentleman's club, but of course there was shady shit that went on. Money talks. The men will go out of here, tell their friends about the dirty pole dancer they hooked up with, which will cause more new faces in the club. It's logic. Disgusting, dirty, filthy logic.

We were just the pawn in this shitty game.

"Just nothing sexual. I don't mind a bit of touching, but no... nothing sexual," I panted out. I was nervous, I didn't want to piss him off. But these were my limits now.

I could see the shock flicker across Jax's face. He would *never* push us into anything we didn't want to do, but at the end of the day, me not wanting to go all the way with these sleazeballs meant less money for Jax.

"Right, okay." He breathed, his hand pushing through his hair "You sure about this, Sage? The money will be good." He smirked, one corner of his lip lifting slightly.

Shit, the money would be good.

But then it hit me, I didn't need the money because I had Rhaegar.

After a few months, I could leave this job, leave my work family and move on from this shitty life.

I swallowed the lump that was lodged in my throat and nodded my head. "I'm sure."

"Okay, baby girl, go get freshened up. I'll get the first man in room one." He leaned in, kissing me on the cheek before he disappeared back towards the club.

I let out a deep breath, relief swarming me. I didn't know why but I thought he was going to kick off, but how could he? My body. My rights.

Jax was a good boss, I had no doubt about that. He always looked after us, but he was still here to make money. Money was always the top tier here. We were just the money spinners.

Brushing the thoughts away, I entered the dressing room, smiling when I saw Shay and Bruce.

There were four dressing rooms, and we all had our own section. I shared with Bruce and Shanay. But occasionally, we would have one of the other girls in here if it was a busy night.

"Damn, girl, you really showed them what ya mother gave ya, right?" She whistled through her teeth as she pulled me in for a hug. I laughed, my shoulders shaking up and down as I did.

"It's them curves, Vix, your legs alone are enough to get the men drooling." She pushed away from me, looking me up and down.

I scoffed.

I was curvy, I wasn't your typical slim girl. I was a size sixteen on my bottom half, my thighs were thick and toned. My waist was small, but I soon filled back out on my top half.

I was grateful for my pole work because it kept me fit.

"Heard you got a few one on ones." She winked at me. "Dirty girl." She sniggered as she sat back down next to me. "What will Rhaegs think?" Her brows wiggled.

"I'm not doing anything that would piss Rhaegar off." I shrugged it off, applying some powder to my sweaty face, trying to set my make-up a little better.

"What?" Shay seemed shocked.

"I'm not doing anything like that, I said I wouldn't." I sat tall, looking over Shanay's head at Bruce who was too consumed in his phone to be eavesdropping. "One of the terms." I lowered my voice as I slouched back down.

"Wow," she whispered.

"Do you not have terms like that then?" I stopped what I was doing as I turned to face her.

"Nope. I told Vance that just 'cos he pays me, I work here because I enjoy it. I am not going to stop what I am doing and what I love for him." She shrugged her shoulders. "He is just work, as is this place."

I sat a little stunned. I suppose her words made sense. It was work either way I looked at it. I got paid to give these guys extra here and I got paid for doing things with Rhaegar.

I didn't have much more time to think about it, Jax was looming in the doorway.

"That's my cue," I said on a shaky voice, pushing away from the dressing table.

"Have fun, boo," Shay called out as I followed Jax.

I walked past Dev and gave him a tight smile, my eyes staying focused on the back of Jax's head as I tried to still my racing heart.

We stopped at the bar, and Jax signalled to the barman for two drinks. Pinching my brows together, I took this moment to look over my shoulder and scan the room for Rhaegs and Mr dark and stormy. I felt my heart drop a little when I didn't see Rhaegs. Maybe he left? Did I go too overkill? I mean, he was lapping it up. All front row and shit. Unless he didn't like what he saw?

"Here, babe, have a drink." Jax smiled, handing me a pornstar martini. I gave him a small smile, unable to stop my thoughts running away from me.

Pouring the prosecco into the sweet cocktail, I nodded at Jax as we clinked our glasses. I knocked it back. I didn't want the pleasantries, I wanted it over with. I wanted to walk the floor like I normally did, I didn't want to have to do my up close and personals.

"Thirsty?" Jax asked, his eyes looking at me over the rim of his glass as it sat pursed at his lips.

I nodded curtly.

Tipping his head back, he finished his drink in one mouthful before putting it back on the bar.

"Ready?"

"Ready as I'll ever be…" I muttered under my breath, so only I could hear.

I wasn't ready at all.

CHAPTER
Nine

You know you're single AF when you start wondering if your stalker is hot.

We stopped outside the lavish purple, velvet doors. I had done this a few times, this was the room I lost my virginity in. I hated these rooms. Tarnished with the memories of my purity being taken.

My heart rate escalated as it thumped loudly in my chest.

"Okay, Sage, the guys in here have been told your limits. If they don't play by the rules, press the black light switch on the wall, and I'll have Tom from security down in a heartbeat." His lips pressed into a narrow line as his hand ran through his auburn hair.

I nodded.

Trying to swallow the bile that was slowly but surely creeping up my throat, I closed my eyes for a moment and inhaled deeply.

It was fine.

Twenty minutes in each room.

Five hundred pounds per room, well, more like two hundred once Jax took his cut.

I felt more anxious now because of Rhaegar. He knew what I did, but it didn't mean he had to like it. Maybe that's why he up and left? Because he didn't like it.

What if he gives me an ultimatum? I would leave this job in a heartbeat, but if things didn't work out or turned sour between me and Rhaegs, I wouldn't have a job. I would be skint, again.

"You hear me, Vix?" Jax's voice startled me, my eyes wide.

"Sorry?"

"I'll open the door in twenty, go get them, my little Vixen." He winked, unlocking the door from the outside and pushing me through into the badly lit room.

I could see a man sitting on the sofa, but the lights were too low to work out his features. I stepped cautiously over to him, my fingers entwining with one another as I tried to calm my racing heart.

"Hello, my little temptress." His voice was low, burly and rough. My skin reacted instantly, my insides coiling, the goosebumps smothering my skin like a cooling blanket, putting out the heat that was coming from my skin.

I knew that voice.

Of course it was him.

Stepping closer and finally closing the gap between us, I let my eyes drink every ounce of him in.

He sat there, relaxed on the low backed, black velvet sofa, his hands sitting over his lap, his legs parted.

His caramel brown eyes looked me up and down, his tongue slowly running across his bottom lip before pulling at it with his teeth.

His large tattooed hands twitched, as if he was trying to stop himself from reacting the way he wanted to. The dark brown hair that fell onto his forehead had a slight wave to it. I wanted nothing more than to run my fingers through it. Tugging and grabbing.

As if he read my mind, he unlinked his fingers and pushed the stray bit of hair away from his face, his eyes narrowing on me.

Pressing his palms flat on his thighs, he stood up slowly.

He was tall. So tall.

Everything about him was large.

I had to quickly pull my mind from the gutter as my thoughts ran away from me.

He must have been at least six foot seven––six foot eight. His shoulders were broad, his arms thick and shaped. I watched as his muscles rippled under his tight white fitted shirt.

I was sure I could see the glorious art that was inked on his skin. My heart tying with his slightly at our one thing in common.

Snapping out of my hypnotic haze, he stepped towards me, his hand coming up to my face as he cupped my cheek. His scent burned through my nose, and I felt a spike of adrenaline hit me as my body consumed the drug that it was being fed.

How could someone's scent do that to you?

"Do you know how long I have wanted to know how your skin would feel under my touch?" His voice was so low, it was barely audible.

I stilled, unable to respond.

He had me completely hypnotized with his gaze.

"So soft, so pure…" His lips edged towards mine, his eyes not leaving mine for a second. His thumb swept over my cheek, my skin pebbling at his touch.

I heard my breath catch in the back of my throat as his free hand gripped onto my hip, his fingers digging into my skin.

"Tell me, temptress, have you been curious about me too?" he breathed, his warm breath on my face.

Swallowing hard and fighting all urges I had to grab his hair and kiss him as if he was the oxygen I so desperately needed in my lungs to breathe, I backed away.

Smirking, I shook my head.

I was hoping to God that he couldn't tell how shit I was at lying. My cheeks blushed with a pinch of red, my chest rising faster as my breathing escalated.

"I'm more curious to know why you're stalking me?" I scoffed out, the nerves that were lacing my not confident voice giving me away.

"Stalking you?" His eyes darkened as he stepped towards me again, closing the gap once more.

I nodded.

"You're everywhere I go. Every morning you're at The Coffee Run, every night you're here... do you follow me home too?" My skin prickled in fear momentarily. If he admitted it, at least I could relax a little even though it was weird as fuck if he was.

I saw a small smirk dance across his lips, one side of his mouth edging up slightly as if he was playing his own thoughts over in his head.

"Now, little temptress, that would be telling..." His hands wrapped around my waist, pulling me towards his warm, toned body. "Wouldn't it?" He winked.

I heard the breath whoosh from my lungs at being in such close proximity to him, and my throat burned at the lack of oxygen flowing through my lungs. Pushing his hands off me, I stepped back, but he only followed, cornering me against the wall.

"Whoops, looks like you're trapped, little one." His eyes trailed up and down my body.

Fuck, I had never wanted someone so much in my life. What the fuck was wrong with me?

Truth be told, I don't think I would even care if he

kidnapped me. Stockholm syndrome? Sign me the fuck up.

If he was my captor, then take me willingly.

My big green eyes looked up through my lashes at him.

Fuck, he was beautiful.

Sinking my teeth into my bottom lip, I slowly dragged them off. I don't know what came over me, my hands touching his hard chest. Trying to hide the gasp that left my lips at the spark that shot through my fingers from touching him, I pushed him back towards the sofa.

The sofa hit the back of his knees, making him fall into the seat.

I stepped back, shaking my finger from side to side at him as he went to stand. Swinging my hips as I walked over to the sound system, I pushed play, letting the first song that was lined up play.

Maneater – Nelly Furtado started playing.

How fitting.

I spun around; my head dipped as I looked up at him through my lashes. I watched him fidget in his seat, his hands grabbing at the tight material over his crotch.

My hands went above my head, my hips moved from side to side as I strutted back over to him.

Stopping in-between his parted legs, I bent down slowly, deliberately pushing my breasts together to give him the best view I could.

"Fuck," he whispered into the air, and my inner self was lying on a chaise lounge, fanning herself.

Placing my small hands on his thighs, palms down, I slowly, teasingly skimmed them up his toned legs, brushing my fingers over his bulging crutch ever so delicately.

I heard his shaky breath hiss through his teeth.

Rolling my body up, I sashayed my hips from side to side, letting the music completely take over my body. My arms were above my head before I let my fingers trace over every single curve of my body. My hips rotated as I let myself get completely consumed. His burning gaze over my body spurred me on.

I ran my finger up my thigh slowly as I stopped dancing for a moment, skimming it across the top of my thigh and gliding it across the front of my hotpants. A moan escaped my lips.

Fuck that felt good.

The buzz was addicting.

I heard a deep, primatial growl come from his throat.

I let my hands continue their trail up my stomach and over my boobs, squeezing them. Letting my head fall back, my breathing became heavier. Snapping my head up, my own eyes were hazy. I felt completely consumed by lust. And I didn't want it to stop.

Reaching out for him, I pressed his legs together before straddling him, my thick thighs either side of his.

"My little temptress," he purred.

Pushing his legs open, my hips dropped slightly. I was sitting over his hard cock.

My hips rocked back and forth, the friction feeling amazing through our clothes as I continued my dance. His hands glided up my bare thighs in the most teasing manner, slow and skilful. My breath hitched, my head falling forward as my hair fell around my face.

I stilled for a moment, his touch taking over my body. I was paralyzed.

"Don't stop, little one, keep grinding on me." He sat closer to me, his hands gripping the skin of my thigh, and the pinch I felt was addicting. I felt the burn. I wanted him to do it all over my body. Marking me. Branding me.

His hands continued their slow torment, my hips gyrating over him. I felt the pleasure rippling through me.

This was so wrong.

So, so wrong.

But it felt so right.

This was my job.

I was a dancer.

A pole dancer.

A stripper.

A *whore*.

That's all I was to these men who wanted extras.

His fingers dug deeper as they reached the top of my thigh, his fingertips edging closer to the hem of my hotpants. I let out a heavy breath, and I could feel the tremble as it left. His once caramel eyes were now dark as they found mine, devouring me with his stare.

My lips parted as one of his hands left my skin, his finger hovering over my core. Reaching behind me, I grabbed onto his knees, lifting my hips slightly, giving him the green light.

At this moment, I didn't care.

I wanted him to touch me.

I wanted every part of him on me.

His eyes, his breath, his lips, his fingers, his tongue.

Everything.

He smirked, his eyes dropping in-between my legs as his fingers skimmed across my clit through the thin material. The electricity coursed through me, my breath hitching, my skin erupting in goosebumps. He lifted his fingers for a second. I didn't want him to.

"Don't stop," I whimpered.

His finger pressed my clit through the material once more, my head falling back when I heard a bang on the door.

"Times up," Jax's voice bellowed.

I scooted off his lap and shut the music off.

"Coming," I called out.

"Not just yet you're not, temp."

Bastard.

I took a moment to compose myself.

How the fuck had I let myself get this worked up with him? How had I let him get so close?

"This shouldn't have happened." I shook my head from side to side, the guilt creeping over me.

"It was always going to happen, we are inevitable." He stood, his hands readjusting his trousers.

"I don't think so…" I scoffed. "Stalker." I couldn't help the slight venom that laced my voice, my eyes narrowed on him.

"And what? You think I am going to stop?" he challenged me as he stepped towards me.

"I'm with someone," I whispered, his hands either side of my head as he pinned me against the wall.

"You think I give a fuck about the saggy balled old guy you're with?" He threw his head back and laughed. "Newsflash, he's not that into you." I could feel the bitterness on his tongue.

I shook my head.

"You're an arsehole." I flipped him off as I ducked under his arms and ran for the door.

"An arsehole who you just dry humped, little temptress, and I am far from finished with you." His head dropped; his eyes burned into me. "See you soon, little one."

I felt a shiver run over my skin as my palm banged on the door for Jax to let me out.

Fuck.

CHAPTER Ten

Newsflash: he's just not that into you. Yeah, right. Dick.

To say I was flustered was an understatement. My eyes were over my shoulder as I took in his demeanour. His fists were clenched by his sides, his head was hung low, his eyes ablaze with rage.

Sighing with relief when Jax opened the door, I flew out of there like a bat out of hell.

"You okay, Sage?" he asked, and I could hear the concern in his voice.

"I'm fine." I nodded, trying to keep my shaky voice calm.

"Need a drink?"

I shook my head from side to side. "No, let's just get the next room over with."

"Okay, sweetheart."

Jax stood outside door number two, giving me a wink as he unlocked it. This room was the same. The lights dimmed, a large figure sitting on the sofa.

I inhaled deeply, bracing myself for what was about to come. Stepping inside the room, the door shut behind me, the sound of the locking mechanism making me jump.

"It's okay, kitten, it's me." I heard Rhaegs' voice, his fingers fiddling with the dimmer switch as the room lit up a little more.

I felt my heart still. Fuck, I was so glad it was him. I ran at him, throwing myself in his arms.

"All okay?" his voice whispered as he cupped my face.

I nodded. "More than okay." I smiled. I didn't want to tell him about Mr dark and stormy next door. I wanted rid of him.

I led him back to the sofa and sat him down as I stood between his parted legs. His hands were on my hips, holding me in place. His eyes scanned over my body, his brow pinching, his jaw tightening as he looked at the red marks on my thighs.

"Who did this?" he growled, his brown eyes back on mine as they darted back and forth.

"Could be the pinch from the pole," I lied. Fuck, I didn't want to tell him it was the guy before, Rhaegs would throw him through the wall.

He shuffled forward, his head lowering as he placed his lips over each mark and kissed delicately.

His lips felt good on my skin. A tingle swarmed through me.

"Do you know, kitten…" His voice was muffled against my skin, and he removed his lips for only a moment to continue. "How hard it was for me to not drag you down from that stage?" He smirked. "All I could think about was pulling you to the edge, spreading your legs and eating your pussy in front of all of those men."

My pussy clenched at his words.

"I would have made them watch as I dipped my tongue into *my* pussy. As I fucked *my* pussy with my fingers. They all want a taste of you, angel, but they can't. Because you're mine."

I swallowed hard, my legs trembling. The thought of Rhaegar doing that invaded my thoughts. His head buried between my legs as his tongue licked and sucked my pussy.

Fuck.

"Dance for me," he ordered softly.

I nodded. I felt numb.

Stepping away for a moment, I walked to the sound system and pushed play.

Pour Some Sugar on Me – Def Leppard played though the speakers.

I loved this song.

Rocking my hips from side to side, I walked back over to him. I stood between his legs as my hips moved, my hands above my head as I let the music take control. Dropping down on my legs, I shook my bum before falling on all fours. My head snapped up as my eyes connected with Rhaegs. Sitting back on my knees, I parted my legs, trailing my fingers from my lips and letting them glide between my breasts, over my stomach and in-between my legs as I rubbed myself, with him watching.

I was turned on.

This song always turned me on. Mr Stalker turned me on something chronic, and me being here on my knees rubbing my clit turned me on.

I was ready to combust at any minute.

"Stand up, angel."

I did as he said.

I always would.

I loved that he commanded me. I was willing to be a submissive for him.

Wrapping his fingers around my wrist, he pulled me down next to him.

"Sit back, spread your legs," he growled.

Sit back, spread legs. Done.

Panting, my eyes watched as his fingers skimmed between my full breasts, squeezing and kneading them with attentive care.

A pang of pleasure shot through to my core.

I whimpered.

"Oh, kitten, I love when you moan." His lips pressed

against my jaw line, nipping as his fingers carried on their trail.

Hooking his long fingers round the side of my hotpants, he pulled them to the side.

"Hold them there."

Hold your hotpants to the side, revealing all. Done.

"Oh fuck, kitten. Completely waxed, my favourite kind of pussy," he growled.

My breath caught as he ran his finger between my slick folds, a moan escaping my lips at how good his touch felt.

But being honest? Anyone's touch would feel good, I was that turned on. My bundle of nerves ready to explode.

He pushed two fingers inside of me without warning, stretching me to mould around him.

"So fucking tight." His voice was low. "Bring your knees up, rest your feet on the sofa, keep them spread. It'll feel so much better for you."

Bring knees up, spread legs wider, feel his fingers fuck you deeper. Done.

Whining, my head turned to look at him. He shook his head.

"Watch me finger fuck you, angel."

Watch your sugar daddy finger you. Done.

My breathing fastened as I watched his fingers slowly pull out then pump back into me. He was warming me up, working me so I was used to the feel of him.

His thumb brushed over my clit softly before he lifted it off me again.

This was erotic.

This was insane.

And I didn't fucking care.

Pumping his fingers into me faster and deeper now, I kept my eyes where he said. I felt my pussy clench around his fingers, the feel of him inside of me bringing me to my ecstasy was more than I could have fantasised about.

He knew what he was doing. Working my body like a pro, as if he knew every fucking button to press when it came to me.

I had never experienced anything as sexually charged as this now.

Who knew fingering felt this good? Because I certainly fucking didn't.

With my free hand, I reached for his shirt, curling my fingers around it as I gripped tightly.

"Oh shit," I moaned, my eyes rolling in the back of my head as he stroked my G-spot.

Bang. Bang. Bang.

"Times up!" Jax's voice echoed loud enough over the music.

Rhaegs pulled his fingers out, pushing them between his cushioned lips and sucked them dry.

"This isn't over. We're going back to my place

tonight," he growled as he stood up.

I couldn't move.

I was in euphoria, my pussy still glistening with my arousal, my fingers still holding my hotpants to the side.

Bang. Bang. Bang.

Startled, I jumped up and covered myself up.

Rhaegar stepped towards me, pressing his lips over mine and fucking my mouth with his tongue.

Maybe this was a little teaser of what I was going to be getting later?

"See you soon, kitten," he whispered on my lips, licking his as he stepped back.

I nodded, rushing to the door and banging so Jax could open up.

What the fuck?

Jax swung the door open, his eyes on mine before they fell to Rhaegar.

I was flustered as hell. I was frustrated. I was like a sexual ticking time bomb. Honestly, if Jax so much as touched my skin, I think I would have come.

I was that wired, that sexually charged, that aroused.

"You okay?" Jax whispered as he closed the door on Rhaegar.

"Yeah, yeah… fine," I muttered. "No way was that twenty minutes…" I groaned.

"The guy in room three paid me five hundred for me to cut your dance short…" I saw Jax wince as I shot him a death glare.

"That five hundred is all yours." He gave me his handsome smile. "Last one, Sage, then you can go home. You look wrecked."

Oh, Jax, if only you knew.

Standing outside door three, my nerves were shot.

Every vibration from the music upstairs was pushing me closer and closer to erupting.

I wanted nothing more than to go home with Rhaegar and continue what we started.

The locking mechanism clicked as Jax opened the door slowly, my eyes adjusting to the dimly lit room.

"I'll knock in twenty…" Jax's voice echoed off down the hallway as I stepped over the threshold, my heart drumming in my ears.

Jumping slightly when the door locked, I seeked him out.

Disguising my loss of breath at the sight of him, I inhaled deeply as I walked over.

What the fuck?

But then again, why was I not surprised.

It was my dark and stormy stalker.

"Well, there you are, my little temptress." His voice was raspy as he edged himself to the edge of the sofa. His legs parted, his elbows resting on his knees. "I didn't think we were quite finished earlier, and to be honest, the thought of leaving you flustered and dripping wet for me seemed a little unfair." Brushing his thumb across his parted bottom lip, his eyes dragged up and down my body.

I was flustered.

My chest heaved up and down as I tried to fill my lungs as quick as I could. Just being around him, I felt the air being snatched from me.

Curling his index finger slowly, he called me over. And like a moth to a flame, I followed.

Every fibre in my body was screaming, but you see, there was something hot but also so infatuating with him. Even if he was a bit of a stalker.

"There's a good girl, so good at following commands." He smirked as he patted the seat next to him. There was music playing softly in the background that he must've put on before I walked in the room.

I sat next to him, I tried to disguise just how much he affected me and just how turned on I was by his presence.

His fingertips softly trailed up my bare thigh, getting closer to the spot I so badly needed touching.

"You're so responsive, so turned on. I know you're trying to hide it, little one... but stop." His lips hovered by the shell of my ear. "Just let it go, feel how good my fingers feel on your skin."

He continued his torment, each stroke closer to where I needed, burning that little bit more into my skin.

"You may not be mine yet, little temptress, but mark

my words..." His voice was barely audible as he whispered in my ear, his fingertips brushing across the front of my hotpants.

He skimmed them across again, but this time, his finger pushed my clit a little harder.

"You will be."

And I came.

My orgasm exploded deep inside of me, and my head fell back as I moaned. Dark and stormy nipped at my ear, his fingers firmly in place as I rode my high, my eyes fluttering shut as he showed me just how beautiful the stars really were.

I felt my body tremble as I came back round, my eyes opening slowly as I looked at him.

I couldn't help but feel ashamed. Standing quickly, I walked the room, pacing back and forth. I needed out. I couldn't breathe in here with him.

He was suffocating.

My fingertips ran across my lips as I replayed what just happened, repeatedly. Walking for the door, I lifted my hand, ready to knock, when he was behind me. His body pressed against my back; I could feel how hard he was.

"You can't run forever, little one. I will get you. I will do whatever it takes." His voice was low.

But though it should, it didn't instil fear in me.

I turned round slowly to face him, my eyes boring

into his. I licked my lips before pulling my bottom lip between my teeth, a smirk playing across my lips.

"We will see about that." A laugh bubbled out of me as I pushed him back and away from me, then banged on the door.

Jax opened it up, and I stepped over the threshold, but not before looking over my shoulder and winking at him.

"You've just started a game of cat and mouse. Tick tock, little one, I'm coming for you."

CHAPTER Eleven

It's okay Mr Dark & Stormy, two can play that game

The rest of the night passed in a haze. Once I had finished with the stalker, I sat at the bar and shotted six vodkas, one after the other. By the time Rhaegar pulled me from the club, I was wasted. Did I plan to get that drunk? Maybe. I couldn't go back to Rhaegar's and spend the night with him after what I did. I felt dirty. Cheap. A whore.

But let's be honest, I was a whore.

I let two men do things to me tonight because I let lust get in the way. Albeit one of them was my sugar daddy, so technically I was allowed to do things with him, but it still felt wrong.

My eyes widened as we approached Rhaegar's building. He was meant to take me home.

My mind was foggy, hazy. I felt unsteady on my feet.

"I wanted to go home," I wailed.

"I know you did, angel, but I wanted to look after you."

Lifting me out of his car, he carried me into his penthouse, walking me straight into his bedroom and dropping me onto the bed.

"I'll be right back." He leaned down and pressed his lips to my forehead.

Oh wow, this bed felt amazing. Not like the piece of shit I sleep on. It's not my mum's fault.

Shit.

My mum.

Sitting up, I searched around the room for my bag. Where the fuck was my bag?

I heard water running, my head snapping in the direction of where Rhaegar disappeared.

"Rhaegs!" I called out, panic creeping over me.

He darted back in the room, his eyes scanning my face.

"Kitten? What's wrong?"

"My mum, I need to speak to my mum."

"Okay, okay," he soothed as he walked to the base of the bed and handed me my rucksack.

Relief swept over me.

Damn alcohol playing havoc with my emotions.

"Thank you," I muttered, grabbing my phone out and tapping a message to my mum to explain I was staying at Shay's and I'll see her tomorrow.

I felt like a shit daughter. I pulled stunts like this.

I fell back onto the bed, my phone still in my hand.

"Come on, Sage, your bath is ready." He stood at the edge of the bed, holding his hand out for me to take. His head cocked to the side, his shirt that was once done up was now open, revealing his toned stomach, his muscles rippling underneath. His brown eyes stayed on me; his lips parted as he waited for me.

He looked completely handsome, and totally fuckable.

I was fucked.

Rhaegs stayed with me in the bath, making sure to wash my skin tentatively, as if he knew what had happened in the other two rooms. Even though what had happened would always stay unspoken between us, I still felt like he knew.

After he washed my hair, his fingers glided up and down my spine so softly, causing my skin to erupt in goosebumps. There was no point denying that me and Rhaegs had a deeper connection, but I still didn't know if it was anything more than sexual.

The way I felt around him is like no other way I have felt before, but I couldn't deny the pull I felt for dark and stormy. It's like I could forget all my morals and rules around him, and I never wanted to disappoint him.

My head tilted back as I looked at Rhaegs, the soft sponge lathering up my body felt good against my skin.

"I love your tattoos." He leaned down and placed a soft kiss on the top of my shoulder.

"Thank you." I hummed, my skin ablaze from his lips.

"You feeling a little better?" Another kiss placed at my collar bone.

Gasping, my breath caught at the back of my throat, and all I could manage was a nod. I had sobered up, not sure how, but I had.

"Good, I am glad, kitten." His arm dropped lazily as it fell into the warm bath water. Reaching across the rolltop bath, his lips moved to the base of my throat. His voice rumbled against my hot skin. "I want to kiss you all over."

Smirking, my head fell back as his lips moved to my chin, nipping and kissing my jaw line. "But not tonight, angel. Tonight, we sleep, but I can't promise that it'll be the same in the morning. I may not be able to stay away from you that long." He smiled against my skin as his free hand moved to my chin, his finger and thumb tilting my head forward. Rubbing his thumb across my bottom lip, his lips slanted over mine. His kiss was soft, gentle. Slipping his tongue between my lips, he teased me. My mouth opened more as his tongue invaded my mouth, mine and his dancing in rhythm with each other.

Dropping his head as he pulled away, his fingers firmly gripped my chin again.

"You're a temptation, Sage." His voice was low and hazy, his eyes darting back and forth between mine. "But you're the best fucking temptation," he breathed before his lips crashed back to mine.

I was completely and utterly lost in Rhaegar.

But my dark, tall and handsome was lingering in the back of my mind, as if my subconscious was reminding me of him.

Honestly, how could I forget?

I woke early in the morning, hot and entangled in a topless Rhaegs. I felt like my skin was on fire.

I was so used to sleeping alone.

I needed to move.

Slowly moving his arm that was draped across me, I delicately placed it next to my body. I sat up cautiously and lifted his leg off me. Turning my head slowly, I looked at him. His lips were slightly parted as the soft breaths escaped them. He looked so peaceful, so calm.

I don't think I will ever comprehend just how handsome he is. His skin had a beautiful glow, his thick silver hair pushed away from his face. He had soft wrinkles around his mouth and at the corner of his eyes. I wasn't sure how old he was, but if I had to guess, he was around mid to late fifties. But nevertheless, he was so delicious.

His muscles were defined under his golden skin, his chest broad and toned.

Sighing blissfully, I folded the duvet back and padded to the en-suite. My head throbbed.

I couldn't remember the last time I had a drink.

I needed to forget dark and stormy, and silly me thought vodka was the solution.

It wasn't.

He was always going to be there; did it bother me?

Honestly?

No.

It should.

Because it's not healthy. It's like he has an obsession... but what if I told you that I liked his obsession? That maybe I may be a little bit obsessed with him too?

The feel of the rush, the buzz that I feel when I am around him.

My skin tingles in the best way, and my heart drums in my chest.

My fingers curled around the edge of the sink as I looked at myself in the mirror, my eyes puffy from lack of sleep, my long black hair pulled into a messy ponytail. A smile appeared at the corner of my mouth as I felt him invade my mind, my mind replaying every heart pounding moment that happened last night.

SOMETHING WORTH STEALING

Did I want Rhaegs to make me come last night? Yes.

Was I happy that it was mystery man instead? Abso-fucking-lutely.

That's when it hit me.

I was addicted to the devil. Even though I didn't know who the devil was.

I liked to play with fire, and he was the definition.

I liked the way he burned my skin from his touch, the way my body responded to his words.

Last night was just a taste of what he could do to me, and now I can't wait to see if he is there tonight, waiting, hiding, watching.

Crawling back into bed and slipping in next to Rhaegar. I laid there. I couldn't sleep. Turning my head, I watched him snooze, there was something so peaceful about it. It wasn't long before my eyes were fixed on the ceiling, and my stomach grumbled. I was starving. I hadn't eaten since breakfast yesterday morning. Normally I can sneak some lunch at The Coffee Run, but there was no chance yesterday with my boss in.

I didn't know Rhaegs well enough to be getting up and wandering around his apartment. I wanted to go home, get freshened up, eat stale cereal with just in date milk and chill for a bit before I had to go to work. I felt out of sorts.

My mind drifted back to last night... what in the

actual fuck was I thinking? I was always told to steer clear from trouble, and Mr dark and stormy was trouble, all wrapped up in a six foot seven, tattoo covered body.

My heart fluttered at the thought of him.

I was dancing with the devil himself last night, I should fear him. Be wary of him. But I'm not.

My skin erupted in goosebumps at the mere thought of him.

All I could think of was how I wished it was him lying next to me.

I turned to look at Rhaegar again when I heard him start to stir, his brown eyelids fluttering open as his pools of dark brown found mine.

"Morning, angel." His voice was raspy and hoarse.

I was doomed.

Once Rhaegar was up, we sat at his lavish dining room table and ate breakfast. There were bacon, eggs, beans, sausage, hash browns, tomatoes, toast… you name it and it was there.

I was sinking down coffee like there was no tomorrow, I needed a kick. The lack of sleep catching up with me.

"How did you sleep?" Rhaegar's eyes popped up from his plate to look at me as he asked the question.

"Well." I nodded, shovelling some bacon into my mouth. I felt awkward as fuck.

"Good, you needed a good night's sleep." Smiling at me, he placed his knife and fork across his half-eaten plate. I panicked and mirrored his actions. His eyes widened before shaking his head. "No, kitten. Eat," he soothed.

Rubbing my lips into a thin line, I gently picked up my knife and fork. "You need to eat."

Giving him a half smile, I carried on eating.

"What are your plans today, Sage? Do I get to spend a little more time with you?"

I felt my insides coil. How could I like both men? Why did I have to like both men?

It infuriated me.

"I have work at one at the coffee shop, then straight on to the club for a late shift," I mumbled through a mouthful of toast.

"That's a shame." His eyes flickered with something, but I wasn't sure what. "What could entice you to stay home with me?" His tongue darted out to wet his lips, his stare penetrative and straight into my soul.

"I have to work, Rhaegs," I breathed.

"Well, you don't have to anymore…" He stood from the table and stalked over to me, his hand running around the back of my head before he tilted it back for me to look up at him.

"How much are you on yearly to work at the coffee house?"

I blushed, I felt embarrassed to tell him.

"Tell me, kitten."

"Fifteen thousand a year," I breathed; my heart raced in my chest.

"Right." He leant down, kissing the tip of my nose. He inhaled deeply as if he was breathing in my scent, and my heart danced in my chest. "I'll be right back." He winked, dropping his hold on me and disappearing.

I sat, stunned. Where the fuck had he gone?

Sitting on my own, I took a minute to have a good look around the lavish apartment I was sitting in. I dreamed of things like this, to live in a place like this with my mum. But that would never happen. Because poor girls like me don't get to live this luxurious lifestyle.

Everything is temporary.

Even Rhaegar.

I know that.

It won't be long before he gets bored with me and fucks me off for someone who has a little bit more ambition in their life than being a stripper.

Reaching for my stomach, it felt like someone had just got a knife and twisted it into it.

I sat back in the chair and let my head drop back, my eyes pinned to his ceiling.

Maybe he was fed up with me already?

No, no, no. Stop being pessimistic.

SOMETHING WORTH STEALING

I hated arguing with my thoughts, but they were always there, pushing their way through and implanting in my brain.

I felt my heart drum when I heard footsteps behind me, and turning in my seat, I saw Rhaegs step closer with a devilish grin on his face.

Oh boy, he was hot.

"That looks like a face of someone who is up to no good," I teased, my eyes following him as he closed the gap between us.

"Hold your hands out." His lips twitched at the corners as he tried to suppress his smile.

I did as he asked.

"Close your eyes." His voice was playful.

I did.

I felt like such a fool. Inhaling deeply through my nose, I waited with bated breath.

"Open your eyes," he whispered.

I looked at him before I felt the weight in my hand. My eyes fell to my turned-up palms when I saw a pile of notes. It had a thick band around it, and my eyes focused as I read it. Two-thousand pounds?!

"What the fuck?" I whispered.

"I want to take you shopping. I called your job and said you had a bug and would be off for the next forty-eight hours."

I started panicking. What the fuck, I repeated to

myself again.

"Rhaegs, you can't do that," I muttered, my throat tight. "They could fire me, then I wouldn't have a job."

I sounded pathetic, but it was all right for money bags just throwing his cash around.

"You don't need a job." He dropped down to his knees, taking the cash from my hand and placing it on the table.

"But, but…" I panicked, it was clear in my voice, and my eyes widened.

"Sage, when will you get it? I will look after you." His thumbs brushed against the backs of my hands, softly.

"But what if you tire of me? This isn't forever, Rhaegs. I'm a business transaction…" I breathed; I felt my heart ache in my chest. It hit me that this won't last forever, and I had no right to feel pained by that, but for some fucking reason, I did. "I don't fit into this world."

"Sage, I wouldn't fuck you over. If, and it's a big fucking if, trust me… If, this didn't work out, I wouldn't leave you with nothing. I would pay you a generous amount of money for your time. You can quit the job at the club, fuck the coffee house off who pays you too little and make something of yourself. When will you get it?" He sighed. "I will sort all your money problems out, your student loan, your mortgage, your debt. Gone." He clicked his fingers. "Don't fight me on this. Quit your jobs, enjoy your time with me and live a little." His hands dropped from my hands and onto my bare thighs.

I was speechless.

My eyes burned from the unshed tears I wanted to cry through fear.

I always said I would never depend on a man after what my sperm donor did to my mum. Ripped her apart inch by inch and left her in a devastation of depression and anxiety.

I wouldn't let that happen to me.

I needed to save myself from that sort of heartbreak, that kind of love. I had to look after me.

And that's why this works, because it is temporary.

"What do you say?" His eyes glistened as he looked at me. "Let me look after you, Sage, like you deserve. I want to worship the ground you walk on."

I nibbled my bottom lip as I contemplated his words.

"Please, kitten," he pleaded.

"Fine, but we both agree this is temporary? And when it's done, it's done. No fucking me over? No leaving me to drown?"

"Agreed." He nodded, removing his scalding touch from my skin and crossing his finger over his heart. "Cross my heart and hope to die." He smirked, winking at me. "And I promise, I will not fuck you over, even if you leave me for another man."

My heart dropped, my stomach knotting. He knows about dark and stormy.

Pushing the invasive thought from my head, I let out the breath I had been holding, nodding my head sternly.

He stood, placing a kiss on my forehead. "Come, let's go get showered. I'm taking you out for the day." He smiled as he turned on his heel before stopping just a few steps away from me. "Oh, and check your bank account." One side of his mouth lifted as he slowly walked away. I let my eyes trail up and down the back of him, because I mean he is fucking handsome. Following him like a little girl, I slipped my hand through his as I caught up with him.

Just temporary.
Once we're done, we're done.
Now let's just hope my heart gets the fucking memo.

CHAPTER
Twelve

Well fuck, I have a sugar daddy.

That motherfucker put twenty-thousand pounds in my bank. *Who the fuck just has twenty thousand pounds sitting in the bank?*

Rhaegar Rutherford, that's who.

Twenty-thousand pounds.

I sat stunned on the bed.

"What the fuck?" I breathed out.

"Everything okay, kitten?" Rhaegs asked as he walked out of the walk-in wardrobe, dripping from head to toe in designer clothes.

I nodded. I couldn't even muster the words. I was in too much shock.

"Is this about the money?" His voice was soft as he sat next to me on the bed, and I slid towards him slightly as it dipped.

I heard his sigh when I didn't reply.

"I did it because I wanted you to see I wasn't fucking

around. I'm not going to fuck this up. I wanted you to use the money to pay your student loan off, at least it's one thing off your debt list." His smile was warm and wide as his eyes burned through to my soul.

I couldn't stop the tears from welling in my eyes, and my bottom lip trembled.

"Sage," he breathed out in a sigh as he pulled me into his arms, embracing me.

"I don't know what to say," I whispered into his black crew neck jumper.

"You don't have to say anything, angel." His lips pressed to the top of my head, a soft kiss planting itself there.

"Thank you." My voice was hushed as he held onto me tightly, as if he never wanted to let me go. But I knew that wasn't the truth. He would let me go in an instant if he needed to.

And that's what I needed to remember.

I was always replaceable.

Once I was dressed in my standard high-waisted jeans and black lace bralette, I slipped my feet into my chunky doc martens. Pulling on a light denim jacket to cover my arms, I met Rhaegar downstairs in the lounge area.

"Sage…" His eyes glistened as he let his eyes wander up and down my body.

"Rhaegs." I blushed under his gaze.

"You look as beautiful as ever." He dipped his head as he held his hand out for me to take, which I did, gladly. "You ready for a full day's shopping?" he chimed.

"I think so," I muttered.

The truth was, I wasn't.

I didn't really do shopping; I would just run into the local charity shop and grab what I needed. I made my bralettes on my mum's old sewing machine, it was amazing what hidden gems you could find in a charity shop.

I pulled Rhaegs towards his driver's car when I felt the tug back. Shaking his head from side to side as he did, a small smirk pinched at the corners of his mouth.

There, sitting in a car space all by itself was a *Lamborghini Urus*.

Fuck. Me.

"Oh my God," I squealed as I pulled my hands out of Rhaegar's and walked around the car, my mouth dropped open as my fingers skimmed over her every curve.

The beauty was matte grey, the wheels, spoiler and door trim were piped in an luminous green paint.

"You like?" Rhaegs strolled towards me, a boyish grin on his face as his hands hid in his pockets.

"Like?" I snapped my head around to look at him. "I fucking love it." I sighed, my eyes moving back to the body of the car.

"Four litre twin-turbo V-eight engine, the torque at eight-fifty, I mean..." I stepped back, shaking my head. "This car is a beast."

"You like cars?" I saw his brows pinch slightly before smoothing them back out, his head cocking to the side.

I blushed. "I *love* cars," I admitted, tucking my long black hair behind my ear. "That's what I studied, cars and everything to do with them. I wanted to be a mechanic, own my own car garage, do custom paint jobs and interiors..." My smile grew as I spoke about my passion.

"Well..." I could hear the surprise in his voice.

"I know, *how can a girl be a mechanic... blah blah.*" I mimicked what I have heard a thousand times over.

"I wasn't going to say that..." He licked his lips as he closed the gap between us. "You just surprise me, Sage James. Every single day you surprise me." His arms wrapped around my waist as he pulled me close.

"So why has this dream never become a reality?" he whispered, his face nuzzling into my hair as he inhaled my scent.

"Because the world is a man's world, it's not for a little girl like me." I nibbled my bottom lip as I felt the tears prick my eyes.

"That's bullshit, this is more a woman's world now than a man's world. I will fucking burn the world to the ground to give you that dream."

"No, it's fine. I believe your life is mapped out for

you, and if I was meant to have that dream, it would have happened by now." I pushed away from him, shaking my hands out to keep them busy.

"Manifest that shit." He laughed, his head tipping back. "You must be into that, right? The stars aligning above you, manifesting your dreams, getting charge from your crystals. Or your mum must have been… to call you Sage…"

"Ha, well, between you and I, she was into all her spiritual shit, until my dick of a dad up and broke her into a thousand pieces." The vile, bitter words spilled out of my lips with no control.

Rhaegs light-heartedness was gone in a second. His whole body stiffened as if he was tense.

Letting out a deep sigh, my head fell forward. "Sorry."

"Don't apologise, I get that you're angry. Fuck, I would be too if it happened to me. But you can't let his cowardly, shitty decisions ruin your pure soul like that." His hand reached out, his thumb and finger gripping onto my chin as he tipped my face up to look at him.

"Your name is Sage, right?"

I nodded, a little confused at his question.

"Well, from my knowledge, Sage is used as part of a spiritual ritual" he winked at me before continuing "it's used to cleanse a space, a person, a soul. It promotes healing and wisdom…"

He stopped, his hand moving to cup my face as his thumb wiped a stray tear that was rolling down my cheek.

"That's you, angel. You have such an aura about you, I for one couldn't stay away from you if I wanted to. Use that energy, cleanse yourself and rid him from your soul." He smiled.

"Because you, Sage James, are stronger than you know, a force to be reckoned with... a diamond in the rough." I felt his breath on my face as he hovered over my lips. "And I'll be fucking damned if I am ever going to let you out of my sight."

Oh, be still my beating heart.

CHAPTER Thirteen

A wise sugar daddy once said…

I fell through the door of Rhaegar's penthouse. I felt dead on my feet.

I had bags upon bags of clothes, shoes, pyjamas, underwear, hats, and accessories.

I don't know why I needed all of it, but I had it.

"I need a foot rub," I joked as I fell onto the sofa, my head falling back as it rested on the back of the lavish leather sofa.

"Let me take care of you." Rhaegar's voice was low and husky as he dropped to his knees in front of me.

"I was joking." I scoffed a laugh.

"I wasn't." His eyes flickered with a certain darkness, a fire burning deep within them.

My stomach coiled.

Unlacing my boot, he slipped it off before his fingers dipped in the top of my sock and rolled them down and off.

Fuck, I hope my feet don't smell.

He moved over to my other foot, doing the same delicate removal.

His hands wrapped softly around my foot, his thumbs pressing into the bridge of my foot as he gently started rubbing my tired feet.

Oh. My. God.

It felt amazing, his thumbs expertly kneaded gently, his fingers wrapped around the top of my foot, holding it in place.

"Feel good, kitten?" His eyes flicked up to look at me.

"So good." I nodded eagerly.

He moved from foot to foot, making sure each one of my tired feet got the attention they needed.

Placing my feet gently down on the carpet, his hands trailed up my thighs before pushing my legs open.

"Kitten…" His voice was low.

Looking down at him on his knees in front of me did something to me. My heart drummed and thrashed against my rib cage.

His fingers trailed up to the button on my jeans, his thumb pushing the silver button through the hole. I watched his fingers disappear into the waistband, tugging them down. Placing my hands either side of me on the sofa, I lifted my bum up so he could pull them off me.

In one swift motion they were off and discarded on the floor.

SOMETHING WORTH STEALING

I knew what was coming.

My chest heaved up and down fast, my eyes fixed to Rhaegar.

The suck of breath he inhaled as his eyes roamed across my lower half. It was as if he couldn't restrain himself any longer.

"Do you know how long I have dreamt about eating your pussy?" he growled, his fingers wrapping around the waist of my black G-string.

Blushing under his filthy mouth, I sunk my teeth into my bottom lip.

Whipping my underwear off in a second flat must have been a new record.

I felt the delicious ache already. I needed him. I needed him to release me.

His hands were on my waist, tugging me to the edge of the sofa. Moving one of his hands up to my stomach, he pushed me back gently, so my back was lazily against the sofa, my bum on the edge with my legs spread.

"Your little cunt is glistening for me already, kitten." His voice was raspy. "And I can't wait to taste you."

He edged forward, his fingers digging and gripping into my bare thigh as his tongue glided up from my entrance to my clit. A rumbling moan vibrated in his throat as he did it again.

I gasped; the air being snatched from my lungs with each stroke.

He looked up at me, a sexy as fuck smirk on his face. Moving one of his hands from my skin, his index and middle finger spread my pussy open, his face lighting up like a Cheshire cat who was about to get the cream.

No pun intended.

His mouth was on me, his expert tongue sucking and licking my throbbing clit.

My hips bucked forward, my hands balling next to me as the feeling of euphoria swam through my veins.

"Oh fuck," I moaned, my greedy eyes watching him.

There was something so erotic about seeing a powerful man on his fucking knees, eating your pussy.

One of the best views in the world.

My head fell back, his tongue swirled around and around before gliding in-between my folds. Pushing his tongue into my opening, his thumb brushed against my clit.

My hand flew to this thick silver hair as I tugged hard.

I needed so much more of him.

Slipping his tongue back up, he whirled and swirled it over my clit once more. He moaned as he pressed harder against my clit, his head moving side to side slowly.

"Oh, I..." I called out; I couldn't even form a sentence.

Fuck.

He didn't let up, and my eyes watched as he ate me,

his tongue lapping at me, his mouth devouring me.

I felt the delicious bubbles expanding in my stomach, my skin covering in goosebumps, my toes curling at the feel of him.

One of his fingers teased at my opening, my hips bucked forward, giving him the go ahead. I wanted to feel him everywhere.

Pushing his finger in, he pumped slowly, stroking my G-spot.

"Rhaegs, I'm going to come," I cried out, my head falling back. My legs trembled and my back arched as I came loud and hard.

But he didn't let up, his tongue moved faster, his finger pumping into me hard as he drank every bit of me.

A shiver danced over my skin, and my chest moved quickly as I looked down at him. Pushing his finger between his lips, he sucked it dry.

Well, fuck.

I tried to lean forward to grab my knickers when Rhaegar pushed me back, shaking his head from side to side.

"I'm not finished with you yet. I've just had that taste, and now I am addicted. I *need* more, Sage. And that's exactly what I am doing now." He groaned, standing up and un-belting his trousers, pushing them down hastily, along with his boxers.

My mouth popped open, my eyes focussing on his

thick cock that was rock hard.

I felt my mouth dry, pressing my legs together.

One corner of his mouth slipped at the side, giving me a wink. Falling to his knees again, he pushed my legs open. Reaching for his jeans, he grabbed a foil packet from his pocket.

I wasn't going to overthink why he had a condom in his jeans.

Tearing the wrapper, I watched as he rolled the condom down his length.

My breath caught as he edged towards me, his hand grasping his cock as he pushed his head at my entrance, nudging softly, but each time pushing a little more of himself into me.

His head fell back, a wide smile spreading across his face as he filled me to the hilt.

A moan slipped past my lips at the feel of him inside of me.

"Fuck, Sage. I knew you were tight, but you feel so fucking good around my cock, kitten," he growled.

I watched as he pulled out to the tip, holding it for a second then slamming back into me.

His fingers dug into my hips as he held me in place, his cock spearing in and out of me.

I knew he was going to be a good fuck, but he was blowing all my expectations.

"Harder, fuck me harder," I whined.

A throaty laugh escaped him. "Your wish is my command, angel. I was just warming you up…" He stilled, leaning down and whispering in my ear.

Whining when he pulled out of me, he stood slowly, his fingers wrapped around himself.

"Turn over, hold onto the back of the sofa and spread your fucking legs."

Well fuck.

Clenching my pussy as I did, I was ready to combust.

I did as I was told, my head turning so I could see him over my shoulder. I nibbled on my bottom lip as he stepped towards me, one of his hands holding my hip, pulling my arse closer to him. His skin on mine, he pushed straight into me without warning. Fast and hard.

The sound of his skin hitting mine was turning me on even more.

He pounded, his grip tightening on my hip, the other was in my hair, pulling at the root and tugging my head back. I felt his body across my back, his lips by the shell of my ear. "This hard enough for you, kitten?" He panted as he filled me to the hilt, his relentless thrusts pushing me closer to the edge of my explosive orgasm.

I couldn't speak. I was completely consumed by him. Leaning up, his grip still in my hair, his cock stretched my pussy.

The burn that coursed through me, the full ache that

was lingering were both signs telling me just how close I was.

"Such a good girl, taking my dick so well while I am fucking you hard." His voice strained as he spoke through gritted teeth. "I want you sore, Sage. I want my mark on you for days," he growled, his fingers pinching into my skin.

I liked it.

I needed more.

My hips moved of their own accord, meeting his thrust each time.

"Fuck," he called out, dropping his grip from my hair. Without warning, his hand slapped my bare arse cheek, hard. The sting like nothing I felt before.

I cried out.

He did it again, this time a little harder.

I felt my pussy clench around his cock as I floated higher towards my orgasm. The sound of our skin hitting together, his grunts and my erotic moans filled the room.

Both of his hands were on my hips now as he thrust his cock into me faster.

"Rhaegs, I'm going to come," I cried out.

"Come, kitten," he whispered, spanking my arse again.

And I did.

I free fell as I came, my orgasm ripping through me like nothing I had ever felt before, and fuck did it feel good.

Rhaegs came with me but pulled out before his full orgasm hit. I watched over my shoulder as he pumped his release into the condom then shuddered.

I couldn't help the sting I felt from watching him do that.

Why wouldn't he finish inside me?

I pinched my brows and quickly turned over, reaching for my discarded G-string that was on the floor. Snatching it up, I pulled it up my legs.

I was throbbing. Rhaegs followed through on his word, one hundred percent.

He walked away before returning with a towel wrapped around his waist.

"Angel, let's go take a bath together... you must be sore." His eyes trailed up and down my body. My hair was wild and had that *just fucked* look, my chest was covered in red blotches from my orgasm, and my skin had a veil of sweat glistening over it.

Rubbing my lips into a thin line, I nodded.

Taking his hand that he held out for me, I followed him into the bathroom where he spent the next hour washing and kissing every part of my body.

CHAPTER
Fourteen

Forty-eight hours of mind-blowing sex and oral… who would want to go back to work?

"Baby, just so you know, we have dinner tomorrow with my son." His eyes lit up as he spoke to me.

"You have a son?" I tried to hide the shock in my voice, but it wasn't convincing.

He laughed, his hand taking mine in his.

"Yup, I have a son." He nodded. "He is really such a lovely kid. Very strong willed though." I watched as if he was remembering a memory. "But he has the biggest heart." He leaned across and kissed me on the forehead.

"Okay," I squeaked.

"He will love you." He leaned back in his car seat. "And you've got this. Get tonight out the way then hand your notice in to Jax." He winked.

I nodded.

I was still trying to get my head around the fact that he had a son. There goes my Friday evening of hot domineering sex with my sugar daddy.

"Have a good shift, kitten. I will see you in a few hours," he chimed, the engine of his car roaring.

I smiled and waved before climbing out of the passenger side.

Letting out a heavy sigh, I muttered under my breath. "Let's get this over with."

Pushing through the heavy doors, I sought out Jax, smiling as I saw him walking towards me.

"Evening, Jax." I wrapped my arms around him as we had a friendly cuddle.

"You okay, Vixen?" he asked.

"I am… sort of." I shied away from him as I fumbled in my bag and pulled out an envelope, my eyes full of sadness as I held it out for him.

"Oh no, no… Vix, please tell me this isn't what I think it is…" He sighed, his head dropping forward.

"I'm sorry, I need to focus on my dream… and I'm not going to be able to do it while I am working here," I lied.

But I didn't want to say I was going to be a stay-at-home sugar baby.

"Fuck," he said, exasperated, his hand pushing through his hair. "I get it, but fuck… the girls and Bruce are going to be gutted." He nodded. "Just know, baby girl, you're always welcome back here. You're family." He pulled me in for a cuddle, squeezing me.

"Thanks, Jax." I sniffled, I didn't think I would get as upset as I have.

Dropping my arm from him, I headed towards the dressing room.

"Nope, you're not dancing tonight. Someone has paid me a generous sum to spend a few hours with you… what a way to spend your last night, aye…" He winked, grabbing my hand and leading me to the back rooms.

I didn't even have to guess.

I knew exactly who was going to be hiding behind that door.

My Mr dark and stormy.

The devil himself.

Walking past the bar, I grabbed the first drink I saw. Tequila shot. Perfect.

Knocking it back without a wince, I followed Jax down the dark corridor. The dark purple door mocked me as I stood outside.

"You good, Sage?"

No.

"Yup, perfect." I nodded confidently, even though my insides were churning. I was fucking nervous.

"All of this money is yours, call it a bonus." Jax winked at me as I heard the door mechanism click. "If you need anything, hit the button."

I swallowed hard, my throat bobbing. My palms were sweaty. My heart jackhammering against my rib cage. I was sure it was going to pump too fast and kill me.

Inhaling deeply, I fluttered my eyes shut for a moment.

Once they opened again, I pushed any feeling I had back down into the darkness. I didn't need anything to distract me.

The room was dimly lit like always. I walked in, the door being pulled behind me.

I always knew what I was walking into with this job. Yeah, sure it was an upmarket gentleman's club… but it was also a whore house. Fuck, I lost my virginity in one of these rooms, just so I could pass my university degree.

I swallowed down the bile that was creeping up my throat and burning.

I hated this job. But I didn't hate the family I had made.

I was in this job because of them.

But after today, I was closing the door on this chapter of my life because I need to make more of myself. I want to become the woman I knew I was meant to be.

And that meant leaving Mr stalker behind too.

Which for some fucked up reason made my heart hurt.

"There she is, my little temptress." He grinned as he stepped out of the shadows. His tight blue shirt clung to his muscles. His dark brown eyes glistened as they trailed over my curves. Fuck, I was grateful for the low lighting so I could hide my blush.

"Sorry about my outfit, I didn't have time to change…" I trailed off, slapping my hand down on my thigh.

"I really wouldn't worry about it, you're going to be naked for me in about five minutes…" He winked, his hands moving round my back as he pulled my body against his.

"Excuse me?" I said breathlessly. "No sex, sorry." I shook my head, a smile playing on my lips as I pushed off him. Turning on my heel, dark and stormy wrapped his fingers around my wrist and pulled me back to him. His hand splayed across my stomach, and his spare one traced the curve of my bum, squeezing and kneading.

"I don't want sex, little one…" he whispered in my ear, then licked the shell.

"No?" I panted.

"No." I felt his breath on my neck as he placed soft, hot, wet kisses on my skin.

"What do you want then?"

Why the fuck am I playing up to him?

Because I am fucking weak.

I'm a weak-ass bitch.

"I want you to dance for me, then when you're turned on and I'm hard as fuck... I want to eat your pussy as if it was my last meal." His voice was more of a growl now than a whisper.

My breath hitched; my chest rose quicker.

"Oh, little temp, do you like that idea? Is it turning you on thinking about my tongue fucking your little cunt?"

I am dead.

"I love eating pussy, I would eat pussy all day if I could. And I could if I wanted to... but you see... there is something about you. Something that I can't shake, and I won't stop until I have you in every single possible way. Sexually, mentally, physically..." His tongue darted out, licking the shell of my ear as his fingers moved from my stomach and down to the waistband of my jeans. "Now, take them off, strip down to your underwear and dance for me, little one."

That's when it hit me, I wasn't sure if it was because I was desperate for the money, or if because this dark and brooding mystery man had more power over my body than I thought.

So what did I do?

I fucking did it.

Mystery man walked over to the sound system, pressing play. The room filled with the slowed down version of Crazy In Love – Beyonce.

Moving to the velvet sofa, he sat down. Legs parted; head tilted to the side as his thumb brushed across his bottom lip. His eyes intensely burned over my skin.

I don't know why, but he gave me a rush of confidence that I have never felt in my life.

Unbuttoning the top of my jeans, I pushed them down my legs slowly, seductively. I rocked my hips slowly from side to side as I shimmied out of them. Kicking them off my feet, I held them up, smirking at him as I dropped them to the floor.

His hungry eyes trailed up and down my bare thighs, stopping at my little white lace thong that was covering what he wanted.

"Leave the bralette on." His voice was husky and slow.

I nodded.

My nipples hardened under the lace of the bralette, straining through so he could see them.

"Turned on already, little one? I haven't even touched you yet…" He licked his lips, pulling his bottom lip between his teeth.

I tried my best to ignore him, pushing the feelings that were swarming deep down inside of me.

Stopping in front of him, I slowly moved down so I was crouching on the floor, my hands on my thighs as I pushed my legs open, letting him stare for just a moment.

Twisting to the side, closing my legs, I body rolled up. My back was to him, his hand reaching out and grabbing me.

I didn't stand a chance.

He pulled me down on top of him, the feel of his cock resting between my legs. The thin material and his suit trousers stopped me from getting the friction I needed.

His hand pushed between my legs, pushing them open so my legs dropped over the side of his. I watched as his fingers trailed up my core. I wanted him to stop, but then again, I didn't. His finger continued its teasing trail before he stopped at my chest. His fingers pinched and rubbed my hardened nipple through the lace material.

My eyes closed for a moment as I rode through the pleasure.

"I think I could make you come by just doing this…" His lips brushed against the shell of my ear.

I hummed in agreement as he continued pushing me towards an impending orgasm. I would be happy to just come now.

It was torture.

Beautiful torture.

"That's enough." He nipped the lobe of my ear, lifting me off him.

I could feel how wet I was, and no doubt he could see my arousal through the thin material.

But did I care?

No.

He stood, readjusting his crotch, his eyes burning into me.

I was like a caged animal; I couldn't control myself around him. He was like an aphrodisiac. I couldn't stay away from him.

I craved him, no matter how bad he was for me.

I never wanted to play with fire until tonight. I wanted to dance with the devil before he dragged me down to hell where we both burned, watching our world and everything we knew burn down with us.

"What's going through that pretty fucking head of yours?" His voice was raspy as he moved closer to me, his hand wrapping around the base of my throat.

But it didn't scare me.

He wouldn't hurt me.

"Just that I can't stop thinking about you," I admitted.

He smirked, his grip tightening. My hand moved to his hand, wrapping my small fingers around his wrist.

"How about I give you something to really think about?" he whispered.

He spun me round, backing me towards the sofa, his hand still firmly around the base of my throat. The backs of my knees hit the edge of the sofa, knocking me back as I fell into the cushions.

Dark and stormy leant down, his fingers slowly

unwrapping from my throat. I instantly missed the feel of him there.

Hovering his lips over mine, he sunk his teeth into my bottom lip, tugging it gently before letting go.

I couldn't stop the whimper escaping my lips at the loss of contact.

His hands skimmed down my bare thighs, goosebumps trailing my skin following his fingers.

I knew what was about to happen. He had already warned me. But it still didn't calm my racing heart.

Licking his lips teasingly, he then rubbed them together before his tongue darted back out.

My eyes were watching his every move, his dark chocolate brown hair falling forward onto his forehead. He looked up through his long lashes, his deep brown eyes seeking mine out. I felt my heart skip a beat, and my blood pumped faster and harder around my body. I'm sure I felt him in my soul, but how was that even possible?

"Fuuuuck." I heard him suck in a breath, his eyes falling from mine to the apex of my thighs.

I trembled. But not out of fear, no. It was out of excitement and anticipation.

His large tattooed fingers wrapped around the thin material that was stopping him from getting to what he wanted, and what I wanted him to get to.

"Look at your pretty, plump pussy glistening for me." His voice was shaking as he tried to contain himself.

My cheeks pinched with a crimson red, I wanted to throw my hand over my face, but I didn't. I didn't want to miss a single thing.

I didn't get another second to think about it. His mouth was on me. A deep moan escaped his throat as his tongue flicked, licked and sucked over my clit.

My head fell back, the pleasure ripping through me. How the fuck was I close to coming already? Reaching out, I grabbed his hair, tugging it hard. He lifted his head, his eyes on mine as he smirked.

"Grab my hair when you like it, little one."

Before I could answer back, his expert mouth was back on me. His tongue trailed in-between my folds, swirling at my soaked opening before gliding over my clit. One of his hands dropped from his tight grip on my thigh, skimming his fingertips over my sensitive skin, teasing at my opening, slowly circling around and around. My hips bucked forward. I needed to have him everywhere. I wanted him everywhere.

"Tell me… tell me you want me to fuck you with my fingers," he said, hushed, his eyes not lifting from my pussy as he continued to tease me.

"I do," I moaned out, nodding my head.

"That's not what I told you to say…" His lips pressed on the inside of my thighs; I felt his finger move.

"Fuck me with your fingers," I whined. Fuck, I hated that I gave in.

"That's a good girl. See? It wasn't that hard, was it?" I felt his smug fucking smirk against my skin.

His lips brushed over the front of my pussy before his tongue was bringing me to new realms of pleasure. He pushed his finger into me, hard and fast with no warning. My pussy clamped around him as his mouth sucked on my clit.

"Have you ever had your pussy eaten this good before, my little temptress?"

I shook my head, my moans echoing around the room, my hips grinding onto his finger, wanting him to go deeper.

"Good," he growled. His tongue slowly flicked across my clit before he bit it softly then sucked it hard. My legs trembled; my pussy tightened as he continued to pump his finger into me quicker. Lifting his lips, he looked up at me. His lips were covered in my arousal, and I loved it. His thumb brushed gently across my clit, his eyes burning into me as I came fast and hard.

I couldn't stop my moans; they were loud and erotic. He didn't stop, his finger still fucking me.

"Come for me again. I'm greedy and I'm not finished with you yet." He shuffled up, his breath blowing over my sensitive skin. His lips pressed to my collar bone, trailing down. With his free hand, he pulled my large breast out of my bralette. His tongue swirled around my hardened nipple before taking it in his mouth and sucking, puckering it.

I felt the delicious shiver rip through me as I felt another sweet, hot orgasm beginning to build.

I knew this was wrong. It was so wrong on so many fucking levels. But was I going to stop? No. I shouldn't want this man, I shouldn't be letting him fuck me with his fingers, I shouldn't be letting him trail his soft, hot as sin lips around my nipple, but here I am. Letting him do everything he shouldn't, and I am loving every single minute of it.

A shiver danced up my spine as his lips brushed across to my other nipple, licking, sucking and puckering again, all the while his finger was stroking my G-spot. I needed more; my pussy ached.

Arching my back, my eyes rolled in the back of my head, his lips locking around my hard nipple. Kneading and massaging my breasts roughly, he squeezed them so he could greedily get as much of them into his mouth as he could. I felt another finger tease at my already soaked opening, pushing the tip in softly and slowly. He stilled, stretching me so I was ready to take another finger. The feeling of him filling me was indescribable. He was an expert, working my body to bring me to the ultimate realms of pleasure. It was good with Rhaegar, but fuck, with him it was so much more. There was a connection that ran deeper than just physical. It was like he was anchored to my soul; I couldn't shake him if I wanted to.

SOMETHING WORTH STEALING

We were one.

The moans escaped his lips as he found pleasure in taking his sweet as fuck time on my body. I felt the burn, the sweet ache that grew as my orgasm sat on the edge, just waiting for that little push. And fuck did he do it. His thumb pressed on my clit, his two fingers pumped in and out of me slowly, and now his third finger was rubbing my tight arsehole, pressing against the place that no man had ever been before.

And instead of freezing and clenching, I lifted my hips. I was offering myself to him and I didn't care.

He was the devil.

I was the sacrifice. I wanted to sacrifice my heart, my soul, my body and my virtue.

I wanted to give him everything.

"Oh, little one. You're so greedy…" His teeth nipped across my hot skin as he spoke. "And I fucking love it." He groaned.

I whined, my hips bucking, silently begging for him to do it. And as if he could read my mind, he did it. His finger pressed into my tight hole and my back arched, my legs trembled, my eyes rolling so far in the back of my head I saw nothing but stars. My orgasm ripped through me, crying out as my whole body began to shake. His mouth was over mine, his lips locking with mine as his tongue invaded my mouth as if he was trying to steal my breath, and I would happily let him take it.

I lay there, panting, my legs spread as he kissed down my sweaty body until he reached my pussy. His mouth was over me as he licked me clean.

I fucking loved it.

His chin rested on my stomach, my hands in his hair as my finger twirled a few strands.

"You taste so much better than how I imagined." He winked, his fingers dancing across my skin.

I blushed, I felt embarrassed suddenly.

"Don't even get me started on your pussy..." he said before mouthing 'oh my God' and rolling his eyes in the back of his head.

A laugh bubbled out of me, my hands falling from his hair as I pushed him off me.

"Leaving so soon?" he groaned, standing off his knees.

I nodded.

"Little one?" he called out as I slipped my jeans back up, fastening the button.

My head snapped up as I looked at him.

"Yeah?" My voice was quiet, suddenly putting my walls back up.

"You belong to me." His voice lowered, his eyes ablaze.

"I already belong to someone else." My voice was strong, even though on the inside I was trembling, my legs about to buckle at any minute.

"Is that so?" He stepped towards me, his large hand pushing through his hair in frustration. I saw a smile creep on his face as he scoffed a laugh.

I nodded, unable to speak. He stole the breath from my lungs.

"Were you with someone when my tongue was in your pussy just a little while ago?" His tongue was sharp and wicked.

I nodded again.

"What about when I fucked you with my fingers while teasing your tight little arsehole?"

My breath hitched as my mind flew through the memories of what happened.

His lips on me, his fingers all over me, in me, filling me...

"You think I am just going to disappear and leave you alone?" He moved closer, his hand grabbing my cheeks and squeezing.

I felt the sting in my eyes, the burn in my throat.

All I can see is red warning flags being waved around us, but will I listen?

Will I fuck.

Because without even realising, I have signed my soul over to the devil.

And there is no getting out of it.

"That's what I thought. I'll be seeing you, Sage." He

dropped his hand from my cheek then stepped around me, knocking on the back of the door.

I heard the mechanism unlock.

"I hope you play the memory of me eating your pussy over and over in your head tonight while your man tries to get you off…" He smirked. "I know I'll be thinking about you." He winked, turning around to face Jax as the door opened.

"I'm biding my time, Sage, I'm not a patient man… it won't be long before I am back to claim what is already mine."

As soon as he was out of sight, my legs gave way beneath me.

I had been a fucking damn fool.

How could I have been so stupid to get wrapped up in him?

I had a deal with the devil.

It didn't matter what I did, he would always find me.

I was doomed.

Chapter Fifteen

Stalker – 1 Sage – 0.

His words echoed in my head; they were on constant repeat. But there was one positive from this, I was leaving the club.

I spoke to my haunting thoughts the whole time I was waiting outside for Rhaegar. I got off early but didn't tell him. I needed to just sit and be left alone with my thoughts. I needed to reason with myself. Sure, he has made a threat, but that was only for my benefit, only for affect.

Yeah.

That was it.

He didn't know where I would be. No more morning coffees, no more late nights hiding in the shadows at work. How would he find me?

He wouldn't.

Relief washed over me; I would be fine.

Looking at the time on my phone, it had just gone

two a.m. Rhaegs would be here any minute.

The cold air nipped at my skin; I left my coat in the club as I ran out in a haze to fill my lungs with fresh air. I was suffocating being around the weirdo I spent my night with. But the truth was, he wasn't a weirdo.

He was a beautiful man who just had some fucked-up stalker issues. I felt the heat over my skin as the memories flooded me from how I spent my last evening at work.

I was pulled from my thoughts when I saw Rhaegar's car approach.

My stomach knotted and twisted.

Did I tell him?

I had to tell him.

Climbing down off the back of the bench I was sitting on, I stumbled over to the car.

"Angel." He smiled as he opened the passenger door for me.

Slipping into the Lamborghini Urus, I hummed as the heated seats instantly warmed me.

"Where is your coat?" Rhaegs' brows pinched as he looked over at me, closing his own door and buckling up.

"I left it in the club." I sighed, shaking my head.

"Well, it's nice and warm in here." He smiled. "Hungry? How about a late-night drive through for a burger and a hot chocolate?"

"That sounds amazing, I am starving," I admitted. I had worked up quite the appetite...

"Did you get what you needed to sort for work?" I asked as I sat with my feet pushed up on the dashboard.

"Kitten, get your feet off there." His voice was soft. "If we have an accident, you will snap your legs and do even worse to that beautiful face of yours."

Rubbing my lips together, I tucked them under me on the warm seat. Rhaegs had given me his coat that he had in the back so I could drape it over me. I just couldn't seem to warm up, even though the car was boiling.

Was it nerves?

"Work was okay, just the usual shit." He shrugged.

I didn't even know what he did. I wanted to ask, but for some reason it felt like I was overstepping my mark a little. I'm sure he will tell me why he has more money than sense one day.

Once he had ordered the food, we sat in light chatter while stuffing our faces with one of the best cheeseburgers I had ever eaten. Screwing up the paper that his food came in, he threw it into the bag. He lifted a leg up and turned in his seat to face me. His smouldering eyes watched my every move as I sipped on my hot chocolate.

"How was your last day at work?" His long fingers tapped on the steering wheel.

Here goes nothing.

I inhaled deeply, playing with the lid of my cup.

"It went quite quick actually." I nodded. "I handed my notice in to Jax, then was ushered straight into one of the private rooms for the evening." My words were rushed, my heart was jackhammering, and the blood was pumping so loud in my ears I could hardly hear my thoughts.

I saw him straighten up and fidget in his seat. "Is that so?" He glared at me for a moment.

I nodded.

"And what did you do? Because we both know what those rooms are for." His brows lifted on his forehead as his eyes burned into me.

"I danced." I licked my lips before my eyes fell back down to where my fingers were playing with the cup.

"Is that all?"

"No," I breathed.

Fuck, I felt like a naughty schoolgirl.

"The man paid for services…" I'm sure my tongue had grown; I was stammering over my words.

"So, you fucked him." The words sliced through me; they were like venom on his tongue. He shook his head slowly in pure disgust, his tongue in his cheek as his eyes moved from mine and to the front of the car.

"No, no, no." I shook my head, my voice a plea. "Since we started our agreement, I said no to sex each time."

His head snapped round to me, his eyes softened, his jaw not so tight.

"Then what did he do?"

"He went down on me…" I felt dirty suddenly. How the fuck had I got so fucking caught up to let him do that to me?

Rhaegs fingers tightened around the steering wheel, his jaw ticking and clenching.

"Do you not understand that you're mine?" he snarled.

"It's work, you knew what I did for work before any agreement."

"You're a dancer, not a WHORE." He raised his voice as he spat the last word at me. It hit me like a knife, slicing me down to my core.

My hands trembled, my throat burned, and my eyes stung.

"Take me home," I whispered, my body turning as I faced out the window.

"My fucking pleasure," he growled.

The car engine vibrated through me as he sped out of the empty car park and down the streets towards my house. The car ride home was filled with deathly silence.

I wanted to speak, but what did I say? He only said the truth.

Sure, I could have lied. But lies always find a way of resurfacing eventually.

Pulling up kerbside, I looked up at my tiny house. It had only been a couple of days, but it felt like weeks since I had been here.

I turned back to look at Rhaegar, his eyes were fixed ahead.

That's that then.

Opening the door, I grabbed my bag from the footwell and closed the door behind me.

Rhaegs didn't stop to see if I got in the door, no, he floored it away quicker than a bat out of hell.

And I just stood on the pavement when the realisation hit me.

I was fucked.

Locking the front door behind me, I walked up the stairs quietly. I wanted a shower, I wanted to wash the night from my skin, but I was so exhausted. I dropped my bag at my feet and fell onto my hard, lumpy mattress.

This wasn't like the bed I was used to at Rhaegar's, he had goose filled pillows and a feather down duvet.

This was just shit compared to his.

But within minutes, I was gone.

-

I woke at eight, not hardly enough sleep but I was awake. I played last night over and over in my head. Could I have done it a little different? Sure, I could have been bouncing up and down on his cock when I delivered the news, or maybe I could have had his cock in my mouth and muffled it out to him.

My eyes were pinned to the artexed ceiling, my fingers knotting together and picking at the skin around my nails.

I hoped to God I hadn't fucked it up with Rhaegar. I was half tempted to message Shay and see if she wanted to meet, but she would be with her guy. There was always Wes, but I wasn't sure if I was ready to go down that road yet.

Puffing out my cheeks, I pulled the covers back from my bed, my feet hitting the un-treated floorboards.

It was cold.

Making my way down the small narrow hallway, I crept down the stairs as I didn't want to wake Mum. But when I looked in our small box kitchen, she was already awake.

"Oh, Sage." Her soft eyes found me, a small smile on her face.

"Hi, Mum." I tucked my hair behind my ears as I stepped closer to her.

"I didn't think you would be home yet… let me make you a tea." Her hands shook as she lifted the kettle.

"It's okay, I'll do it." I nodded, walking over and taking the kettle from her hand.

She stood, her back against the worktop as she

watched me.

"You okay?" I asked as I flicked the switch.

She nodded. "You look different."

"Do I?" I furrowed my brow as I threw two tea bags in the bottom of the cups, then added our sugar.

"Yeah, you look older somehow." She walked towards me and wrapped her arms around my waist.

I felt my heart burst, I couldn't remember the last time she cuddled me like this. Guilt slashed through me at the thought of leaving her here alone.

My eyes scanned the room, it wasn't as bad as I thought it would be. She actually managed, which I felt hurt me more. She could cope without me. Maybe I needed to give her a few days respite?

She took my face into her hands and kissed my forehead. "I missed you." She smiled before disappearing into the living room.

My heart swelled.

I finished the tea and followed her into the living room.

"Here we go." I smiled down at her as she took the cup from me. I sat on the tatty sofa; my legs curled under me as I sipped on my tea.

I sat for a while, trying to work out what I was going to say to her about having some time on her own, not that I had anywhere to go anymore. I am pretty sure me and Rhaegar are over.

"Mum…" I bit the bullet.

Her head turned to face me.

"How did you get on while I wasn't here?"

"I got on well." She smiled. "I felt like a had a little bit of purpose again."

My heart broke.

"Well, how would you like if I let you have some time to yourself a few days a week?" I asked, starting to see that little glimmer of hope.

"I would like that." She pushed her brown hair away from her face.

"Yeah?" I smiled at her, my fingers wrapping around my hot cup.

"Yeah."

"Okay, that's good."

"Where will you go?" she asked, her brows furrowing.

"I'll find something to occupy myself." It wasn't a lie, but it wasn't exactly the truth. I didn't know what I was going to do. But I would figure it out, I always do.

We sat in silence as we finished our tea, my mum standing and taking my empty cup out my hands and walking to the kitchen.

I snorted a laugh as I stood up and made my way upstairs.

I needed to dye my hair, the pink was fading, and I felt like a change. Plus, I needed to keep myself occupied so my thoughts weren't plagued with Rhaegs.

Sitting on the hard, cold floor of my bedroom, I looked in my little mirror and applied the dye. I had to wait for it to take, and pushing off the floor, I made my way back downstairs. There was a small bowl of washing up which I started to do. I just needed to keep busy.

There was a knock at the door, making me jump; I looked at the time. Who would be knocking at eleven?

"Mum, can you grab the door?" I called out, but no answer. Sighing, I pulled my gloved hands out of the boiling water and stormed to the door. Undoing the catch, I twisted the handle and pulled the door open. My eyes widened as I took in a handsome as ever Rhaegs.

"Rhaegar," I breathed. "What are you doing here?"

"Coming to see my girl." He looked at me as if I had spoken another language.

"Your girl?" I whispered as my fingers wrapped around the door. I took a moment to take in his appearance. He was wearing dark blue jeans and a tight fitted tee that clung to the muscles in his arms. His hair was pushed back and away from his face.

"Sage, did you call..." My mum's voice trailed off as she stood frozen behind me.

"Mum." I turned, taking her hand. She looked terrified. "This is Rhaegar."

"Her boyfriend." He smiled, but his smile faltered for a moment, his eyes flickering with something I hadn't seen before. It took him a moment for his eyes to move from my mum to me, his hands resting in front of him, overlapping each other.

Well, shit.

"Boyfriend?" my mum whispered in my ear, her hands on my shoulders as she gripped tightly.

"Seems that way," I whispered back. "Go sit down, Mum, I'll make a tea." I turned my head and placed a kiss on her forehead. She was much smaller than me, and I was short.

She scurried off into the living room, not looking back.

"She okay?" he asked, his eyes following my mum.

"Yeah," I breathed. "She is just very cautious of men." My eyes dragged up and down his body, my voice a little condescending.

"I get it."

"Do you?" My hand reached across to the door as I blocked Rhaegs' entry to my home.

"Sage..." His voice was low.

"Sorry, are you back to calling me my real name now? Or are you still stuck on whore?"

I didn't even care what I looked like. All around my hair line was black, and the back of my neck was also covered in dye.

I watched as his head dropped. I hoped he felt bad.

"Sage, I didn't mean it..." His voice was broken.

"No, you did," I said bluntly. "If you're big enough to say it, then be big enough to own up to it. Because, Rutherford, if you didn't mean it, you wouldn't have said it." My voice was icy.

I heard him sigh.

"I'm sorry."

And I don't know why, but I stepped aside and let him in. I dropped my eyes as he stepped towards me, and he stopped for a moment before gripping my chin and lifting it, so I had to look at him. "I really am." His lips moved closer to me as he planted a soft kiss on my cheek.

I felt my skin react, but it didn't react like it did before.

I moved away, walking him down the short hallway. My lungs breathed in the electric fire that was on but it wasn't cold.

Whenever she felt uncomfortable, she put the fire on.

"Mum, I'm just going to wash my dye off. Rhaegs will come up with me, okay? I'll boil the kettle… will you be okay?" My voice was soft and low.

Her eyes darted from me to Rhaegs before she nodded and faced the television again.

"Okay, I won't be long."

I turned on my heel, brushing past Rhaegs and into the small kitchen. I heard him approach, closing the space between us. He looked ridiculous in this tiny house. Six foot three of him and he was ducking as he walked under the door frames.

"Will you want one?" My tone was sharp.

He shook his head.

I would be lying if I said I didn't want to jump his bones, because I did. But I was pissed with him.

"Good, because I wasn't going to make you one anyway." I shrugged my shoulders and barged past him.

Climbing the steep stairs quickly, Rhaegs was on my tail. As soon as I was on the landing, he grabbed me by the wrist and pulled me to him.

"Are you planning on being petty for the rest of the day, kitten?"

"Absolutely," I breathed as he pushed me back into the wall.

"Is that so?" His lips hovered over mine.

Do. Not. Give. In.

I nodded.

His hands moved either side of my head, pressing flat against the wall. He trapped me.

"I've apologised, don't do this…" he pleaded.

"I'm not doing anything. I'm allowed to be pissed at you!" I snapped at him. "You knew what I did when we met, you knew what my job was, yet you treated me like most men do, like nothing more than the shit on the bottom of their expensive shoe. You called me a whore, Rhaegs…" My voice tremored. "It's not okay."

"I know it's not, Sage," he breathed, his eyes moved back and forth to mine. "I know this is no excuse, but the thought of another man's hands, mouth... just anything on you... it set me off. If I could go back in time, I would change my reaction."

I could hear the sincerity in his voice, his lips parted as he waited for my response.

"Okay," I breathed. "But let it be known, I'm still angry with you," I sniped.

"I know, kitten," he whispered, relief washing over him. Moving his hand from the wall and to my face, he cupped my cheek, lifting my lips towards his. My breath hitched as his lips slanted across mine. His kiss was soft and gentle. No tongues, no hunger. Just a simple kiss.

"I'm sorry," he whispered, his breath on my lips as he pulled away.

I nodded, rubbing my lips together.

"I really need to get this dye off..." My voice was low.

He stepped back, pushing his hand through his thick silver hair.

"Go sit in my room, I won't be long." Giving him a tight smile, I pointed to where my room was. I watched as he stepped over the threshold, his eyes widening as he took in my box room.

Welcome to poor-ville. You're going to hate it.

Walking back in the room, my hair dripping wet, my

eyes found Rhaegs. He was sitting on the edge of the bed, holding up the box that had the vibrator inside.

"Not even opened it?" He huffed, shaking his head from side to side. "Shut the door." His voice was low, his eyes burning into mine.

"Rhaegs," I breathed, my eyes pulling from him as I looked over my shoulder at the open door.

"Do it," he ordered. Looking back at him, I nodded. Stepping back, I shut the door gently.

He undid the box slowly, pulling out a nude vibrator with a small clit vibrator attached.

"Take your bottoms off, then sit on the bed, legs spread."

I inhaled deeply, the blood in my veins burned.

"I want you to forget about what he did to you last night, I want your mind filled with me and only me. Do you understand, kitten?"

I nodded, unable to speak. I licked my lips slowly as I stepped towards the bed.

Pushing my bottoms down and letting them fall to the floor, I sat on the edge of the bed. Rhaegs fell to his knees, pushing my legs apart before his fingers found my clit, rubbing gently.

I gasped, moaning softly as I watched.

"I want you to watch everything, do not take your eyes off of me," he whispered, his lips pressing to mine.

I moaned in agreement. His touch felt so good.

My mind filled with a haze of dark and stormy. Forcing my eyes shut for a moment, I needed rid of him.

"Look at me," Rhaegs snapped.

My eyes flicked open, my chest heaving up and down.

"You're so wet." He groaned, his fingers moving from my clit as they glided through my folds and straight into me.

"This is mine," he growled, his fingers pumping hard into me.

"Yes," I panted.

"Say it."

"Yours."

"Such a good girl." He licked his lips, his eyes pulling from mine before they fell to the large vibrator in his hand. Clicking the button, the toy hummed, the small vibrator attachment buzzing with it.

"I'm going to fuck you with this, I want your tight little cunt to come all over it, then I'm going to lick you clean." His tongue ran across his bottom lip.

Slipping his fingers from me, he ran my arousal that was on the tip of his fingers around the top of the lifelike vibrator. Letting it press against my clit for a moment, the pulse that crashed through me stole my breath.

"Oh," I cried out.

Rhaegs knelt up. "Quiet, kitten, we don't want your mum to hear you now, do we?" he whispered, pressing his free hand over my mouth.

Gliding the vibrator through my folds, he pushed the tip at my opening, teasing me by pressing the tip in then pulling it out.

Bastard.

"Rhaegs," I moaned, but it was muffled as my words were wasted.

He smirked, his eyes flicking down to my pussy.

"Watch me, princess." His lips curled as he pushed the vibrator into me. The vibrations changed, instead of a constant vibrate, it now pulsed.

"Oh, look at your greedy little cunt taking every inch of this vibrator." He tsked, licking his lips.

The clit attachment danced over my swollen nub, my skin covering in an ice blanket as the shivers crashed over me.

He pulled the vibrator out before pushing it back in, each time the small attachment hitting my clit.

This was hell.

Erotic hell.

I needed to come.

"See how frustrating it is?" His voice was low. "This is how you made me feel last night. This is how I felt knowing another man has touched and tasted what is mine." His voice was louder now, spite lacing it.

I see how this was going down.

My pussy hugged the vibrator as Rhaegs continued

fucking me with it. I watched… I watched as the nude shaft was pulled to the tip, covered in my arousal, before being pushed deep into me, hitting my G-spot over and over.

Once the vibrator was deep inside me, Rhaegs pushed one of the buttons and the pulses sped up, as did the small clit stimulator, my clit sensitive.

"Come, Sage," he commanded, gently pulsing the vibrator in and out of me.

And I did.

I came so fucking hard, my eyes stung from the frustration, Rhaegs' hand still clamped over my mouth as my moans drowned.

He played me.

Then he ate me like he promised.

Told you I was just the pawn in this wicked game.

CHAPTER
Sixteen

How do I look? Step mum in the making or?

Sitting at the large dressing table, finishing my make-up off, I was nervous. My eyes moved from the mirror to the toy train I picked up. Rhaegs told me Dex, his son, liked trains. He would spend hours playing with them. So what better way to get the kid to like you? Buy him toys.

A small smile crept onto my face before turning and finishing my look off with red lipstick. Pushing my hands into my hair, trying to keep the volume, I took a deep breath. Pushing off the chair, I stood and looked at myself in the full-length mirror.

My freshly dyed hair was jet black, sitting in loose curls. I wore a pillar-box red, tight fitting wrap dress. It clung to my curves, it's low-cut V-neck plunged, pushing my large breasts together. Perhaps my outfit was not the most appropriate choice for the occasion, but Rhaegs is my sugar daddy, not my husband. And Stepford wife is definitely not my style. And being honest? I chose the dress for Rhaegs, not his son.

Grabbing the toy train, I dropped it into my bag and walked down to meet Rhaegar by the front door. His beautiful eyes roamed up and down my body, as did mine on him. He looked handsome standing there in black fitted, skinny legged suit trousers and a crisp white shirt tucked in. He had the top two buttons undone, showing some of his sun kissed skin. Holding his hands behind his back, he leaned in and kissed me on the cheek.

I still hadn't quite forgiven him, but I'm sure by the end of the night he will have shown me just how sorry he really is. I blushed at the naughty thoughts of Rhaegar eating me, fucking me... showing me who is boss.

"What's got you blushing, kitten?" he whispered as he hovered his lips over mine.

"Just thinking of what you *might* do to me later." I breathed, my skin smothering in goosebumps.

"Oh, there is no might about it. I'll be doing it all." His teeth sank into my lips as he tugged. "Now come on, Dex will be at the restaurant." He kissed the side of my head, his arm wrapping around my waist as he pulled me to him. We walked quietly to the car; my eyes lighting up when I saw the Urus.

"Want to drive? Just a little step to show you how sorry I am." His hand dropped from me as he fished in his pockets for his keys, dangling them in front of me.

SOMETHING WORTH STEALING

"Of course!" I squealed, moving my feet quickly on the spot. I was so grateful that the car was automatic, I should be fine driving in my killer Jimmy Choos that Rhaegs bought me a couple of weeks back.

I rushed quickly to the driver's door, opening it and sliding in.

I was pretty sure I just orgasmed.

I was in heaven.

My fingers skimmed over the dash before they wrapped around the steering wheel.

"It suits you," Rhaegs said as he sat in the passenger seat.

"It does?" I smiled at him, my eyes glistening.

"It does." He reached for my hand, bringing it to his lips and brushing it across the back of my hand.

"Start her up," he coaxed, a glimmer in his eye, my hand still in his. I started the car, and the engine roared, vibrating through to my core.

"Oh my God." I giggled like a schoolgirl. I know people don't get it; they see it as *just a car*. But it was so much fucking more. People want to spend money on expensive bags, phones, shoes, and clothes. But spending that money on a car meant so much more. A car would always have your back if you looked after it. Not even people would do that.

Pushing it into sport mode, the exhaust went from hot to panty melting within seconds, the low rumble echoing in the underground car park.

"You ready, kitten?" he asked, a certain glee to his voice.

"I was born ready, baby." I winked, pushing my foot down on the accelerator and wheel spinning out of the car park.

Rhaegs was thrown back in his seat, his hand holding onto the handle above the door.

"Stop it!" I snorted a laugh.

"Fucking hell, Sage." His eyes widened as I slipped through the traffic.

"What's wrong, baby? Don't like going fast?" I teased, licking my top lip slowly.

"Only when I'm in control," he growled.

"You can show me just how fast you like to go once we are back home," I purred as I opened the car up on an empty strip of road. I wanted to see how close I could get to her top speed. One-ninety on a London Road was impossible, or was it?

"Sage, fuck's sake, you're gonna kill us!"

"Don't be silly." I shook my head, a laugh rumbling out of me. Easing off the accelerator, I slowed outside the restaurant. We pulled up outside The Gherkin.

I had seen it when travelling to work.

I had heard about it.

I had never been here.

"I think I'll drive home." Rhaegs smirked, leaning

over and kissing me on the cheek.

"Spoil sport," I teased, pouting my lips.

"Only joking, angel." His hand slipped in-between my legs, squeezing my bare thigh. "I want you to have it, you drive it so much better than me."

My eyes widened.

"No, I can't. Don't be silly." I shook my head from side to side quickly.

"I'm not. Take it, please." His voice was a plea. "A gift from me to you." His hand moved from between my legs, his thumb brushing across my bottom lip.

"Rhaegs, it's a two hundred grand car. I can't."

"You can, and you will. Not up for discussion, kitten." He shrugged his shoulders, grabbing my Chanel and opening the door then slamming it.

Holy fucking shit, he has just given me his fucking car.

What!?

Turning the engine off, I clambered out the car as best I could in my tight dress and killer heels. Locking the car behind me, I walked quickly to catch up with Rhaegs.

I would pay him back, somehow. I couldn't just accept it.

I would slip money back into his account without him knowing. Yeah. That'll work.

"Ready?" he asked, his fingers slipping through mine. I nodded. Taking a deep breath, I followed him into the building. The lift doors pinged open, and I held onto his hand tightly as he led the way.

"Why are you nervous?" He laughed softly.

"Because I am meeting your son, it's a pretty big deal."

I felt Rhaegs squeeze my hand in a reassuring way. I was anxious because Dex's mum was probably sitting there, and how awkward that the father of her son was bringing a sugar baby. I just wanted the ground to swallow me up.

I wasn't with my thoughts long when the doors pinged open, my eyes widening, my jaw dropping as I took in the beautiful restaurant. I stepped out the lift, still clinging onto Rhaegar. I wasn't paying much attention to anything else but the stunning views that were ahead of me.

"Wow," I whispered as my eyes scanned the room.

"Impressive, isn't it?"

I nodded, even though he wasn't looking at me. He was talking to the server.

Well, at least I could tick this one off the bucket list of *expensive places I would never go to... until I got a sugar daddy.*

Tick.

I followed Rhaegar through the busy restaurant, and I felt so small and out of place here. Not that you would think it with the designer clothes I was wearing. But under all of this, I was a little poor girl.

"Stop fidgeting, you look beautiful," Rhaegs whispered in my ear. "If you carry on, I'll lay you across our table and eat your perfect pussy."

I slapped my hand across his chest, and his arm wrapped around my waist as I giggled at his dirty words.

"Here we go, Mr Rutherford, your table." The server brought me back round to the room... my mouth was dry, my heart thumping in my chest.

What in the actual fuck?

CHAPTER Seventeen

Well, this is awkward.

Mr dark and stormy.

Holy.

Fuck.

Is it hot in here? Shit. I can't breathe. How bad would it be if I ran for a window and jumped? I would die.

Stupid girl.

The puzzle pieces started joining up. This is why he looked so familiar. He was a younger, hotter version of his dad.

"Sage, I would like you to meet my son…" Rhaegs ushered me forward. "Dex, this is Sage. My girlfriend."

My eyes flashed from Dex to Rhaegs.

This was not happening.

I watched as all six foot seven of him stood from the chair, pushing his button to his royal blue suit jacket up, his eyes burning into mine as he stepped towards me.

"What a pleasure to meet the girl that has caught my

father's heart. You must be something special." Dex winked at me, leaning in and kissing me on the cheek. My cheeks flushed a crimson red, his lips brushing against my ear, whispering, "Don't let on, little one. This can be our little secret for a while." Stepping back, he embraced his father. "So, when can I start calling her mum?" He winked at me before tipping his head back and laughing, Rhaegs joining in.

Dick.

I smiled tightly as Rhaegar pulled my chair out. Sitting down, I dropped my bag to the floor. How the hell was I going to get through dinner? I darted my hand out, grabbing the stem of a wine glass and drinking the cool water that was in. It could be toilet water for all I cared. I was burning up from the inside, and I felt like I was blushing all over my pale skin.

Could I sneak out?

Of course I couldn't.

I sat staring at Dex. Why did he have to be so handsome? All I could think about was his lips, his mouth, his tongue…

"Baby…" Rhaegs voice snapped me out of my fantasy.

"Sorry." I smiled, shuffling in my seat as I sat up.

"Drink?"

"Vodka cranberry."

Rhaegs nodded at the waiter, who scurried away

quickly.

"So..." Dex's voice ripped through me, the hairs on the back of my neck standing tall. "How did you two meet?"

I coughed, clearing my throat and drinking another mouthful of water.

"Through a friend." Rhaegar smiled at me before averting his eyes back to his son.

"That's nice, you two look good together." The corners of his lips curled. "I don't know why but you look familiar..." Dex said, leaning forward so his arms were on the table, his fingers reaching for a breadstick.

"Do I? I get told I have one of those faces." I shrugged, reaching for my own breadstick. I needed to keep my hands busy.

"Really?" His brow pinged high for a second before smoothing back out quickly.

I nodded, humming.

"Where do you work? Maybe I have seen you there?" He sat back in his chair; he was fucking loving this. He was fighting a smile. The bastard.

"I'm in-between jobs at the moment," I admitted. Okay, it wasn't the whole truth, but it also wasn't a complete lie.

I side-eyed Rhaegs. Would be so nice for him to jump in the sinking, burning ship with me.

"I see." His elbows rested on the table, his right hand

running over his left knuckles. "What would you like to do?"

"Have my own car garage." *Alert. Broken record. News flash, sweetie, it isn't ever going to happen. Especially if Rhaegs finds out his son's tongue was buried in your pussy last night.*

My heart skipped at my subconscious.

I wish I could take a photo of his face, because it would make a great picture. Surprise slipped over his normal façade.

"I wasn't expecting that." His voice broke, and his eyes softened as he stared at me.

"Not many people do." I shrugged. "People don't expect a girl like me to work in that industry."

"But like I told you a while ago, angel, the world is your oyster. If that's your dream, I will get you there, kitten." Rhaegs smiled, turning his body towards me, his hand cupping my cheek as he kissed me softly on the lips.

This felt wrong.

He smiled as he pulled away, twisting back in his seat.

My eyes immediately flicked to Dex. His whole demeanour had changed. His shoulders up and tense, his eyes glowering at me, his jaw tight and ticked.

"I have a friend that can get you a job." His voice was cold as he shot his words at me like bullets.

"Really?" My brows raised, my eyes on his as I

searched his face for any sign of the old Dex returning.

"Really." His low voice was gruff.

"Well…" I breathed, but before I could finish, he swooped in.

"I'll sort you out an interview for Monday, don't be late. It's my name on the line as well as yours."

"Dex, no need to be like that." Rhaegs shuffled in his seat.

"I'm not being like anything, just letting your little *kitten* know the deal."

And I've just come.

The way he said kitten.

Seductive.

Sultry.

Hot as fucking sin.

I wanted his mouth all over me.

Biting. Sucking. Licking.

The apex between my legs ached and I pressed my thighs together to try and suppress it, but it didn't work. I would do anything now to slip my fingers into my thong and relieve myself a little. But I couldn't.

Dex and Rhaegs were chatting about work. I didn't even know what they did, so it was easy to zone out of the conversation. I sat and people watched, it was one of my favourite things to do. You had all walks of life in here, and sure, I was one of them. But they didn't know that.

I was an elite compared to them. I was sitting with

two rich as fuck and sexy as hell men. Only needed two more and I had my own harem.

Oh.

A harem.

Or just a Dex and Rhaegar sandwich. Now that is a fantasy. These two men sending me to seventh heaven. Worshipping my body in ways it has never been worshipped before. They would bring me to new levels of pleasure. And I was here for it.

I wonder... I smirked at my ludicrous thoughts. There is no way Rhaegs is going to fuck me and let his son join in.

Nope.

Rhaegs is possessive as fuck, and Dex, well... he is Dex.

He is the type of guy that would burn the world down if anyone even stepped anywhere near me.

"Angel, are you okay?" I heard Rhaegs ask.

"Mmhmm." I nodded. "Oh, and Dex... I brought you something when your father insinuated that you were a little younger and told me how much you liked trains." I rolled my eyes, reaching into my bag and placing the black toy steam train on the table.

"Well..." Dex picked the small toy up in his large hands, holding it up to look at. "It's a lovely train..." He smirked, placing it back on the table.

"Can I have a bottle of champagne, please?" I asked,

smiling as the waiter approached the table.

"Of course. Dex, what would you like?"

"An old fashioned, please." He licked his bottom lip before pulling it in with his teeth.

"Can we order food? I am starved." I groaned a little louder than I wanted.

"Do you know what you want?" Rhaegs asked.

"Anything, honestly, I'm not fussy. You've been here before, right?" I leaned into Rhaegar.

"I haven't, no." He shook his head. "But Dex has." He cocked his head over in his direction.

Brilliant. Of course he has.

"What would you recommend?" I asked, wrapping my arm and hand around Rhaegs lower arm.

"The steak. You can't beat a bit of plump pink meat. All the juices running out as soon as you touch it..." His voice was raspy. "Melts on the tongue as soon as it hits it." He winked.

"Dex." Rhaegs shook his head.

"What? I'm talking about steak. Not my fault your mind went to the gutter." He tsked, laughing at his father as he looked over his menu.

"You knew what I was talking about, didn't you, Sage?" Dex's voice sliced though me.

I swallowed hard.

I am certain Rhaegar could hear my heart thumping in my chest. And if he couldn't hear it, he could see it.

I nodded quickly, not looking up from the menu.

"I think I am going to go for the chicken stuffed with ricotta, please." I shut the menu quick, pushing it into the middle of the table. I needed more alcohol.

The waiter arrived back with our drinks, finally.

Yes.

Alcohol.

Once our order was put in and light chatter resumed. I was feeling braver after each sip of drink, and more and more turned on towards Dex. How was I meant to stay away from him?

I couldn't.

It was impossible.

"So, Dex," I said loudly, taking my glass and washing down the nerves with a big gulp.

"Sage." His voice was unravelling what I felt for Rhaegs.

"Don't you have a girlfriend?" I asked, holding my glass as I swigged the champagne.

"Nope, but I have my eye on someone." He winked, smirking at me.

"How lovely." I couldn't help the roll of my eyes and shaking my head from side to side.

"The thing is, I know she has her eye on me too... problem is, she is with someone else, and it definitely isn't for love."

I choked on my mouthful of champagne at Dex's words.

What the fuck is he on?

He warns me not to say anything, yet he is dropping bombshells like that.

"You okay?" Rhaegs asks, but I can see the cogs turning in his head. His eyes are moving from Dex to me. Like he is trying to piece the missing pieces of a jigsaw puzzle.

"I'm fine, the bubbles went down the wrong hole." I nodded, reaching for a napkin and pressing it against my mouth.

Silence fell over the table while we waited for our food. Dex's eyes were on me, Rhaegs were on Dex, and mine were on my lap.

I let out a sigh of relief when the waiter placed our food down. Mine smelt divine. My mouth watered at the sight of food. Chicken, mash and green vegetables. My stomach growled in hunger.

I didn't wait, I dug straight in. I saw Dex smile as he watched me eat my food like I was some zoo animal. But I didn't care. I was too hungry to give a shit.

Once dinner was finished and my belly was full, I sat and listened to Dex and Rhaegs talk about their work.

I was intrigued.

"As I was saying to you yesterday. The club in Belgium would be perfect. Prime location, don't you think?" Dex asked Rhaegar as he sat back in the chair and sipped his old fashioned.

"What sort of club?" My mouth moved before my brain caught up. I felt so rude. Leaning forward, I grabbed my glass, knocking the remainder of it back before pouring another glass full to the brim.

"Gentleman's club," they both said in unison.

Those sneaky fucks.

"Oh, isn't that convenient." I slammed my glass down. That sentence was made for one man only. Dex fucking Rutherford.

"We don't own your club, well, not yet anyway. That was one of the reasons I wanted you out." Rhaegs' voice was cautious, and so it should be.

"That's why you look familiar!" Dex's voice boomed across the restaurant.

Rhaegar's eyes flew at Dex before they narrowed on me.

Petrol. Match. Fire. Me.

Grabbing Rhaegs' arm, I turned and pulled his mind away from what he was thinking. He knew. Of course he knew.

"Back on track." I clicked my fingers, so Rhaegs looked at me. "Why did you want me out? I wouldn't have done anything, just would have plodded along." I sighed.

"I know you would, but we don't want a girl that's with us to be used as collateral," Rhaegar said, and Dex narrowed his eyes on me.

"Why would I be collateral? I'm just a whore." My tongue was sharp as I spat my words at Rhaegar.

"Sage," he said in a warning tone.

"I'm just telling you the truth." I shrugged, reaching for another glass. My head was fuzzy, my words were a little slower as I swayed slightly.

"I think you've had enough," Rhaegs snapped, taking the drink from my hand.

"I'm fine!" I slurred a little.

"Dad." Dex's tone was harsh.

I jumped when I heard a phone make a noise.

"That's mine," Rhaegs said. Reaching into my bag, I pulled out Rhaegs' phone and saw *Shanay* on the screen.

I pinched my brows as I focused on the name.

Why was she calling him?

"Sorry, didn't mean to look," I admitted as I handed the phone to Rhaegs. *Yup, totally did.*

I watched as he stood from the table, listening to what was being said.

I tried my hardest not to look at Dex, because once I looked, I knew I would be gone.

Wanting to pat myself on the back after managing not to look at said 'hot-as-sin-fucker,' Rhaegs stepped back towards the table.

"I'm sorry, I need to go."

His voice was rushed as he kept his eyes on the floor.

"Why?" I asked, sipping my drink as I did.

"There has been an issue between Vance and Shay, she needs my help."

I sighed.

"Okay," I muttered. "Let me get my bag, I'll come with you." Bringing my glass to my lips, I drank a mouthful.

"No, no, it's fine. Stay here, finish your bottle then Dex can drive you home." He stepped behind my chair, his hands on my shoulders. Tipping my head back to look at him, I couldn't help the pout.

"Don't drink any more," he whispered against my forehead as his hand cupped my chin, holding me in place. Craning his neck, he placed his lips on mine and kissed me softly, his tongue slowly pushing its way in.

I moaned.

He was such a good kisser.

"I'll see you soon, kitten. I'll pick you up tomorrow, then I want you naked in my bed." He licked his lips, winking at me.

I smirked back, his lips pressing to my forehead before he straightened himself up, pulling the cuffs of his shirt down.

"Dex, put it on the company card." He nodded at his son, bending and grabbing the keys out of my bag and walking out the restaurant.

This could get bad.

Dex didn't move his eyes from me, they were dark and haunted. The once dreamy brown was now a daunting black.

Knocking my drink back, I grabbed the waiter as he walked past and ordered myself another bottle of champagne.

"Want another?" I asked Dex as I sat back in my chair, crossing my arms.

He shook his head, his index finger pressed to his lips, his eyes narrowing on me as his glass was held by his other three fingers.

Why did I find him so hot?

Why couldn't I just ignore the feelings that stirred deep in my stomach?

"Just the bottle for me, please." I gave the waiter a toothy grin as he nodded and walked away.

I watched as Dex's eyes fell to my chest, my arms still in place. I knew full well that I had a good bust, my cleavage pushing together so he could get an eyeful.

His tongue shot out, wetting his bottom lip, then pulling at it with his teeth.

"Are you playing a game with me, little one?" He leant forward, his glass hitting the table. His elbows were resting on the white tablecloth as he edged closer to me.

So what did I do?

I did it back.

Dropping my arms, I smirked at him and leant

across the table. Our faces were so close I could feel his breath on my skin. The alcohol laced it, intoxicating me. I needed more.

"No games here, what you see is what you get…" I licked my lips. "Well, in your case, what you don't get." I scoffed a laugh as I sat back, watching the young waiter popping the bottle and pouring it out for me. I thanked him and brought the glass to my lips as I took a sip, the bubbles slipping down my throat like pure silk.

"Will that be all?" the guy asked, his eyes glued to mine.

"That will be all." I nodded sweetly, my fingers tightening around the stem of the delicate champagne glass.

"Perfect." He hummed as he walked away.

"Don't be fooled, little temptress. If I wanted you, I would have you. I don't play games," Dex snarled at me, sitting back in his seat and a little more flustered than before.

I smirked, batting my eyelashes before my eyes burned into his.

"I don't think so." I winked. "The only person that gets to have me is your dad. He fucks me so good; I don't even think you could match up to him." I shrugged my shoulders then pushed myself away from the table.

"Please excuse me, I need to use the ladies." I reached down and grabbed my bag before turning on my heel and walking to the toilet. I rocked my hips from side to side, and my heel clicks echoed round the restaurant. I looked over my shoulder to see Dex's eyes on my arse. Flicking my hair over my shoulder, I laughed to myself.

Fucking cheek of him, thinking he can dictate when he wants me. Not going to happen.

Even if he did make my panties melt. I was horny as fuck and it was all for him, but I would never let him know.

Chapter Eighteen

Sugar Daddy's Son = panty melter in every sense of the word

I stood and looked at myself in the mirror, I was flustered. I wanted to say it was the champagne, but I knew it was Dex Rutherford that had me feeling like this. He made me feel so brazen and bold. I knew with him by my side I would be invincible. That's truly how I felt. Me and him against the world.

We would have it all.

The hot as fuck sex.

The lavish life.

The two perfect children.

I sighed, shaking my head from side to side as I rummaged in my bag for my red lipstick. Smiling to myself when I found it, I unscrewed the top and applied a fresh coating. Rubbing my lips together gently then pouting, I dropped the lipstick back in my bag and ruffled my fingers in my hair to try and give it a bit of a lift.

Turning the tap on, I washed my hands, jumping when I heard the ladies toilet door slam shut. For the size of the restaurant, the toilets weren't massive. I felt claustrophobic suddenly.

My eyes darted up, my head turning to look to the side of me.

And there he was.

Of course he was.

He strolled towards me like he owned the room, his eyes burning into my soul, one of his hands fisted deep in his suit pocket, the other just hanging by his side.

I swallowed down the butterflies and the soul consuming feelings he made me feel. Straightening myself up, I turned my head to look at myself in the mirror. I could do this. Of course I could.

"I think you're lost; this is not the little boy's room." I smiled as I cocked my head to the side, my own eyes trailing down my body in the reflection.

"Oh no, I'm not lost, little one." His lips pressed to the shell of my ear, his large tattoo covered hand splayed across my stomach as he held me against him. My breath hitched, my skin coming alive from his touch. Every inch of skin smothered in goosebumps, and I loved how he made me feel. I was like an addict, craving anything from him. I knew he was bad news; I knew he was dangerous, yet I couldn't stay away.

His lips pressed against the skin on my neck, his soft

lips trailing down as he stopped at my collar bone, and I felt the smirk on my skin.

I wanted to pull my eyes away, but I couldn't. I just watched.

"You see the thing is, Sage, you think by quitting your jobs, by running away from me that I wouldn't find you?"

I stilled, my heart racing in my chest.

"But that's where you're wrong. I would have always found you and look how easy it was. You're with my father. I get to see you whenever the fuck I want now. No more hiding, little one, I won't stop until you're mine." His lips kissed my skin again, and a shiver danced up my spine, my eyes fluttering shut.

"And you will be mine. Take that any way you want, either as a threat or a promise," he snarled, his hand that was once on my stomach was now skimming its way up my body. I could have stopped him at any minute, but I didn't. I wanted his fingers on me. He stopped at the base of my throat, wrapping his fingers around my neck.

"I would love nothing more than to make you come here, watching as my dick stretches you in the most delicious way. Feeling your tight little cunt squeeze my cock as I fuck you raw." He stopped for a moment, sinking his teeth into his bottom lip as if he was trying to restrain himself.

"Fuck, Sage, you would be so sore. I would be imprinted on your brain, on your skin…" His eyes flicked up and connected with mine. His fingers unwrapped from my throat, gliding up to my chin as he tipped my head back.

"Just remember this… When you go back to Daddy dearest's house" his lips nipped at my ear lobe before he continued "and he tries to fuck you, all you're going to see when you close those pretty green eyes is me. You're going to fantasise that you were coming all over my cock and not his." He smiled against my cheek. "I'll be the best fuck you ever have." He kissed where his lips were, pressing his hard cock into me.

Fuck.

I was horny. I couldn't stop myself, my hips grinding and rubbing over his bulge, a quiet moan slipping past my lips.

"Oh, little temp, don't tease me. I would destroy your perfect little cunt; I don't think you're ready for just how much I would ruin you."

His free hand grabbed my hips as I moved away from him, pulling me back to him so our bodies slammed into each other.

"You want it? I'll give it to you willingly, it's only you that is stopping what's inevitable between us." His words crashed through me.

I did want it.

I wanted him. So fucking much.

But I was with his dad.

SOMETHING WORTH STEALING

This was all fifty shades of fucked up.

"That's what I thought, little one, all mouth and no show... well, technically you do show it because your nipples are hard and pushing against the material of that sexy dress. Plus, I would bet you a thousand pounds that if I ran my finger through your pussy, you would be fucking dripping."

I swallowed hard; he was so right. I could feel how damp my knickers were, I was soaked.

"Let me see..." he whispered, both of his hands gliding down my curves and stopping at the hem of my dress. He looked at me in the mirror, his eyes searching for the go ahead. I didn't do anything, but he knew I wanted him to.

"Good girl," he groaned as he pulled my dress up over my hips, his fingers skimming gently over my skin, his fingertips trailing shapes as they made their way down in-between my legs. His hand tapped my inner thighs, my breath caught as I opened my legs for him. I couldn't take my eyes off the large mirror as I saw his fingers trail up the inside of my legs before skimming over the front of my nude thong.

I was ready to combust, my stomach coiled, I clenched my pussy as he hooked his finger round the side of my thong and pulled it to the side, his breath hitching as his greedy eyes fell to my bare pussy.

"Look how wet you are." He groaned as his finger

slipped between my folds, dipping into my pussy before he dragged them up and rubbed over my clit softly.

Moaning loudly, my fingers wrapped around the edge of the vanity unit that was in front of me, my head falling back onto his chest.

"I love being right." He grinned against the skin on my neck. As soon as the words were off his tongue, he pulled his finger from me and pushed them into my mouth.

"Taste yourself, just see how fucking good you taste." He watched as I sucked his finger dry. "That's why I am addicted to you, your taste is like nothing I have ever had before," he whispered, slipping his finger from my mouth and dragging it down my bottom lip, pulling it down and running it past my chin.

"Take them off, I want your knickers."

My eyes widened. All of a sudden, I was sober and no longer high off of him.

"No." I choked out a laugh, the shock lacing it.

"Don't make me rip them from you, Sage." His eyes darkened.

I turned slowly, holding the unit behind me. "You want them?" I questioned him, my voice shaky.

He didn't respond, he just stood in front of me like the fucking God he was.

I lifted myself up on the edge of the unit and sat, spreading my legs for him.

"Come and get them." I dropped my chin, my eyes burning on him as I waited.

He smirked at me, giving me a wink as he stepped towards me, and his large fingers grabbed my chin, tipping my head up. "Oh, baby, I like this side of you." His lips hovered over mine, my breath was on his face as I tried to control my heavy breathing, but it was no use. I was gone.

His lips pressed to my jaw, soft lips on my skin as his teeth grazed and nipped at my sensitive skin. But he didn't stop there. He moved his lips down my neck, brushing them across my collar bone then stopping them in-between my breasts, and this time, he licked and sucked on my skin… I was sure he marked me.

I was going to be in so much trouble. But I didn't care.

He moved across to my other breast, sucking and licking and leaving his mark.

I watched with eager eyes to see what was going to happen next. His beautiful brown eyes found mine as he fell to his knees, his hands gripping onto my bare thighs as he spread my legs further.

"I want nothing more than to eat your pussy." His voice was low as his eyes stayed on mine. "But if I start, I won't stop. Your pussy is like a drug, and I am already addicted." He groaned, one of his hands moving to the material that was covering me from what he wanted.

What I wanted.

He pulled my thong away from me in such a teasingly slow manner. Once they were off, he stood, then scrunched my thong in his hand and brought them to his nose, inhaling deeply.

"These will keep me going until I can bury my tongue inside of you to get my hit." His voice was slow, his eyes hazy.

There I was, panting, legs spread, pussy wet and horny as fuck.

I was ready for him. I didn't give a shit now, he could take me, own me and completely ruin me.

But it wasn't going to happen tonight. Because as soon as his hungry eyes fell on me, there was a loud bang on the door.

"What a shame, little one, you'll just have to get yourself off tonight seeing as Daddy dearest won't be there..." He tsked, shaking his head then stuffing my thong into his pocket. He held his hand out for me take. It took me a moment to come round from whatever the fuck I was high on.

Bang bang bang.

My head turned to face the door.

Shit.

Sliding off the unit, I pulled my dress down, grabbed my bag and took his hand.

Unlocking the door, he opened it, looking at the

woman who was standing with her jaw on the floor. He smirked, tightening his grip. He stopped beside the woman, lowering his lips to her ear.

"I would avoid the vanity unit if I were you, I just fucked her on it." He spoke quietly, but loud enough for me to hear.

Oh my fucking God.

I blushed a crimson red, my skin on fucking fire from the embarrassment. We were already on the move by the time the poor woman registered what Dex had just said.

Pulling my hand from his, I stormed towards the table, my eyes narrowing on the receipt. Good. He had paid.

I turned on my heel, pushing past a smug as fuck Dex as I walked for the elevator.

I was fucked.

Chapter Nineteen

Yup, my stalker and sugar daddy's son has taken my knickers.

I stood outside, my eyes darting up and down the street, praying and hoping a taxi was going to fly by at any moment. But of course, I am Sage James. I'm not that lucky.

I heard his shoes hit the concrete before I saw him. Turning my head quickly to look over my shoulder to see Dex standing there, his eyes devouring me on the spot.

"I'm waiting for a taxi," I snapped at him, my eyes back on the road.

Please, if someone is looking over me, let a taxi arrive at any second.

"Sure you don't want to jump in with me? My father did say I had to take you home." He closed the gap between us, his warm breath on the back of my neck. It was a mix between whisky and mint. A weird but wonderful combination.

"My car is just around the corner, I would rather you ride home with me, and I am sure my father would feel the same." His hands moved around my waist, holding me up. "I promise I won't touch you until you're begging me..." he whispered, licking the shell of my ear.

"Fine." I groaned, grabbing his hands and peeling them off my skin. I couldn't have him close to me, I needed to put some space between us. Turning on my heel, I walked towards the crossing.

"Wrong way, little one!" Dex shouted out. I rolled my eyes, cussing him under my breath.

"Coming!" I called back, walking back towards him.

"Stubborn little thing, aren't you?" He nudged into me, lacing his fingers through mine. Gasping at the shock that just bolted me, I pulled my hand out.

"Stop fighting it," Dex growled, grabbing my hand again.

"I'm not fighting anything," I sulked, not looking in his direction. I would rather look at my pretty shoes hitting the concrete.

"And a liar, as well as stubborn." I heard the snort of a laugh that left him. I couldn't help the small curl at the corner of my lips, but I wouldn't show him that.

"There she is." Dex dropped my hand, fishing for his keys. My eyes lifted from the floor as I looked up, and holy fucking shit... a Lamborghini Aventador. Her bodywork was covered in the same grey as the Urus.

This car.

Oh my God.

I did not expect Dex to have a car like this.

"Oh my God," I breathed out, Dex stepping forward and opening the suicide doors.

"Now I know you like cars, I wanted to show you my girl." He winked, holding my hand as I stepped down into the car.

"She is a beauty." I hummed as my fingers skimmed across the dashboard.

"She is." He dropped down, crouching, his fingers trailing across my bare skin. "And I can't wait to fuck you in here." He licked his lips, standing and shutting the door down.

The flame in my cheeks showed him just how much I wanted to be fucked in here. But this little game we were playing had to stop. I wasn't just playing with fire, no, I was dancing in the flame.

Sucking in my breath, I averted my thoughts to the car. This is what I wanted in my life. Cars like these that I could spend all day with. Sad, I know. The interior was every man's wet dream. Well, in my case, a girl's wet dream too. The steering wheel alone was hot as fuck. I wanted to skim my fingers over the badge, because let's be honest, I would never actually own a car like this. I was grateful that the centre console ran down from the dash and sat high as it sloped into a console, putting something between me and Dex.

I watched as Dex slipped in the car elegantly.

"I would have thought a man of your stature and build would have gone for something a little... bigger." I smirked as he shut the suicide door. "Is it true what they say? Guys who buy flash cars have small dicks?" I snorted. "You know, overcompensating." A laugh bubbled out of me.

I felt Dex's icy glare boring into the side of my head. Covering my mouth with my hand, I needed to stop myself from bursting into a fit of giggles.

"Oh, little one, no overcompensating here. My dick will rip you to shreds, and now I can't wait to show you just how big I am," he snarled. His eyes moved from mine and to the buttons that were sitting between us. His long index fingertip swirled around the red case that covered the start button, his eyes flicking across to look at me. He was trying to tease me. Bastard.

His finger dipped into the small hole, teasing before pulling it out and skimming around the casing again.

My breath hitched.

Turning his finger over and curling it, he flipped the switch open and pushed the button, starting the engine.

"Even cars like to be turned on, just got to find the right button to push." He winked before looking in his wing mirror and pulling out. The car fucking roared down the quiet side streets of London.

My fingers gripped into the side of the leather seats.

This car wasn't just fast, it was fucking lethal. A six-point-five litre with a V-twelve engine. But fuck did he drive it well. To be honest, this car wasn't made for roads like this, it was made to be cruising through the quiet roads of France, or a fucking grand prix track.

I felt the spike of adrenaline course through me, my skin prickling with excitement. Letting go of my grip, I started to relax. Dex knew how to drive this car.

He bombed across tower bridge, my eyes lighting up at the iconic tourist spots. Not that I spent too long looking because before I knew it, we were sitting at a red light.

Joys of London.

"Have you ever driven this car out of London?" My brows were sitting high as I looked at him.

"Yeah." He laughed. "A few times. I hardly drive her to be honest. But I knew you liked cars, so I wanted to bring her for your sake." A small smile played across my lips.

"How did you know? I only told you tonight..." I shook my head as my eyes fixed on the red light, counting to see how long it would take to change.

"Oh, Sage, give me a little credit, baby." His voice rumbled through me. "I know a lot about you... I've been studying you for a while shall we say..." His eyes averted from me and back to the road as he crawled through the lights.

"Stalker." I rolled my eyes, looking out the window.

"Don't be like that, baby." His large hand came across and squeezed my bare thigh. "You love it." His voice was a whisper.

I didn't respond. I kept mute until we got home. Being that close to him was suffocating, it was like he sucked the air out my lungs, causing me to gasp for breath.

My heart raced as we pulled down the road that led to my house. I felt my skin prickle, and my palms started sweating as he slowed the car outside my front door.

Turning slowly to look at him, my brows furrowed. He didn't look at me, a boyish grin spread across his face as he cut the engine, the roar quietening instantly.

"How did you know where I live?" My voice faltered slightly.

"I just do." His brown eyes finally met mine, my heart thumping against my chest.

"Convenient." I rolled my eyes, shaking my head from side to side. "Thanks for dropping me home." I gave a small smile; I tightened my grip around my bag. Dex was out of the car quickly and opening my door. He held his hand out for me to take. I didn't want to take it, but being honest, I don't think I would have got out of this car without him. It was low to the floor, plus wearing heels and a tight dress wasn't working in my favour at the moment. Pushing my thighs together as I clambered out the car and being mindful that I was commando. That was a task in itself.

"Thank you for the ride." I smiled at Dex, dropping my hand from his. "I got it from here." I stood, turning to face him.

"Nope, I'll walk you to your door." He winked.

Course he would.

"I'll see you soon, Sage." His voice was low as it rumbled through me, each of my nerve endings buzzing from his words.

"I have no doubt about it, stalker." I winked, slowly turning and walking the steps to my door. I fought the urge to look back as I let myself inside my house and closed the door quickly.

I pressed my back against it, my hands pressed to the door as I tried to still my racing heart.

It took me a few minutes to calm myself down. Locking the door behind me, I reached for my phone and told Rhaegs I was home. I waited a minute or two, but I had no response.

Tiptoeing upstairs, I got myself undressed and ready for bed. I felt exhausted suddenly.

My dreams were filled with a dark eyed, tatted hunk who seemed to invade more than just my dreams.

-

Four weeks had rolled round quickly. I missed working at the club, but I was kept busy with Rhaegar. I was a little bummed out that my interview was pushed back, Dex didn't say why, just told me that he would be in touch with a new date. I had to cover a couple of shifts at The Coffee Run after Wes begged and begged me. To be honest, it was welcomed. I felt like I was going brain dead being a stay-at-home sugar baby. Rhaegs seemed disinterested over the last week, as if his mind was elsewhere and like he was too busy for me.

I felt stupid even thinking it because the sex was still phenomenal. Well, it was up until a week ago when Rhaegar suddenly stopped wanting sex with me. Every time I tried to initiate it, he pushed me away with some fob off excuse, but what I didn't get was he was still happy to go down on me at every given chance. I felt like we still had that sexual connection, but it felt as if everything else was fizzling out around us.

Pushing the intrusive thoughts from my mind, I finished getting ready. It seemed that everywhere I had been lately, Dex was. Whether it was just a pop in to his father's apartment or a needed cup of coffee, you name it, he was there. The truth was, I liked it. I felt some sort of comfort knowing he was there, always a few steps behind me as such.

I hadn't felt like I was being followed for a while, no more strange shadows lurking, and I was grateful for that. Maybe it was all in my head? Maybe Wes was right with the tiredness? I was working all the hours under the sun with little sleep or food.

Running my fingers through my hair, I broke through the small knots. The sun had been shining all day which made me happy, not so much my almost translucent skin but the sun always felt good on my skin. I sat down on my bed and slipped my feet into a pair of black heels before standing and giving myself an approving nod of my outfit. I had a short, thigh length black racer back dress on. It hugged my curves, and I was hoping Rhaegar wouldn't be able to keep his hands off of me.

After mine and Dex's little encounter in the bathroom at the restaurant, we hadn't had the chance to be near each other. One night when we were at dinner at his dad's, he tried to corner me in the hallway while Rhaegar was on a business call, but I ducked under his arms and hid in the lounge and staying in Rhaegar's sight.

I couldn't keep playing with fire. We had already had too many close encounters and I didn't want to fuck what I had with Rhaegar up.

Dex was a bad idea.

A hot as fuck bad idea.

But I had to steer clear.

Grabbing my bag, I kissed my mum goodbye and ran for the door. It wasn't a Rhaegar day, but I needed to make sure he was okay. He was leaving my messages on read, and when he did reply or answer his phone, he was cold and blunt. It made me anxious in thinking that I had upset him somehow and I had no clue why. Was it because me and Dex were growing closer as friends? Shaking my head, I stood kerbside, waiting for the taxi I had ordered. I missed driving. I hated getting taxis, but I didn't have the car. The Urus stayed at Rhaegar's, and even though it was technically mine, I couldn't park it here. I would come down to my car on bricks.

Smiling as my taxi rolled to a halt, I jumped in and gave Rhaegar's address. I don't know why but I felt nervous or was it excitement? No, it was definitely nerves.

The taxi ride was short, the roads quiet, we were just before rush hour which worked well. The taxi driver slowed outside Rhaegar's apartment, and throwing him the cash, I climbed out the car and began walking towards the elevator. I felt a hand on my lower back as I stopped outside the elevator. I ignored the buzz that ran through me, my eyes wandering to the side to see Dex standing next to me, smiling down at me. I was trying to push the wanting feeling down, the crave and hunger that he caused. I had to.

"What are you doing here?" I asked as I pushed the elevator button, and the doors pinged open instantly. Stepping in, I broke the contact and stood with my back against the handrail of the elevator, my eyes on the doors as I watched them close.

"Just thought I would pop in to see Daddy dearest. What about you? I didn't think Thursdays were a sugar baby day." His tone was mocking.

I rolled my eyes. "I wanted to come and see him, I am allowed to see him on other days," I snapped.

Dex stood beside me, trying to hide his smirk, his hands in front of him.

My heart raced having him this close to me.

"Do you know how much I want to kiss you?" he whispered; I could feel his eyes on me. But I didn't give in. I didn't turn my head to look at him, nope. I stayed staring at the doors in front of me. Because I knew that if I looked at him, I would kiss him. And kissing Dex was not good, for either of us.

My heart raced as the doors pinged open, I just wanted to get to Rhaegs so I could get rid of Dex now. Just that short lift ride with him had been too much.

"Rhaegs!" I called out, my heels clicking against the high gloss tiles. I pulled my black hair over my shoulder, looking at Dex as I did.

"Maybe he isn't here?" I said quietly as I walked into the empty dark lounge.

"His car is here, maybe he is in his office?" he suggested.

"Stay down here, lemme go check the bedroom," I said quietly as I kicked my heels off and headed towards the stairs.

SOMETHING WORTH STEALING

Dex was behind me, of course he was.

"Why can't you listen to a simple instruction?" He infuriated me. I could feel my blood boiling as I climbed the stairs one at a time, slowly. Something felt off. I could feel it in my gut. Something wasn't right.

"Because playing by the rules is boring."

I rolled my eyes at his childish comeback.

Tiptoeing along the hallway, I could hear Rhaegs growling. I stilled outside the room, Dex was next to me, his sorry eyes on mine. If I didn't know what was going on, I did now with that one look in Dex's eyes.

I inhaled deeply, pushing the door open hard so it smashed against the wall. Storming into the room, there Rhaegs was, laying on his back with motherfucking Shay bouncing up and down on his cock.

My eyes widened, my mouth agape, and my legs buckled. I reached out to grab the wall, but Dex was there, holding me up, and at this moment, I was so glad he was.

I watched as Rhaegar's eyes widened when he noticed it was me.

"Sage, kitten." His eyes darted from mine to Shay's.

Shay turned her head, her eyes finding mine as they engulfed in guilt. Rhaegs pushed Shay off him, grabbing the white bedsheet and wrapping it around the lower part of his body, trying his best to cover himself up.

He stepped towards me, but I shook my head. My throat burned; the lump lodged in my throat.

I knew we weren't official as such, but it still fucking stung. I was his, sure, I have done a pretty shitty job... his son is my fucking kryptonite.

"Don't you dare take another step," I warned Rhaegs, making him stop dead in his tracks.

"Kitten, let me explain..." His head turned and looked over his shoulder at a clambering Shanay. "It isn't what it looks like."

"No?" My brows furrowed. "Because I'm sure you were fucking her, or more to the point, she was fucking you... pretty shit might I add." My voice was full of venom. He lost his grip on his towel, letting it slip slightly.

"Oh wow..." I stepped out of Dex's grip, hysteria ripping through me. "So you won't come in me because of some fucking issue, but it's fine to fuck her, who let me add is probably infested in all sorts of STD's, without a condom?"

I was fucking angry.

He never told me why he did that, but it fucking stung that he chose not to wear one with her, but with me, he wouldn't do anything without one.

Rhaegs dropped his head in defeat. "Because of Dex's mother, she trapped me... and I... I couldn't have that happen again... but with Shay, tonight... it all just got a little heated."

"You're an arsehole." I closed the gap between us and slapped him around the face hard but instantly regretting it as my hand stung. Rhaegs' head whipped round, his hand shooting out and grabbing my throat as he pinned me against the wall.

He didn't have a chance to do anything more, Dex was there, grabbing his dad and throwing him to the floor.

"Keep your fucking hands off of her," Dex's voice rumbled. Shay screamed, and I stood fucking anchored to the floor.

What in the actual God was going on? I wanted to move, I wanted to run out, but I couldn't. Dex was on top of his dad, laying punch after punch into his face.

Adrenaline spiked through me, waking me the fuck up from the haze I was clouded in.

"Dex!" I screamed, running at him and trying to pull him off. "Please, Dex..." I sobbed as I fell to the floor.

It was too much.

It had gone from ten to a hundred real fucking quick.

"Sage?" Dex's voice hummed through me as he pulled me to him.

"Please stop fighting," I wailed.

"We've stopped, we've stopped," he reassured me, his arms squeezing me tight. Pulling away from him and wiping my black-rimmed eyes, I looked over at Rhaegs.

His nose was a little bloody, but apart from that, he didn't have a mark on him.

"Sage, can we talk?" Rhaegs kneeled up, his sheet wrapped tightly around him.

"I don't want to talk." I shook my head from side to side. "What is there to talk about? You're shagging my friend." Shrugging my shoulders, the words that came from my mouth tasted bitter. Well, I suppose that's because they were. They were real fucking bitter.

"It's not like that," he repeated himself.

I held my hand up. "Please, give me a little credit… stop bullshitting me… I can't do this." My voice was exasperated. I stood up on shaky legs, holding onto the wall for support as I walked out the room. I didn't get very far when I heard Dex rip into Rhaegs. Sliding down the wall, I couldn't help but listen.

"You're a real prick, do you know that?" Dex growled. "No wonder Mum left you, and there you are giving your bullshit story that she trapped you? More like dumped your arse when she found out how much of a cunt you were."

I gasped. I shouldn't be eavesdropping, but here I am.

"That's the thing, Dex, she spun you a web of lies," Rhaegs spat out. "She was the one acting like a whore, she wasn't interested in you. But then again, Mummy dear done such a good job of fucking you up…" Rhaegs stopped for a moment. My heart was drumming in my chest. "I guess the apple doesn't fall very far from the tree… your mother was a whore, and now you're chasing after one."

My eyes stung with tears. Why was he being so cruel?

"Says the guy who paid for her and who was, only a few moments ago, balls deep in another whore yourself," Dex spat. Did he think I was a whore? I mean, who am I kidding... I was. Or am.

I threw my head into my hands.

"Do you think I am stupid, son? Do you not think I knew what was going on?" Rhaegs' voice grew louder. "Anyone could see it from a fucking mile off, you, pining and simping over what was mine."

"She was never yours," Dex argued back.

"Oh, you silly boy. She was. She still is. She signed a contract."

Fuck, the contract. He isn't going to pay me.

"What's the matter, son? Did she not tell you about the contract while you were fucking her?"

I pushed off the floor and stormed back into the room. I wasn't having that. No way.

"We haven't slept together!" I screamed. "I, unlike some people, didn't break the contract," I seethed, my eyes narrowing on Rhaegs.

"Well..." Dex's voice went higher pitched. "Technically you did."

I snapped my head towards his direction, glowering at him.

"What the fuck are you on about?" I screwed my nose up. "We didn't sleep together. The only person I have slept with is Rhaegs."

"What about at the club? You had your pussy fucked by my tongue." Dex's eyes darkened, his tongue darting out and licking his lips.

"That was work. Rhaegs knew what happened at work." I was trembling, my voice was quivering. It didn't matter how much I tried to stop it, I couldn't. I was angry.

"Was he the guy from your last day at work? Who paid you for hours on end?" Rhaegs bellowed, towering over Dex.

"That was me." He fucking stood there, grinning like a Cheshire cat and proud as fucking punch.

Rhaegs flew at him, pushing him against the wall, his forearm pushing into Dex's throat.

And what did Dex do? Just fucking smiled.

"Her pussy was worth every fucking penny. How does it feel to have lost her, aye, Dad?"

Rhaegs pushed harder into his throat.

"Go on, do it. Kill me," Dex growled. "Or would you rather just break me? Like you broke Mum, pushing her to overdose!"

I froze, a chill running up and down my spine, and my blood ran cold. I had to move my eyes away from what was happening and focus on Shay. She was just standing there, completely gobsmacked.

"What's the matter, Father? Cat got your tongue?" Dex snarled, pushing Rhaegar off him and storming out the room.

SOMETHING WORTH STEALING

The room fell eerily quiet, the tension thick and continuing to grow.

"Shay, I think it's best you go..." Rhaegs didn't even finish his sentence, she was up and out of the room like a bat out of hell.

I watched a defeated Rhaegar walk over to the bed before he sat on the edge. His head fell into his hands, he didn't move.

I stood for a moment, and part of me wanted to go over there and comfort him, but the other part of me couldn't give two shits.

Sighing, I turned on my heel and walked towards the door.

"I'm going to go..." My voice was barely audible, cracking at each word.

"Sage..." Rhaegs called out. Looking over my shoulder, his brown eyes met mine. "I'm sorry."

I gave him a weak smile before walking out the door. I didn't go to find Dex, I didn't give two shits about Shay.

I just needed out.

Grabbing my bag, I headed for the door.

I didn't look back.

I was done.

CHAPTER
Twenty

When it all goes to shit, what do you do? You run.

I half expected Dex to be running behind me, but he was nowhere to be seen. They had both crossed a line tonight. I was infuriated with them. Pulling my phone out, I tapped a message to my mum; I wanted to let her know I was staying at Wes's.

Or so I hoped.

I called his phone once, twice, three times before he answered.

"Sage, I'm kind of busy. What are you calling me for? Is everything okay?" He was groggy. He wasn't the best when I interrupted him, or more so when I interrupted one of his booty call sessions.

"Can I come stay with you? I need to lay low…"

"Fine. Let me get rid of Edward." I heard his deep huff.

"Thank you," I whispered, cutting my phone off. I

kept my head down and walked. I walked until my feet were blistered and my toes were numb from the heels, but I didn't stop. I just wanted to get to Wesley's.

An hour had passed when I turned up on his doorstep. I felt battered and bruised.

Pressing the buzzer on his flat, he unlocked the door instantly.

I could just about smile when I saw him. He was wrapped in a duvet with the most ridiculous bag puss slippers on.

"Hey, peach." He sighed, holding his arms out for me to fall into. He was wearing an old faded *Busted* tee. Man, we loved that band.

Shutting and locking the door behind him, he led me towards the lounge area.

"Want to talk about it?"

I shook my head from side to side.

"Let me get you some clothes." Wes disappeared into his bedroom, and I stood in the middle of his small living room just staring into oblivion.

How the fuck did I get here?

I should have never listened to Shanay. I should have steered clear. Who the hell in their right mind would sign a fucking contract to become someone's sugar baby?

Me.

That's who.

And why the fuck did this all hurt so much? I felt the

tears prick my eyes. I had tried my hardest to keep them in, but I couldn't anymore. So I let them fall.

Wes re-appeared holding a faded dark grey *Busted* tee.

I laughed through a sniffle, palming my tears away from my blotchy cheeks. "How many of them have you got?"

"You don't want to know." He smiled, wrapping his arms around my shoulders. "You take my bed; I'll sleep on the sofa…"

My eyes widened as I shook my head from side to side quickly. "No, no, Wes. I'll take the sofa."

He held his hand up and closed his eyes. "I will not argue with you on this, get your hot little tooshie into that bed, now." He closed his hand into a fist and pointed towards the direction of his bedroom.

I smiled, clinging onto the tee he gave me and walked towards him.

"There's a good girl, we can talk in the morning. I don't have work till three." He placed a kiss on my forehead. "Let me get some snacks and we can watch a film." He beamed before disappearing into the kitchen.

I sighed and sunk into his bed. *What the fuck was I going to do?*

Wes was back within seconds, with a handful of goodies that he dumped in front of me.

"How to Lose a Guy in Ten Days?"

SOMETHING WORTH STEALING

"Sounds perfect," I said quietly. I felt numb.

Wes smiled, clicking the TV on and pressing play on the film. I didn't want to watch it, but I also didn't want to be alone.

Once the film finished, Wes wished me goodnight and closed the door behind him. I would be lost without Wes.

Lying in bed, my mind started racing with questions that I didn't have the answers for. Then came the intrusive thoughts that consumed me.

Will Rhaegar still pay me?
Will I see Dex again?
Will Dex still be willing to let me start my new job?
Please let me see Dex again.
I'm going to have to go back to the club.
What about The Coffee Run?
Will I see Dex again?
Will I see Dex again?
Repeat.
Repeat.
Repeat.
I'm a failure.

Grabbing a pillow from beside me, I smothered it over my face. I needed to quiet my mind, I just needed to sleep.

Tomorrow is a new day. Well, technically, it's already

tomorrow.

Ugh.

Lifting the pillow, I stared at the ceiling. I watched Wes's star ceiling twinkle above me. Hundreds of small LED lights all flashing and dimming at different times.

It was calming. It was beautiful.

I started counting them. One, two, three... thirty-one, thirty-two, thirty-three...

And I was gone.

My dreams were filled with Dex and Rhaegs. Screaming, fighting and sex.

Hot, passionate sex.

I was awoken by the smell of coffee wafting through my nose, and it was enough to wake my grouchy soul from her not so peaceful slumber. Opening my eyes slowly, I winced at how bright the room was. Wes was sitting on the edge of the bed, his legs crossed underneath him.

"Good morning, my little ray of sunshine." Wes beamed at me.

"How are you so happy?" I groaned, sitting up and shifting towards the headboard so I was leaning against it.

"I got a good dicking last night." He shrugged his shoulders, handing me a cup of coffee which I gladly took.

"A night of good dick brings a day of content." He smiled proudly.

A deep belly laugh came out of me.

SOMETHING WORTH STEALING

Oh, Wes.

My beautiful red-headed friend.

Bringing the cup to my lips, I took a mouthful of the coffee he made. It was so good.

"Ready to talk about it?" he asked, sipping his own coffee and looking at me over his cup.

"I suppose, it's so stupid though." I shrugged. I looked at my feet, they were blistered to shit.

"Nothing is ever stupid." He shook his head.

I inhaled deeply, puffing my cheeks out with my breath before blowing it out.

"Where do I begin…" I laughed, but it was nerves. Crossing my legs under the duvet, my coffee sat in the middle of them, my head falling forward as I looked at the caramel-coloured liquid.

"From the beginning, I guess?" Wes's smart comment made me smile. He smiled back at me, reaching across and rubbing my leg through the duvet.

Inhaling deeply, my eyes were on him. I felt anxious, but I had no need to be. Wes was amazing, he never judged.

"So, I was working at the club a couple of months ago and Shanay…" I had to stop for a moment, there was a bitter taste in my mouth at her name.

"Eww." Wes turned his nose up. "I never liked her. Sorry, babes, but I didn't." He shook his head in complete disgust.

I scoffed a laugh, licking my lip as my smile grew.

"Anyway" I lifted my eyebrows "she said that she had a sugar daddy."

He gasped, his hands flying to his mouth. "No fucking way!" He was gobsmacked.

I just nodded, swallowing the large apple like lump in my throat back down.

"She was telling me how great it was having an older man look after you. You laid down your rules, your terms and conditions etcetera…" My palms were sweaty. Rubbing them on his duvet then bringing my cup to my lips with trembling hands, I took a mouthful, trying to wet my tongue.

"Go on…" He tilted his head down, but his eyes stayed pinned to mine.

"She asked if I wanted her to pass my number on to one of her sugar daddy's friends, so of course, in the moment, I said yes." Wes's eyes widened, his lips parting ready for him to speak, but I shook my head, placing my finger over my lips.

"A couple of weeks went by without a word. At first, I wasn't keen and thought I had made a massive mistake, but then he messaged me." I sighed, I couldn't help but feel hurt when I thought back to mine and Rhaegs' first date. "He came and picked me up that night, we went for dinner and then back to his. I was hypnotized by him, addicted to him somehow, even though I had only just met him. Once we were back at his, we could have easily fucked, the tension was that strong, a connection like a forcefield surrounding us and pushing us closer together. But we didn't. He made me sign a contract stating certain terms that *neither* of us were to see other people. I was still able to keep my jobs, he still went about his day doing whatever the fuck old, rich men do."

Wes's perfectly shaped brow pinged up. "How old?"

I rolled my eyes, leaning across and swatting him in the arm.

"Things were good, and the sex was off the charts." I fanned myself with my hand as I felt my skin burn. "Then it all got a little more complicated…"

"Give me your cup." Wes stood from the bed abruptly, holding his hand out. I furrowed my brow, looking at him confused as I handed over the cup. He smirked then turned on his heel and disappeared.

I just stared at the door until he returned with our cups, both refilled with coffee.

"Sorry, we needed more, do continue." He winked as he handed the cup to me then waved his hand at me to continue my story.

"You're enjoying this, aren't you?" I pouted at him, my fingers wrapping around the hot cup of fuel.

"Just a little bit." He smirked, holding his thumb and index finger up, showing a gap.

Tosser.

Taking a mouthful of my coffee, I hummed in appreciation. "Okay, where was I?" I sat for a moment, replaying our conversation over in my head. "Oh yeah, it got complicated…"

"This intrigues me." Wes wiggles his eyebrows.

"Shh." I shook my head. "Anyway, I was at the club, doing my set. Rhaegar said he wanted to come every night I was working…"

"I'm sorry, but his name is Rhaegar?" He curled his tongue as he sang his name. "It's so sexy." His eyes narrowed, giving me this seductive look. Such a dick.

"Anyway… Rhaegs was there, and after my set I was pulled from the stage and Jax said that I had some private clients for a dance. I laid down the law and said I wasn't sleeping with anyone, but anything else was fine. So fast forward, and behind door number one was dark, tall and handsome from the coffee shop."

Wes screamed. "Shut. The. Fuck. Up." He looked shocked, his eyes widening, his coffee cup moving downwards in slow motion and into his lap.

"Yup." I blew my cheeks out, my own eyes bulging out my head as I pursed my lips, pouting.

"Then what?"

He was fucking loving this.

"Then once I was all hot and heavy from him, it was on to door number two, and yup… you can guess, right?"

"Hot as fuck sugar daddy Rhaegar… Oh, giiiiiirl." He

sat back, fanning himself.

"Mmhmm, he finger fucked me, and just as I was getting to my explosive orgasm, Jax knocked on the door. No way in hell was the time up, sneaky Dex paid for Jax to end it early..." I rolled my eyes. "Wes, when I say he literally touched me, I mean it. He literally touched me. And I fucking came like I never came before. I saw stars and shit." My cheeks blushed, my mind taking me back to that night. Fuck, I would do anything to go back there now.

"Sage?" Wes snapped me out of my daydream.

"Mmhmm?" I hummed.

"The contract... you broke it?"

I shook my head from side to side. "Not exactly, it was agreed that work was work."

"Right..."

"Anyway, Rhaegs wanted me to give up my jobs and focus on doing my dream, which is when it all went downhill... on my last night at the club, Dex paid to have me to himself. He went down on me, it was the hottest thing I have ever seen..." My voice trailed off a moment as I took a mouthful of coffee. I don't know how, but my mouth was dry. "Fast forward to a few weeks ago, I think, fuck, I don't know... the weeks feel like they've rolled into one." One of my hands flew above my head. "We went for dinner, me and Rhaegs. He wanted me to meet his son..."

Wes already knew what was coming. "The way he

was talking, well, it was as if his son was a kid… so I went out and bought a train because Rhaegs said he loved trains…"

"Shut the front door. No, no you didn't… you went out and bought a fucking toy train." Wes tipped his head back as he laughed. Laugh it up.

"I bought a train, yes." I looked down, picking an imaginary piece of fluff off the duvet. "We went for dinner, and who was sitting at the table basically eye fucking me?"

"Dex!" Wes squealed with excitement. "This is amazing." He sighed, his eyes rolling up as he fixated them on his ceiling as if he was talking to someone else.

"I'm glad you think so." I snorted a laugh. "Rhaegs had to go, Shay messaged him… said there was an issue…"

"Uh-oh, I smell a dirty fucking rat." He tsked.

"He went and left me with Dex. We flirted, I suppose, if that's what you want to call it. I went to the ladies, and he followed. I mean, of course he did… he was obsessed. Damn, I was obsessed."

Wes was grinning like a cat who had just got the cream.

"Nothing happened," I snapped. "At work, yes, but we never fucked. I only slept with Rhaegar, but Rhaegar seemed to have other plans… cut a long story short… I walked in with Dex last night, to see Shay bouncing up and down on Rhaegar's dick…"

I exhaled deeply, bringing my cup to my lips and

drinking my coffee. Wes didn't say anything. Fuck, I don't even think he moved.

I was adamant you could hear a pin drop, that's just how quiet it was. I wouldn't even be surprised if a tumble weed blew pass. He would talk in a second, I think his pretty little head was just trying to process the word diarrhoea I just offloaded to him.

"That fucking slut," Wes fumed.

"Hold on." I shook my head, holding my hand up. "There was two of them, Rhaegar is just as bad as she is."

"This is true." He huffed. "What a dirty old dog... please tell me Dex stuck up for you..."

"He did, but then it just went to shit. Something about Rhaegs killing his mum or something." I placed my cup on the bedside unit before putting my head in my hands. "What the fuck am I going to do? I'm going to have to go and work back at the club. Dex got me a job, well, sort of. He cancelled the interview and hasn't given me a new date, and after all of this, I doubt he will now. And if by some sort of miracle he does, how the fuck can I go there and just sit there knowing what went on between us all?"

"You're not going back to the club; I won't let you." Wes placed his own cup down now, and he shuffled closer to me, pulling my hands from my face. "You are going to get yourself dressed up, you are going to go to that new job once Dex gives you a new date, and you're going to show them who the fuck Sage James is," he said with assertiveness in his voice.

"You're not some weak little girl who needs a man. You're a fucking lioness. You're going to own this and shoot for those stars, baby girl, because let me tell you, no one is more deserving of living their dreams than you are."

I hadn't realised, but I had hot, burning tears rolling down my cheeks.

I didn't know if it was sadness, anger or pure happiness at me having a friend like Wes.

Pulling my sorry arse out of the shower, I got dressed back into my *Busted* tee and a pair of Wes's jogging bottoms that were a little on the tight side. He was like a bean pole, toned and sculpted, but tall, long and skinny. Then there was me, curvaceous from my bottom half down. I was envious of girls that didn't get chub rub, but this was the body I was given, and I learned to embrace it. Sometimes.

I brushed through my damp hair and stuffed my clothes from last night into my bag. People were going to think I was doing the walk of shame. Well, fuck them.

I kissed Wes on the cheek and thanked him again for last night and this morning. I didn't know what I would do without him.

Once I was outside on the street, I couldn't bear to walk in my heels, so I took them off, holding them in my hand and walked down the road bare foot. I wouldn't walk all the way, I was hoping that I would be able to grab a taxi, I wasn't in the mood for the tube today.

Walking aimlessly to one of the stations where I knew taxis would be waiting, I fished around in my bag for my phone. I switched it off last night once I spoke to Wes. I didn't want to talk to Rhaegar. And I definitely didn't want to talk to Dex, not that I thought he had my number, but then again, this was the guy who knew where I worked, and no doubt knows where I live. The thought just made my blood cold.

As soon as my phone was on, it vibrated again and again.

Rhaegs.

Rhaegs.

Rhaegs.

Unknown number. Most probably Dex.

Rhaegs.

Yup, it's Dex.

Dex.

Dex.

Dex.

Dex.

Dex.

Shaking my head, I had to applaud them for their determination.

Silly boys.

Dropping my phone back in my bag, I smiled when I saw the taxi rank. I held my hand up, getting one of the old-style London taxis attention as I walked towards them.

Climbing in and slamming the door, I told the driver my address and headed home.

The taxi ride was short and sweet, and luckily for me, I had a driver who didn't want to talk. Perfect. Throwing him the little cash I did have, I hopped out and let myself through the front door.

"Mum, I'm home," I called out, dropping my front door keys on the old, shabby table that sat in the narrow hallway.

I heard a childlike giggle come from the living room. My mum? Laughing? I scoffed.

Walking cautiously down the dark and damp hallway, my heart was thumping.

A chill crept up my spine, my skin tingling as it smothered in goosebumps. Slowly looking around the door frame, there he was sat.

The motherfucking devil himself.

My breath caught; my eyes widened.

"Mum?" I whispered. My mind started racing with questions. *Did he threaten her? Did he force his way in? What if he broke in while she was still asleep?*

"Hello, darling." She smiled at me, standing from her

chair and walking towards me as she pulled me in for a motherly embrace.

Where is my mum and what have you done with her?

"Hey…" I said, a little confused, pulling back from her and furrowing my brow.

"You know Dexter Rutherford, right?" Her eyes glistened as she looked over her shoulder at him. My eyes moved slowly… *did I know Dexter Rutherford?*

"Mmhmm, yup." I nodded. "He is my boss."

Lie.

Boss of my vagina maybe.

"I'll go put the kettle on." She kissed me on the cheek and walked out of the room.

My stony glare moved back to Dex after my mum left.

"What in the fuck are you doing here?" I whisper shouted, pointing my finger at him.

"Can't a boss come and see his best employee?" He winked at me, his fingers drumming on the arms of the high-backed chair he was sitting in.

"Answer me," I snarled as I stepped towards him.

"I'm just doing a little charity work." He shrugged his shoulders, his large tattooed hands linking and sitting on his lap, his beautiful brown eyes not leaving mine.

"Don't you fucking dare even think of using my mum and charity in the same sentence," I spat through gritted teeth. I didn't give two shits how hot he was or how he made my body purr by just looking at me. Nobody, and I mean nobody disrespects my mum. My blood boiled; I felt the anger rising in me.

"I didn't mention your mum…" His brows pinched together, his glare burning through me. My anger sizzled out, like two wet fingers over a burning candle.

He was the fingers.

I was the flame.

Dex stood from the chair, closing the small gap that was between us, his neck craning down so he was looking over me.

"Don't get worked up, little one," he whispered. "Once your mum is back, maybe she can tell you why I'm here." His scent drifted through my nose, intoxicating me. He always smelt so nice.

Minty breath that was somehow always laced with the soft smell of bourbon. Then there was his cologne, it was powerful but not intense. It was juicy, spicy, fresh with a hint of vanilla. The whole combination was delicious.

His fingers gripped my chin, tipping my head back so I had no choice but to look at him. "You're coming with me once we're done here." His tone was low, chilling, domineering.

He dropped my chin as quickly as he took it when Mum stepped back into the room with a tray. Her *not to be used* tea pot sat on it, a little pot of sugar, three cups and a plate of biscuits.

To say I was confused was an understatement.

I knew I hadn't been home much in a week or so, but how could she have changed this much?

"Take a seat, Sage." Dex's voice was smooth like silk as he sat back down in the chair. I rubbed my lips together, forming a tight line. I sat next to my mum, watching her with beady eyes as she poured the tea. There was no tremor, no shakes, no nervousness at Dex's presence. She would find someone of Dex's demeanour terrifying, surely?

Shit, she ran when Rhaegs turned up at the door, and Rhaegs is a kitten compared to Dex.

My mum smiled as she held Dex's tea out to him, which he took gladly, giving her the most sickening smile I had ever seen.

"So, Sage, I know you're wondering why I am here…" He smirked, bringing his cup to his lips.

Fuck, to be that cup of tea right about now…

Returning from my perverted mind, I nodded.

"I am actually, because being honest, *Dexter*" I licked my lips, crossing one leg over the other as I leaned forward "I don't trust you."

"Ouch." Dex fell back in his chair, placing one of his hands over his heart as if I had just shot an arrow through it. The rumble of his laugh filled the room as he sat back on the edge of his seat, his eyes, which I'm sure were undressing me, were looking me up and down.

"You can trust me." His voice cracked slightly. Did it actually hurt him that I said that? I felt my own heart hurt, a pain searing through.

I swallowed hard.

"The reason I am here, Sage, is because I have been helping your mum…" His eyes fell from me to his cup, then they flicked back up to mine with a glimmer of sadness.

"I have been paying for therapy for your mum, she has been going twice a week for the last three months…"

My eyes bulged out my head. *Three months?* I had literally only just met Rhaegar.

"Three months?" I choked on my own words.

"Yes, Sage." His voice was low, quiet. He was treading carefully; he knew I was close to blowing my top.

"How have you known my mum for three months?" You could hear the confusion that was lacing my voice. What in the fuck was going on?

"I've actually known Dex a lot longer than three months…" My mum's voice squeaked beside me as she looked at her hands.

My head spun to her; my heart was racing. I had no clue where this conversation was going.

"Me and his late mother, Jackie, were old school friends… we were always together, but as always, you grow apart, start a family. Then I found out the news that Jackie had lost her life to a drug overdose; it broke me. Then your father disappeared... but it wasn't that he just disappeared. He had another family. So not only had I lost my best friend, I lost my husband too. He didn't care that I was pregnant, I begged him to stay, if not for me, for you. He tried, he stayed... but he wasn't in love with me anymore. To fall out of love with someone is painful, but to have that someone that *you* love with you because they have to be, as if they're forced to... well... that's excruciating. But once you turned three, I told him to leave. I would have rather brought you up on my own than with him." My mum's voice began to tremble. "Sage, what I'm about to tell you will upset you..." She turned in her seat, her small, cold hands taking mine in hers. "Your father used to beat me, abuse me... then he would get his friends round to sexually assault me while he watched." I watched the tears prick her eyes. "It wasn't just your father leaving that made me like this." She let out a choked laugh through her tears. "There was so much more, and when I saw Rhaegar turn up, I bottled it. I knew of him with Jackie, he wasn't the best to her, claimed that she trapped him with Dex which is complete bullshit. He was never committed to her, but she was to him... no matter what he says." She sniffed. "But this conversation isn't about Dex's father. I know you are with him, and I respect your choice, but it'll take me a while to get to know him..."

She stopped, giving me a tight smile.

The air was ripped from my lungs, it was as if someone had swung a baseball bat across my back and winded me. My hand pressed to my chest as I tried to absorb as much information as I could.

"Sage?" I heard Dex's voice. He was on the floor in front of me, holding my hand. "It's okay." He smiled.

I nodded, closing my eyes as I inhaled deeply, slowly.

"I'm not with Rhaegar anymore, Mum," I managed, shaking my head. "And I won't be, it's over between us. It just didn't work out, we didn't work." It stung saying the words, but it was the truth. We didn't work. "I'm so sorry." I sobbed, pulling my hands from Dex's and throwing myself at my mum. My poor mum.

There's me thinking she just couldn't get over the heartbreak of my dad leaving, but it was so much more. What a horrible, vile human being.

"It's okay, darling," she soothed, her hand stroking my head. "I'm getting better."

I pulled away, looking at Dex then back to my mum. "You are?" I sniffled.

She nodded.

"Dex?" Her head cocked to the side, inviting him to take over the conversation.

"She is." He smiled at me as he stood slowly, but not moving, he stayed close. "Before my mum died, she would talk to me about her friend Lisa and how she wanted to do all she could to help her out of this situation. I just listened; I was still young at the time. But when my mum passed, I vowed I would always look out for Lisa from afar. She never wanted my pity or my money." Dex laughed softly. "So I just watched, I followed, and I made sure I knew what was happening. I have tried finding your deadbeat dad, but it is as if he has vanished." He sighed. "That's when I saw you... and I couldn't stay away. I needed to make sure you were safe too, because these men that used to come for your mother know where you both live, and I was worried they were going to come for you too... and Sage..." His eyes softened as he looked down at me, but I mean, he really looked at me. I felt our souls entwine as he did.

"I couldn't have them hurt you..." He sounded choked; his jaw clenched. "You became an obsession..."

My eyes widened at his confession, my head turning to look at my mum.

"Once you were in the picture, I upped my game. I put your mum into therapy, and trust me, it took a lot. I said if she couldn't do it for herself, then to do it for you. Because you both deserve so much more than this." His hand waved around our tiny living room. "So, from this moment on, your house is paid off, your loan is gone, your bills taken care of..." He smiled proudly. "Your mum is going into a therapy scheme, sort of like rehab, a live-in as such, and you will be coming with me until she is ready and back home." His eyes darted to my mum, my head spinning to look at her. The admiration in her eyes while looking at Dex was enough to tip me over the edge as I cried. They were tears of relief, sadness, guilt and happiness all rolled into one.

Pushing down the feelings I felt about leaving with Dex, I turned my body towards her.

"I am so proud of you." I smiled the biggest smile I could.

"This is all for you." She nodded, taking my hands in hers. "I want to be better for you."

CHAPTER Twenty One

So, it seems my stalker has been around a lot longer than I thought.

It wasn't long after our conversation that Mum was put in one of Dex's cars and whizzed away. I felt lost and alone. It had always just been me and mum, but now it was me and Dex.

This wasn't going to end well.

Or was it? How the hell was I going to cope living with Dex? Did he look at me different now? More like a little sister?

"You okay, little one?" he asked, his head lifting from his phone.

I nodded.

But was I okay? I don't think so.

The car ride wasn't long, we had just pulled into Kensington. This place dripped with money.

We pulled up outside a prestigious house, my jaw laxing slightly. The house was finished in white render, the large impressive pillars sitting either side of a dainty black gate. It was truly stunning.

"Come on, let's go indoors." Dex smiled as he opened the door and stepped out, rushing to my side and opening the door.

His driver was already by the boot, grabbing my bag of clothes.

Dex looked at the contents. "Is that all you have? Have you forgotten anything?" he asked as his hand touched the small of my back, leading me into the house.

"Nope, I'm not rich. I only have a bit."

"What about the clothes my dad bought you?"

I felt the bile rising.

"Left them. I don't want anything to do with him." I shook my head.

"Then we will go shopping tomorrow, before you start your new job." He nodded firmly, unlocking the door to his swanky pad.

"No, honestly, its fine…" The last word came out a whisper as I took in the entrance hall to this house.

Greys and whites wrapped around the room, decorated with shiny chrome furnishings and accessories.

It was truly stunning.

"Wow," I managed.

"Nice, aye?"

"Very." I smiled. Dex removed his hand from my back, causing me to frown. I liked the feel of his skin on mine. I like the way my skin pebbles and prickles, the way my hairs stand on the back of my neck before an eruption of goosebumps smothers me from head to toe.

I followed him up the black painted wooden stairs, my hand gliding up the black painted handrail, my eyes wandering around. I couldn't get over how beautiful this house was. The stairs twisted slightly at the top as we stepped onto a large gallery landing. The outside of this house was very deceiving. You wouldn't think it was this wide and deep from standing on the front step.

"This will be your room." Dex smiled as he opened the door to a large, airy room. The floors were thick pile white carpet that your feet sank into. The bed sat in the centre of the room as you walked in, sitting underneath a large sash window that overlooked a beautifully maintained garden.

The room was painted in a beigy grey. It was light and bright. Unlike my dingey, dark box room. This bedroom was probably as big as the whole upstairs in our house.

"You also have a walk-in wardrobe to the left, and then if you carry on through, you'll see the en-suite which has a bath, shower and sink." He smiled.

"I won't ever want to leave." I sighed, smiling as I walked towards the bed, my fingers running across the white soft duvet. The large window was framed with long, thick white curtains that finished the room off, and a stunning crystal light sat centre of the room.

"Then don't." Dex shrugged his shoulders. "I won't be pushing you out the door, little one." His voice was low.

Thump.

My heart banged against my chest, combusting in my ribcage.

"Dinner will be served at seven. Go and enjoy a bubble bath and do some reading or listen to *Busted*." His eyes narrowed on my tee that I was still wearing from Wes'.

I blushed as his eyes trailed up and down my body.

"Thank you, Dex,"

"No need to thank me, little temp." He nodded, stepping back and closing the bedroom door behind him.

Once I was sure he had gone, I ran and dived on the bed. So this is what it's like to have expensive bedding and a proper mattress.

I was never leaving my bed.

That was my decision.

I would become a bed whore.

I was sad to see I was eating dinner alone, but his housekeeper Bridget told me he was on a business call and to send his apologies. I sat quietly and ate my dinner, and once I was finished, I placed it in the sink. I lingered for a little while, hoping he would turn up, but he didn't, so I took myself to bed. I would be lying if I said it didn't sting a little.

    I felt exhausted, it had been a long twenty-four hours and I had a lot of stuff to take in. Of course, as soon as my head hit those wonderful duck feather pillows, I was in a peaceful slumber.

CHAPTER Twenty Two

Two guys, one whore.

I was awoken by the bed dipping, and rolling onto my back, I opened my eyes. I could see two figures... was I seeing this right? Sitting up slowly, I rubbed the sleep out of my eyes then gave them a minute to re-adjust to the dimly lit room. I felt my heart race when I saw Dex and Rhaegar sitting on the bed, smirking at me, eyes alight with desire.

"What's wrong?" I asked, my voice hushed, my fingers gripping the heavy, plush duvet.

"Nothing is wrong, little one..." His voice trailed off as he turned to look at his dad. "We just want to make it up to you. Apologise, as such..." Licking his lips, his hand glided towards me.

What in the actual fuck?

I leapt from the bed, standing by the entrance to my walk-in wardrobe.

"What's wrong, kitten?" Rhaegar's voice was smooth

and silky, his eyes trailed up and down my body, taking every inch of me in.

Dex pushed from the bed, strolling towards me, his hand cupping my face and pushing me into the doorframe. A gasp escaped me when it hit my back.

His lips brushed against mine. "You're telling me you haven't ever thought about this?" he whispered, his breath on my lips.

My eyes darted past his, looking at Rhaegar who was now walking towards us. He stopped at the side of me, one of his arms wrapping around my waist, the other hand gliding over my oversized tee. His fingers pinched and rolled my nipples through the material, and a low hum vibrated in my throat.

"You're telling me that you wouldn't love to be filled with mine and his cock?" Dex groaned, his lips pressing to my collar bone, his hands on my hips, holding me in place. Rhaegs' fingertips continued to roll my now hardened nipple, tugging slightly. My breathing was harsh.

Dex's lips moved from my collar bone, trailing down between my breasts before falling to his knees. Pushing my tee up over my hips, his lips kissed over my naval, his tongue dipping into my belly button. My greedy eyes fell to watch him, his eyes meeting with mine.

Standing up slowly, he pushed into me. His body on mine. Craning his head, his hair fell onto his forehead. It always looked so soft, I wanted to run my hands through it. I was desperate to see what it felt like.

"Come to bed, little temptress. Let us show you how sorry we are." His tongue darted out as he licked his lips.

Dex stepped away from me, walking backwards towards the bed, Rhaegs following him. They both sat on the edge of the bed, legs parted and their eyes devouring me.

"I just need a minute," I whispered, slipping into the walk-in wardrobe and straight into the en-suite.

I stood over the sink, looking in the mirror.

Could I do this? The thought replayed over and over in my head. Grabbing my toothbrush, I smothered it in toothpaste and brushed my teeth.

I couldn't have bad breath.

Popping my toothbrush back in the cup that sat on a holder on the wall, I wrapped my fingers around the edge of the sink. I closed my eyes and inhaled deeply.

You have thought about this, you have one hundred percent thought about sleeping with Dex and Rhaegs.

You just don't want to admit it.

Sighing, I stood tall. Fuck it.

I'm not with either of them, they're willing to do it and so am I.

You only live once... well, that's a lie. Technically, you live every day, and you only die once.

"Shut the fuck up," I snapped at my thoughts. Jeez.

Shaking my hands out and exhaling deeply, I turned

on my heel and walked back into the dimly lit bedroom.

They were both still sitting there. Dex was wearing a tight tee with grey jogging bottoms, relaxed and casual. Rhaegar was in his signature open collar white shirt and tight in all the right places suit trousers.

I stalked over to them, standing in-between both of them. Dex's greedy hand reached round and palmed my bare bum cheek under my tee, while Rhaegs' hand gripped onto my thigh.

"You ready for the best night of your life, little one?" Dex asked.

I nodded.

No going back now.

Dex stood from the bed, his hands pushing around my waist and spinning me, so we had swapped places. His hands move from my waist, slowly gliding up the side of my body until his fingers wrapped around my shoulders. Giving me a gentle nudge, he pushed me back onto the bed.

He smirked down at me, his tongue running across his bottom lip. My belly flipped, a delicious ache growing in my pussy.

My eyes darted to Rhaegs who was standing next to Dex. His eyes were devouring me. My skin heated up, my lips parting. I knew how good Rhaegs was in bed, he was a good fuck, but Dex... he was who I was excited for.

I couldn't help but stare as Rhaegs shrugged his shirt

off and let it fall to the floor. Next was his belt. Slowly, he unbuckled it, then whipped it from the belt loops and held it in his hands.

"What I would pay to spank your perfect, peach arse with this belt." He growled, tightening his grip around the leather, the veins popping in his forearm.

My breath caught as he dropped it to the floor, the thud echoing around the room. His trousers were off in a flash, his boxers too. There he stood, completely naked. His large cock hard and in his hand as he pumped his closed hand up and down himself.

Dex crawled up the bed, still fully clothed, annoyingly. He kneeled next to me, so he was looking down on me. One of his hands flew to my hair, gripping and tugging it back so I had no choice but to look up at him.

He grinned at me, his lips curling into a sinister smile. It turned me on. I don't know what came over me, my hand slipped in-between my legs as I rubbed my clit through my thong.

A gentle moan passed my lips which caused a growl from Dex. The bed dipped, and Rhaegs was in-between my legs within seconds, snatching my hand away.

His fingers tucked into the side of my thong, tugging it down my legs and bringing it to his nose and inhaling deeply. Discarding them to the floor, his fingers dug into my bare skin of my thighs, pushing them wider.

"Fuck." He sucked in a breath. "I have missed this pussy," he groaned, lowering his head down as he flicked his tongue across my sensitive clit, then sucked hard.

"Oh," I breathed, Dex releasing my hair so I could watch.

"Watch. Watch as he eats your pussy and makes you come." Dex's voice was a whisper, his fingers still entwined in my hair, tugging occasionally.

I did as he asked. My eyes were glued to my pussy and the man that was eating me as if it was his last meal.

My head fell back, it felt amazing. Rhaegs had a wicked tongue, gliding in-between my folds, swirling it at my opening before dragging back up and flicking over my clit.

Rhaegs looked up at me and smiled, a small glisten to his lips from my arousal.

My head turned as I looked at Dex, one hand still firmly in my hair, the other pulling his jogging bottoms waist band down, fisting his cock and holding it tightly.

My eyes widened; my jaw lax as I took all of him in.

Holy fuck.

He was long and thick. So thick.

I clenched, trying to press my legs together so I could protect myself. There was no way he was going to fit.

Nope.

Wasn't going to happen.

"Don't worry, kitten, he isn't going anywhere near

you." Rhaegs winked, his hands pushing my legs open, his finger gliding down my core and pushing into my soaked entrance.

The breath left my lungs as he pumped his finger in slowly, filling me in the most delicious way.

"We already agreed, I get your pussy, Dex gets your mouth." Rhaegs grinned, slipping a second finger in now, stretching me. Moaning out, my hand flew to grab onto Dex, my fingers clutching onto the leg of his jogging bottoms.

"Oh, little one, you missed." Dex smirked, grabbing my wrist and placing my hand over his cock.

My eyes found his, focusing on him as he moved my hand up and down his length.

I was no naive girl, but he hypnotized me. I felt lost.

I followed his lead, my eyes moving to Rhaegs who was still finger fucking me. I was so overwhelmed. I had never been so turned on in all my life.

Rhaegs pulled his fingers out, bringing them to his lips and pushing them into his mouth, sucking them dry.

A small whimper escaped me at the sight of him doing that. I don't know why that turned me on so much, but it did. My orgasm was teetering on the cliff edge, ready to tip and send me free falling into the cold ocean.

Rhaegs dipped his head back between my legs, licking and flicking over my clit, his fingertip teasing at my opening.

SOMETHING WORTH STEALING

That was all it took to send me into oblivion.

Dex hadn't even touched me yet and I was free falling through the stars as my orgasm crashed through me.

Rhaegs kneeled up, grinning down at me. I was spent, my legs were still trembling, my chest heaving up and down.

Rhaegs's hands reached up, grabbing my hips and flipping me over so I was on my front. Lifting my arse in the air, his palm rubbed over my bare bum cheek before slapping it.

"What a fucking view." Rhaegs growled, moving closer to me, his dick pressing into me. Dex smirked, edging closer to me, his dick still hard. I could see the pre cum on the tip of his head. I wanted to lick it, let my tongue swirl and taste him.

Dex moved in front of me, his dick lining up against my lips. Oh, I saw how this was going to go.

Licking my lips, I looked up through my lashes at Dex, a small smirk curling on my lips.

"Suck it." He growled, holding the base of his dick as he pushed through my lips, the taste of him on my tongue. I moaned in appreciation of just how good he tasted. My lips tightened around his cock, my mouth moving up and down slowly. Dex smiled, groaning as he watched me suck his cock, his head tipping back.

"That's it, temp, keep sucking."

I did as he asked, I wanted to do everything he asked

of me and more. Rhaegs' hands were all over me, touching, gripping, pinching.

My skin was alight, my desire burning deep inside of me.

Dex was gentle, letting me take control as my lips moved up and down slowly.

I felt Rhaegs rear up behind me, his dick lining up at my soaked opening before pushing it into me without warning. I cried out; it was muffled around Dex's dick. I had never felt as sexy as I did now. Rhaegs was slipping in and out of me fast, his hands tightening around my hips as he ploughed into me harder. The sound of his skin hitting mine was making me tingle in all the right places.

Our moans and groans filled the room. Dex's thrusts sped up, his cock hitting the back of my throat. I gagged at first, my eyes watering, but after that, I controlled it. Rhaegs's hands moved round, rubbing over my clit. My hips rotated and ground into him. I needed more.

Dex's hand gripped onto my hair, pulling at the root as I continued to deep throat him. I felt the bubbles popping in my stomach, my pussy clenching around Rhaegar.

"Are you going to come for me, kitten?" Rhaegs gritted out through his teeth.

Moaning, I arched my back a little, my hips meeting Rhaegar's harsh poundings.

I felt the saliva dripping down the corners of my

mouth, Dex's dick throbbing on my tongue as I continued my sucking.

"That's it, little one, I am so close." He groaned, his head tipping back, his grip tightening in my hair.

Dex's cock pulsed as he came down my throat, and I swallowed every drop of him. Dex pulled out of my mouth, smiling down at me. "That's a good girl."

Rhaegs sat back on his knees, pulling me on top of him. He spread my legs wider, letting them sit over the top of his muscular thighs.

He stilled his movements as I rocked over his cock, slow and deep. Dex sat in front of me, his hand gripping my cheeks as he tipped my head back, his lips hovering over mine as his tongue swiped in-between my parted lips.

"I can't wait to have you to myself," he whispered.

I feel myself quiver with anticipation, my thrusts slowing as pleasure starts to consume me. Dex's free hand skims down my breasts, kneading them and rolling my nipples between his fingers. Moaning out, my eyes glued to Dex's, Rhaegar's cock pushing in and out of me gently.

I wasn't doing any of the work anymore, I was too consumed by Dex's trailing fingers, his nipping at my chin. Rhaegar's hands held my hips in place as he rocked himself into me... this was too much... I felt like I was going to explode, to combust. Like a volcano ready to erupt. Dex's fingers brushed against my clit, rubbing softly. My pussy tightened around Rhaegar, my moans filling the room as pure ecstasy ripped through me.

Rhaegar roared as his cock pulsed, pulling out of me and filling the condom.

My shoulders fell, and all of a sudden, I felt sluggish and exhausted.

Dex moved me, laying me down on the bed and kissing my forehead.

My heavy eyes moved to Rhaegar as he tied the end of the condom then headed towards to bathroom to discard it. I don't know why but it stung that he still did that with me and not with Shay… Fuck… Shay. *What had I done?* Guilt began to consume me. I was as bad as them. I should have never given into temptation.

I turned my head to look at Dex. I know they made a deal for him not to fuck me, but I couldn't wait.

I needed to know what he felt like inside of me, what we felt like together. Sitting up slowly, I climbed over Dex, my legs either side of him.

"Baby…" Dex's voice was low, his large hands moving to my waist as his fingers dug into my skin. "What are you doing?"

"What does it look like?" I winked, cocking my head to the side. "I need you. I need you to fuck me," I whispered, my hands pressing against his rock-hard chest.

"Little one…" His own voice was hushed now, his

head lifting slightly as he looked to where his father disappeared to.

"It's only fair." I pouted, not taking my eyes off of him. "Please, Dex, don't make me beg anymore."

I heard a rumble that vibrated through his throat. His cock twitched underneath me. He was hard. I moaned, even just feeling him underneath me felt amazing. Pressing to his chest, I lifted my hips. One of his hands lined his thick cock at my opening. I was nervous, I was worried that he wasn't going to fit.

"Relax, I need you to relax," he whispered. I nodded, sliding myself slowly down his long, thick cock as my pussy stretched around him, the feeling of fullness consuming me.

"Oh God," I breathed out, my head tipping back.

"Fuck, you feel so good." Both of his hands were back on my hips as he began moving me, my hips thrusting back and forth over him. My skin tingled, my stomach knotting as it coiled. I wasn't going to last long. This is all I have thought about, all I have wanted in what felt like forever.

My head snapped round to see Rhaegar stroll towards us, and his eyes darkened as he smirked.

"Greedy little girl." Rhaegs head shook from side to side. "Couldn't resist?" he asked as he knelt on the bed, sitting on the edge as his hands moved to my breasts. His fingers rolled my nipples as I continued grinding over

Dex's cock, my moans filling the room.

Rhaegs' lips pressed into my neck, my breath hitching. I felt myself fall sluggish. Dex rocked his hips up into me, his cock stroking my G-spot over and over. My pussy tightened around him, my hands moving to my hair as I gripped it. I didn't know what to do with myself, the pleasure ripped through me. Rhaegs' fingers dropped from my aching breasts, gliding down my stomach to the apex of my thighs. His fingers rubbed my clit, matching his son's thrusts which were now hard and fast. I was so wet, his cock slipping in and out of me with ease as I began bouncing up and down on his cock, his fingers gripping onto my hips much harder now.

"Fuck, Sage, keep fucking me like that. Your little cunt is so tight." He groaned, his head lifting before his eyes fell to in-between my legs, watching his cock fill me again and again. The delicious build continued to grow, the bubbles bubbling deep inside of me, a shiver blanketing my skin as my orgasm ripped through me.

"Oh, Dex, I'm coming, fuck," I cried out, my head falling back, Rhaegs' lips locking around my nipple as his fingers rubbed my clit hard.

"Yes, fuck, Sage," Dex growled, finding his own high as he came.

My heart raced, I wanted to call out, but I couldn't. I felt exhausted suddenly.

It was as if I was paralysed. That's the only way I

could explain it.

"Sage..." I could hear Dex's voice echoing.

My eyes struggled to focus. I tried with all I had to focus on Dex, but I couldn't.

"Hey, little one..." I heard his voice again.

I tried to call out again, but there was no use.

He couldn't hear me.

"Sage, baby..."

"Sage..."

My sight plunged into darkness, my body relaxing as I gave in to exhaustion.

"Are you having a nightmare?" His voice ripped through me again, and this time I could hear him a lot clearer, and I was adamant he was touching me.

"Dex?" I murmured grouchily, happy that he could hear me.

"Yeah, Sage, I'm here." His voice was quiet but clearer.

My eyes opened, and blinking, it took me a minute to adjust.

"Where's Rhaegs gone?" I asked, confused.

Dex's brows pinched as he looked at me strangely. "My dad isn't here..." Dex shuffled forward on the bed, holding his hand to my head. "Are you feeling okay?" he asked.

I nodded.

"You look flushed, clammy, and a little shell

shocked." Dex scoffed a laugh.

"Well, we just had a threesome... I would be more concerned if I didn't look like this." It was my turn to let a laugh escape me.

"A what?" Dex's eyes widened. "Little one... once I have you, there is no way in hell I would let another man near you." He smirked.

"Did it not happen?" I was confused, I had just been through it, I had just come, three times.

Oh my God.

"Sage?" He smirked. "Did you have a sex dream?" He chuckled.

I blushed.

"Holy shit." Dex's head fell back as the most beautiful laugh escaped him.

"Stop it, you're embarrassing me..." I swatted him away.

"Don't be embarrassed... just let me know, was it me fucking you or..."

I stilled, shaking my head.

"You wouldn't, you were *too big*..." Grabbing the pillow from behind me, I held it over my face. "But then I climbed on top of you... and you know..." I spoke, my voice muffled.

"Uh-uh, nope. I don't think so," Dex growled, pulling the pillow away from me. "One, how do you know how big my dick is?" His brow pinged up. "And secondly, I feel robbed. I can't wait to see just how good we are together." He winked, leaning towards me and pushing me down. "But for the meantime…" His fingers trailed up and down my bare thigh.

My clit throbbed; my pussy pulsed.

Were me and Dex finally going to sleep together?

Chapter Twenty Three

When dreams become reality

I watched as Dex pushed off the bed. He was only wearing a tee and matching short set. Gripping the hem of his top, he lifted and pulled it over his head before he dropped it to the floor. My eyes bulged as they roamed over his toned torso. Every inch of his skin was covered, apart from just under his hips. That area was bare.

He was a God. He must have been crafted by the God of Gods, because I mean, how is it possible for him to look this good? I wanted to run my hands across his pecs, trailing them down his six pack. I wanted to feel every line, every curve... I wanted to feel every bit of him under my fingertips.

Kneeling on the bed, he crawled towards me.

"As much as I want to fuck you, I need to wait. Take my time. I don't want the first time I sleep with you to be rushed. I want to enjoy every single inch of you, tasting you, feeling you..." He leaned down, his lips brushing against the shell of my ear.

I shivered. But not in a bad way, no. In a very, very good way. He made me feel alive, my skin prickled with goosebumps, the promises he was whispering in my ear were enough to tip me over the edge.

"How about we take care of each other... a little taste?" He leant back, smirking as his hands trailed across my bare thighs, his fingertips drawing shapes into my skin.

"Okay." I licked my lips. "But I think it is only fair that I go first... you have already tasted me, yet I am still waiting to see how you taste." My voice was silky, my hair framing my face as I sat up, placing my palms on Dex's chest and pushing him back onto the bed.

His eyes lit up, his lips curling into a smile.

"Oh, I like this... you want to be in control, do you?" He licked his lips.

Nodding my head eagerly, I climbed over him, my legs sitting either side of his waist. Dex pulled his bottom lip in, his hand flying to wrap around the back of my head, pulling me towards him. Our lips locked, his tongue invading my mouth. Our kiss was rough, heated and full of want. I felt his lips break into a smile, his tongue slowing as he caressed mine before sucking my tongue into his mouth.

Holy fucking hell, that's hot.

The moans that vibrated through me echoed in his

mouth. Dex pulled away, biting my bottom lip as he did, tugging it hard. I whimpered.

So much for me being in control. He was trying to take back the power.

Nope.

Don't think so.

He pulled away from my lips, his beautiful eyes falling to my mouth as a smirk played across his lips.

His hands tightened around my waist, but I wriggled back over his bulge, shaking my head from side to side.

"I don't think so." Now it was my time to smirk. Lifting myself off him, I shuffled down his body, and falling in-between his legs, I sat on my knees. Cocking my head to the side, my raven black hair fell to the side, cascading past my ribs.

"Look at you, looking all seductive and sexy as fuck," Dex growled.

I smirked, blushing a crimson. Dipping my fingers into the side of his shorts, I tugged them down. His cock sprung from the tight waistband. I gasped and licked my lips.

"Oh," I breathed, my breath catching as my eyes widened.

"Don't be scared, little one." Dex winked at me.

Sucking in my breath, I wrapped my fingers around the base of his cock tightly, an approving groan slipped from his lips, his head tipping back slightly before he looked at me, his head tipping to the side as he pinned his eyes on me. His hand ran around the back of my head, gripping tightly.

"Suck it," he ordered, his eyes full of want and need, his voice masked in a hazy, lustful tone.

Tingles swarmed me at the words he just said, they were the same as my dream.

I lowered my head, Dex's hand staying firmly in place as I parted my lips, pursing them at the tip of his cock, licking the pre cum that sat beaded on his tip.

He groaned, his fingers entwining in my hair, gripping tighter.

I took that as my cue to slip my mouth down his long, thick cock. I moaned as I took him deep into my mouth, and when it got too much, I slowly pulled him out, swirling my tongue at his tip before running it down from his head to the base of his cock. The most satisfying, erotic groan left his throat, his hand tightening in my hair.

"Don't stop." He begged, lifting his shoulders up and tipping his chin down to look at me, thrusting his hips, silently begging for me to put him back in my mouth.

I swirled my tongue over his head again, letting my tongue lay flat and run down the base of his cock as my mouth took him deep.

"That's it, baby, take me deep." He groaned, thrusting his hips into my mouth. I took him slow, but I wanted to meet his needs. I wanted him to come and have the most explosive orgasm of his life.

My fingers wrapped around his thick cock, and moving my hand up and down, I mirrored my sucking with my hand.

Sliding down his cock, he hit the back of my throat, holding my head there with his hand. At one point, I thought I was going to gag. But I stopped myself. My spare hand slipped underneath him, rubbing his balls. His hips twitched, his cock pushing deeper.

"Fuuuuuck, Sage." He sucked in a breath, my eyes flicking up to look at him, his breath hitched.

"Look at me, keep looking at me," he begged through pants. His cock pulsed in my mouth. Fuck, that was a turn on.

I did as he asked, I made sure I kept my eyes on his the whole time, slowly pulling him out to the tip, pursing my plump lips around his thick head then slipping my mouth down to the hilt.

His head fell back into the pillow then quickly snapped back up again.

I did it again and again until I felt his cock pulse, his grip tightening on my hair as he rocked his hips into my mouth.

"I'm going to come. Fuck, Sage, let me come in your mouth." He growled, pumping his hot cum down my throat, swallowing every bit of him.

Sucking him clean, I sat back on my knees, smiling

as I wiped the corner of my mouth with my ring finger before sucking it.

"Oh, little one, I am going to devour you." He groaned, pushing me back on the bed before he fell in-between my legs, sending me to infinity and beyond.

Twice.

-

I woke from a peaceful slumber, stretching out. My head turned slowly, a smile gracing my face, but it soon faded when I saw the bed was empty. It stung, my heart falling into the pit of my stomach.

I was stupid to think he would be here, no doubt once he gets me fully, he will kick me out and leave me on the street. He isn't the kind of guy who settles down. He owns gentleman's clubs for fuck's sake.

Talking of gentleman's clubs, I need to talk to him about that little bomb that they dropped at dinner the other night.

That dinner felt like weeks ago, when in reality, it had only been two nights. Crazy.

I debated getting up and having a nosey around the house, but then again, I didn't want to face Dex just yet.

Last night wasn't just oral, it was so much more. I felt like we connected, our bodies becoming one even though we didn't sleep together.

My skin tingles even thinking about him, my heart fluttering like mad in my chest as if I have a thousand butterflies swarming in there.

He made me feel things I didn't know I could feel. Setting off a fire deep inside me that only he could light and extinguish.

My mind flickered back to last night.

His lips were soft, his kisses gentle as they trailed down my belly. The feel of his kisses on my skin were tantalizing. They were addicting and I wanted them all over me. I was sure I was going to come just from his mouth, but every time I got close to that sweet release, he smirked and pulled away while shaking his head from side to side. His beautiful chocolate brown hair fell forward onto his forehead.

He was high off the lust and no doubt the post-bliss from an explosive orgasm I gave him with my mouth.

He wanted to return the favour, but he took his sweet time making sure he savoured and covered every part of my exposed skin. My skin was covered in a sheen of sweat, the moonlight lit the dark room so we could only see so much. There was something erotic about sexual situations in the dark. Only seeing the odd lip press to the skin, the small tongue strokes while his fingers trailed along my glistening skin was a turn on in itself, sending my hormones into overdrive, while the dull ache grew in-between my legs. I needed Dex to see to me, to take the burn away and send me to paradise.

My breath caught when I heard the door go, pulling

me from my flashback as Dex strolled into the room, only wearing low hung grey jogging shorts. My eyes trailed up and down his body as I took his appearance in. How could he always look so hot? I felt self-conscious all of a sudden, even though we have been intimate before, it had never been like it was last night. Last night was completely different. I fell for him.

I know that sounds stupid, and even I'm internally cringing as I think it, but it was true. I had completely fallen for Dex Rutherford.

Hook, line and sinker.

Utterly, obsessively and truly fallen.

Hard.

I felt as if I had tripped into Dex's world and now I didn't want to leave. It was fucked up, it was messy, but it was beautifully messy, and I couldn't wait to drown in him.

"Like what you see?" he asked as he leant against the door frame, his muscles rippling under his skin as he crossed his arms over his chest. There was something so sexy about a man with good arms, and Dex's arms were hot as fuck.

I wanted to watch him grab the bed sheets over and over again just to watch the veins pop under his skin. I wanted to know what they looked like while grabbing my hair and tugging my head so far back that my neck was close to snapping. I wanted him grabbing my tee tightly, yanking me up while his thick cock filled my pussy, repeatedly making me come. I wanted his hands wrapped tightly around my throat, like a necklace while he ploughed into me.

My eyes widened when I finally came back round. *What in the motherfucking God was wrong with me?*

"What are you thinking about?" Dex asked as he strolled towards me.

"Nothing." I smiled sweetly, grabbing the duvet and pulling it under my chin.

"Don't lie."

"I'm not." I fidgeted on the spot, blushing under his intense stare as he climbed onto the bed.

"You're a terrible liar, Sage James." He smirked, placing a kiss on my forehead. "Let's eat then go shopping. Then I was thinking we could chill out before you start your job on Monday."

"Interview," I corrected him.

"Job." He winked.

Climbing off the bed, he stood, holding his hand out for me to take.

I let out a small, blissful smile as I threw the duvet back and took his hand.

We sat in the car, sitting in bumper-to-bumper traffic as we headed towards the shopping centre. I really didn't need any new clothes, but Dex insisted on buying me some new bits, seeing as I left all my stuff at Rhaegar's, and despite my dirty, filthy dream, I don't want to actually see him.

I shuddered as the memories flashed through my mind.

"You okay?" Dex asked, his hand reaching across, squeezing my leg.

"Yeah, fine." I smiled.

His brows pinched. "Sage, I know you a lot better than you know yourself, I have watched you for the last couple of years. I know your body language. What did you just think about?" he asked, his eyes not leaving mine as we stayed stationary.

I sighed. "Ugh, it's nothing." I waved my hand in the air, dismissing him. But his burning eyes didn't leave mine. I swallowed hard. "Fine..." I rolled my eyes, looking out the window for a minute before our eyes connected again. "I was just thinking that I didn't want you buying me new clothes, and that's not me being ungrateful because I am extremely grateful to have you. But I just..." I stopped for a moment. "I could easily go and get all the clothes Rhaegar, I mean your dad, it wouldn't be an issue. But the problem with that is, I don't want to see him, despite my dirty dream of the three of us... the actual thought of seeing him makes my skin crawl." I winced at my own words, listening to how harsh they were.

"I get that, I do." Dex nodded, his eyes moving from

mine to the crawling traffic in front of us. "But I wouldn't want you going back there anyway, plus, I want to buy you new clothes." He smiled.

Was it wrong that I didn't even feel a bit concerned that he had been watching from a distance for two years? Absolutely. I just didn't get the danger feel from him, I felt safe with him. I truly don't believe he would do anything to hurt me…well, not intentionally. *I hope.*

"That's kind of you." I nibbled on my bottom lip. Before we could speak about anything else, my phone buzzed. I smiled at the name that flashed on the screen.

Wes.

"Shit, Wes," I breathed a whisper.

"What's wrong?" I could see the concern all over Dex's face.

"Oh, it's nothing. I was meant to text Wes yesterday after I left his and I forgot." I shook my head softly from side to side in annoyance.

"Do you mind if I quickly call him?"

"Of course I don't." Dex smiled, sighing in relief as we broke through the traffic, taking the slip road and booting onto the A-road.

Chapter Twenty Four

Today's the day. One step closer to living my dream.

I woke early, my stomach in knots and riddled with nerves and anxiety. First day jitters. That's all.

Sitting in the large dressing area of the walk-in wardrobe, I brushed through my long hair. I didn't exactly know what I was going to be doing today so that didn't help. Dex told me to wear something casual and comfortable, so after a lot of 'uuming' and 'ahhing,' I chose high waisted skinny jeans and a basic tee.

I couldn't see me going straight into the garage, and if I did, they would have overalls.

"Morning, beautiful." Dex's voice was soft as he padded through to where I was sitting, handing me a cup of coffee.

"Morning." I grinned as I took the cup off him, taking a mouthful and smiling. I moaned in appreciation, the froth from the coffee sitting on my top lip. "If you ever decide to give up the club gig, I think you could give The Coffee Run a run for their money."

Dex let out a soft chuckle, dropping his head as his eyes fell to the floor before he met with mine again. Stepping towards me, he leant down, rubbing his thumb across my top lip then pushing the pad of it into his mouth and sucking it clean.

I blushed.

"You had a little milk moustache. But fuck, I can't wait to hear you moan like that when I fuck you." He winked.

"Thanks." I giggled, trying to ignore his last comment. I couldn't get distracted now. Turning away from him, I placed my cup on the dressing table as I finished my make-up off.

"How are you feeling?" he asked as he sat on the floor next to me, his legs crossing underneath one another.

"Okay, I think." I furrowed my brow. "A little nervous, but that's expected, right?" A laugh bubbled out of me.

"A hundred percent." He nodded slowly, closing his eyes. "But I will be there too, I won't leave you on your own." The corners of his mouth turned slightly as he looked up at me.

"No you won't." A nervous laugh slipped out of me as I turned to look down at him, and at that moment, I could tell he was completely fucking serious.

"Dex..." I shook my head.

"Sage..." He mimicked me.

"You can't," I stammered.

"Oh, I can." He nodded enthusiastically. "And I will be. I am not letting you out of my sight." He growled like some possessive animal.

I rolled my eyes. I didn't even have it in me to argue with him. Let's face it, he has followed me before, why is this even a shock to me?

Rise above it, Sage, rise above it.

I inhaled deeply as I finished my mascara off then pushed off the chair and grabbed my coffee. I heard Dex clamber to his feet behind me, following me like a lost puppy dog. I don't know why but it irritated me that he felt he could just decide to up and follow me to work, as if it was his given right.

But it wouldn't matter how much I flew at him, he wouldn't listen.

I didn't even know him that well, yet I felt like I could read him better than I could read myself.

I felt the rage start to fizzle as the thoughts continued. I liked that he wanted to be around me that much, that he wanted to protect me, keep me in his sights. But then it caused a small bit of anxiety to ripple through me. Did he know something? Or was it just that he wanted to be as close to me as he could?

I was at the bottom of the stairs, grabbing my rucksack and throwing it over my shoulder.

"Give me five minutes, little one." His voice was hushed as he disappeared into the kitchen. Shaking my hands out, I tried to push the rage out of my body that was still rearing its ugly head.

Dex walked in moments later, holding a pink glittery unicorn lunchbox.

I couldn't help but snort out a giggle, tipping my head back as my giggle turned into a deep laugh.

"Lunch." He smiled, handing me the small square box.

"Thank you." I beamed at him, taking the lunchbox, letting my bag drop off my shoulder and slipping it into my rucksack. Dex opened the front door, the sun beating down on us. Holding his hand out, gesturing for me to walk out the door first, I bowed my head as I walked past him, silently thanking him as I stepped down the three steps that led to the black iron gate. I didn't get a chance to open it, Dex was there opening it for me as he let me pass through again.

"Thank you," I muttered, standing kerbside. I furrowed my brow as I saw the *Lamborghini Urus* sitting outside the house.

I looked over my shoulder at Dex who stood there looking proud as punch.

"How did this get here?" I asked, the confusion

evident in my voice as my eyes volleyed between him and the car.

"I went and collected it early this morning from my dad's, he gave it to you, so I thought it was only right you had it," he said, his voice cool like the nip in the air. "Oh," I breathed out. "I didn't think it would still be mine after what happened, I am surprised he didn't give it to Shay instead of me." I shrugged my shoulders, not wanting to sound bitter.

"No, no." Dex shook his head, his hands fisting deep into his charcoal grey, fitted and tight in all the right places suit trousers. I couldn't stop my tongue from poking out and licking my top lip, the taste of him still evident on my taste buds. He was addicting, I wanted to taste him all the time. How sad was that?

I was addicted to my stalker. He was fast becoming my obsession which scared me, I felt like the roles were reversing. I wouldn't know what to do if he decided he didn't want me around anymore.

"It was your car, my father gifted it to you... he may be a dick, but he isn't heartless," Dex said as he stepped towards the Urus, taking his keys out of his pocket and throwing them at me. My right hand flew up, grabbing the keys that came towards me.

"Good catch." He winked before strolling towards the Urus and waiting at the passenger side.

Unlocking the car, I watched as he slipped in, me

slipping in next to him.

"I love this car." I sighed, pushing my foot on the break as I started the engine.

"Me too." He nodded. "Oh, and before I forget..." His voice cracked slightly as he opened the glove box and handed me a white envelope with my name written on it.

My breath caught at the back of my throat.

"You don't have to read it if you don't want to, but my dad asked me to give this you." I could hear the sincerity in Dex's voice.

I nodded numbly, turning my head to face forward as I looked out the wing mirror and pulled off.

I jumped when the satnav started talking to me, instantly grateful that Dex had put the address in otherwise I would have been driving aimlessly around London.

"I want to read it." I swallowed the apple sized lump down in my throat.

"Okay." Dex's voice was blunt as he threw the letter back into the glove box.

Shit, was that the wrong thing to say? Should I have said no?

My head pounded as I let the thoughts swim around, over and over. Fuck it.

"Sage, shit!" Dex called out, reaching across, grabbing the steering wheel, pulling me back into line.

"Fuck, sorry!" My eyes widened as I turned to look at

him quickly then let my eyes fall back to the road.

"Where were you? Were you thinking of my dad?" His words sliced through me.

"No." I huffed. "I was thinking that I had upset you by saying that I wanted to read the letter."

I heard Dex inhale deeply, his eyes closing for a moment.

"You haven't upset me; I just want us to be able to move forward without Daddy dearest lingering around in the background." I don't know why but his voice was cold as he spat the words out as if they were poison on his tongue.

"I do too..." I breathed out, my heart jackhammering in my chest.

"I am glad we are on the same page at least..." His eyes burned into the side of my head. I couldn't bring myself to look at him because if I did, I would lose myself in his dark brown eyes and I would never want to pull myself back out again.

The rest of the car journey was quiet, every time I went to speak it was as if my throat tightened and began to close so the words just wouldn't come out.

I pulled into the spot that Dex pointed out, cutting the engine and tipping my head back, letting it rest on the car chair.

"You ready?" Dex asked, turning in his seat, one leg sitting under the other.

"I think so." I gave him a weak smile that didn't quite hit my eyes.

"You are going to smash this, Sage." He reached across, taking my hand in his and rubbing his thumb over the back, a tingle spreading from my fingers all the way to my toes. I gave him a curt nod, pulling my hand which only caused him to tighten his grip. My head snapped back round to look down to where he had his fingers wrapped around my wrist before they lifted to look at him.

"Let me go," I whispered.

He shook his head. "I can't do that until you get out of your mood..." He licked his lips, his free hand pushing through his hair.

"Dex..." I groaned, his fingers wrapping tighter. "I'm not in a mood," I growled at him.

"No?" His brows sat high on his forehead.

I huffed.

"You started it," I said defeated as I sunk into the chair.

"I did." He smiled. "I didn't mean to come across as I did. It just... it grates on me. The thought of my dad trying to take you back..." He breathed harshly out of his nose.

"Dex, he isn't going to take me back. It's over between us. He fell for Shay, it's fine, I get it. I was just a contract, a job, a charity case." Even saying the words hurt, tears pricking my eyes. It was still the case now, but

SOMETHING WORTH STEALING

I wouldn't say that to Dex. Swallowing down the burning lump, I started to feel a little overwhelmed. It had been such a crazy few weeks, everything was so up and down.

"You're mine, Sage. I can't let him or anyone near you..." I saw him tense.

"No one is going to, but you took me from him, technically." I turned my face to the side to look at him, my head resting on the back of the car chair.

"I don't think so." He gasped, dropping my hand and laughing. I laughed with him, but the silence soon blanketed over us. "The thing is, little one, sometimes, something is worth stealing... and that's how it was with you. From the moment I saw you all grown up and shit, something changed. It was like we were destined to be together. I *needed* you, I have never needed anyone or anything like the way I needed you." He breathed, his fingers stretching and reaching for my hand before he pulled them back.

"I had to humour yours and my father's relationship, I had to bide my time." His eyes fell to where his hand sat splayed flat on the arm rest that sat between us. "Then the silly bastard cheated on you and that was my moment to take you, to keep you safe. I have been watching you for as long as I can remember. Before I knew it, you were all grown up and a temptation that I couldn't stay away from. Then once you started at the coffee shop, that was my meet cue, my moment. But truth be told, I could never muster the courage to speak to you about anything other than my cortado coffee order." He scoffed. "Then one night, I went to the club, had some *business* to take care of. You see, no one really knew who me and my dad were. Just knew we injected a lot of money into that club, they didn't know that we were going to buy it. We had dog's bodies running it, we just used to pop along for shits and giggles." He smirked as if he was remembering a memory. He quickly snapped back round. "I heard them talking about this *little vixen*, some green eyed, curvaceous beauty... so of course I had to check out the woman that was going to own my soul." He winked. "That's when I saw you again. Call it what you want, obsession, stalker, fate... we are written in the stars, destined, little one. I know you believe it too. Sure, we haven't had the best start, things have been awkward as fuck... but let me make it up to you. Let me court you, date you, whatever the fuck you want to call it, but let me date you. Let me have you, even for just one night, and I promise you won't want to leave me, because you see, Sage, I know you want me too. I can see it; I can feel it. The way you look at me, touch me, even the way you talk to me. Our hearts are already in love, your brain just needs to catch the fuck up and get back from whatever holiday she has fucked off to." His fingers tapped on the leather arm rest before they reached out for my hand. This time they made it to my skin, the electric rush that coursed through me made my breath catch and my heart race at a million miles per hour.

Everything he said was true, but to put everything in his hands and hope he doesn't break me is scary.

He was a tornado, me a volcano.

Each one of nature's destructions.

Both set to destroy whatever was in our paths. Yet we gravitated towards each other like we needed the colossal, catastrophic disaster to happen.

That's what we were.
We were destruction.
A beautiful fucking disaster.

CHAPTER
Twenty Five

Work, work, work, work.

"You've got nothing to say?" Dex asked, and fuck if his voice didn't break me. His low, gruff voice cracked as he asked the question.

"It's just a little overwhelming," I admitted. It was the truth, he fucking floored me.

But I just couldn't muster the words to tell him.

"I see." Dex licked his bottom lip, pulling it in-between his teeth, his eyes moving slowly to look out the window.

I inhaled deeply, breathing out my nose.

I took that as my cue to leave, nodding to myself. Opening the door, I didn't turn to look back at him. So much for not leaving me on my own.

Dick.

Walking towards the large car garage, I clung to my rucksack strap and took a deep breath as I stood outside the office door.

SOMETHING WORTH STEALING

"Come on, Sage, you can do this." I closed my eyes, re-assuring myself over and over.

Stepping forward, my hand reached out and grabbed the handle to open it.

I saw a young man sitting behind the desk, wearing dark navy overalls, grease all over his hands and a few smudges on his cheeks.

"Can I help you?" the man asked. I stared for a moment longer, and his dark brown eyes trailed up and down my body. He stood slowly, towering over the desk. The arms of his overalls were pushed up, revealing his caramel skin and muscular arms. Oh, I love a good set of arms.

Snapping out of it, my eyes met with his. His black ringlet hair was longer on top, but skin faded at the sides. Just as I went to answer, I heard the door chime with someone walking in.

"Her name is Sage, Sage James." Dex's voice splintered through me, my hairs rising on my neck.

"Oh, shit, yeah, of course." The guy behind the desk fumbled with paperwork.

"And, Hugo?" Dex called out, his hand snaking around my waist as it splayed across my stomach, pulling me to him.

"Yes?" Hugo asked, his eyes pinned to Dex.

"Don't even fucking look at my girl, do you understand?" Dex snarled, pulling his hand from my stomach, lacing his fingers through mine and dragging me into the garage.

What in the actual fuck?
I was ready to go home.

My body hummed; my blood pumped. The smell filled my nostrils, like a drug it hit me different. I know people didn't get it, but I buzzed. My skin tingled as my eyes widened looking round the garage. There were old bangers, newer cars, then I noticed a Rolls Royce nineteen-twenty-five Phantom. My eyes bulged as they glued to the stunning car that sat proudly higher on a stage over the back of the large airy garage.

The shiny black paintwork looked brand new; I could hear muttering next to me, but I was zoning out.

"Sage." Dex nudged into me gently.

"Yeah?" I whispered, pulling my eyes and looking up at him.

"Bryce is talking to you." He leant down, whispering in my ear. I felt the nerves creep up me. I turned to look at the older man, he must have been late forties, early fifties. His black hair was greased back, his eyes a light green. They were mesmerising.

"Sorry, Bryce. Please excuse my rudeness." I blushed. "I was just admiring the phantom over the back," I admitted.

"She's a beauty, right?" Bryce looked over his

shoulder, my eyes trailing back across.

"She really is." I sighed.

Our conversation died out for a moment while we both studied the car that took focal point in the garage.

"Let me show you around." Bryce smiled at me before his eyes lifted to Dex, giving a curt nod to acknowledge a silent conversation they have had between themselves. Dex was such a shit.

I followed Bryce through the garage where he introduced me to Hugo, Dave, Ryan and Travis. I greeted them all, giving them a smile. Their eyes all lifted from mine to Dex who stayed close behind me.

Brilliant.

This was going to be like hell on earth. How was I supposed to work here and get to know the guys when I have this idiot standing behind me, staring them down? I need to prove that I deserve to be here, not because Mr Possessive got me a job.

"Gentleman, can you give us a minute? Bryce, I will catch up with you in five." I gave him the best smile I could. Bryce's lips curled as he looked down at his feet, I'm sure I heard a cluck of his tongue on the roof of his mouth. The rest of the guys scampered back to where they came from.

"Baby…" I plastered a sweet but sickening smile over my face, stepping closer to Dex, my fingers fiddling with the buttons on his shirt.

"I need you to stop being a big grizzly bear and being all protective and let me find my place here." My eyes widened as I tried my best to give him an intimidating look. "And they're not going to respect me while you're being all big and burly. Let me do this. You want to hang around for the day? Fine. Just don't cause me any shit, I can do this. I *need* to do this." I sighed, and my fingers fell from his shirt. "For me, Dex."

I heard him breathe in, his eyes not moving from mine. I could see the cogs turning in his head, playing it over.

I wanted to beg him, but I wasn't going to. He needed to know how serious I was about succeeding and doing this on my own.

If he couldn't do this for me, then I would no longer want him in my life.

He stepped towards me, his fingers wrapping around my wrists as he placed them back on his shirt, his lips hovering over my head before he pressed them to my skin, lingering for a moment and inhaling deeply.

My eyes stayed fixed on his throat bobbing slightly as he swallowed down my scent.

"Have a good day, little one," he whispered before breaking away from me, turning on his heel and walking out the door.

I stood, stunned.

I didn't think he would have done it, and a small

smile crept onto my lips as I watched him sit in the car.

Okay, so he didn't go completely, but he did listen. I held my hand up and gave him a wave, a ghost of a smile on his lips before he turned his head away from me.

Sage, one.

Dex, nil.

Today was going to be a good day.

The hours slipped past like minutes. Bryce spent the remainder of the morning showing me where all the tools were, how the office ran and what needed to be done daily. We both agreed I would man the office Monday to Thursday, then on Fridays I would shadow an experienced mechanic.

I knew my cars, I knew the basics of an oil and filter change, a change of a tyre and a car overheating, but it was more the electrical side of things in the newer cars that I needed a little help with. Sure, most of the work was done by the computers and diagnostics now, but you still needed to know what to do when your hands needed to get dirty, and I couldn't wait. I was dismissed for lunch, and sitting in the office, my body hummed at the chatter of the guys. I was half expecting them to be seedy and perverted with half naked girls pinned up around their garages, but Bryce assured me it wasn't that *type* of garage.

Smiling a goofy grin, I reached down for my lunchbox out of my bag. It was purples and pinks with a white unicorn on the front, surrounded by glitter that moved when you pushed the gel layer that was on top. A snort of a giggle came out of me. Who knew Dex could be sweet?

Undoing the zip, I gasped to see a little note sitting on top of my sandwiches.

Sage,
Be mine?
Today, tomorrow, always.

Dex X

Woah. It's soon, too soon... but is it? Really? I know what I feel for him. He makes my heart flutter every time I see him, and my tummy flips in excitement before swarming with excited butterflies that can't seem to stay still. My skin smothers in goosebumps before tingling with anticipation of when he will kiss me again. My body reacts to him, my heart sings for only him, and my soul? It fucking aches for him.

Of course, I wanted to be his.

Today. Tomorrow. Always.

Holding the note in-between my fingertips, my eyes lifted to the door to see Dex standing there, his head cocked to the side, one corner of his lips lifting.

"Dex," I breathed as he stepped in, closing the door behind him.

"Sage." His brows raised, a playful grin now spreading across his beautiful face.

"Do you mean this?" I turned the note for him to see.

"I didn't write that." He furrowed his brows, looking at me all confused, like he had no clue what I was going on about.

"You didn't?" My voice laced with a sting, my heart dropping into my stomach.

"Nope." He darted his tongue out and ran it across his bottom lip as he took a seat opposite me on the other side of the desk.

How could I have been so stupid?

"Oh," I just about managed. "I see." My voice cracked, my eyes pricked with tears that were ready to cascade down my cheeks.

"Fuck, Sage." His voice cut through me. He pushed away from his chair and was by my side within seconds, his thumb brushing away a stray tear that managed to escape.

"You silly girl." He choked out a laugh. "Of course I wrote it." He sighed, his eyes softening as they gazed into mine.

"You did?" I sniffed, all of a sudden feeling like a prick.

"Yes!" Placing his other hand on my cheek, he pulled my lips closer to him. "It's always been you, I just wanted to see if you wanted me back..." He pulled his bottom lip between his teeth, the look of guilt smothering him. "Okay, so I could have gone about it in a different way... that was actually quite cruel." His eyes moved from mine as they focused on the wall that was next to me.

"It was cruel." I pouted, my brows pinching together.

"I'm sorry." He moved closer to me, his eyes falling to my parted swollen lips. Placing them over mine, he kissed me softly, delicately, lovingly. I melted into him, his hands still clasping my face as he held me in place.

Pulling away, he inhaled deeply.

"Your kiss is like a drug; do you know that? I never want to stop." He groaned, his thumb brushing over my bottom lip. "Forgive me."

"We hardly know each other," I argued back, my voice feisty.

He placed small pecks on my lips. "Sage." *Kiss.* "Please." *Kiss.* "Forgive." *Kiss.* "Me." *Kiss.*

A laugh bubbled out of me, my hands moving to his face as I held his head in my hands.

"I forgive you." I smiled sweetly.

"Be mine?" he asked once more, his eyes burning

into my soul, his hands still firmly in place.

"Today. Tomorrow. Always," I whispered against his lips.

"Bingo." He smirked before kissing me once more, his tongue pushing through my lips as it danced with mine.

The workday ended quickly; my head felt ready to explode with the amount of information I was given today. My smile grew with each step I took closer to the car, Dex sitting in the driver's side.

"Missed you," he whispered as I slid into the passenger seat.

"I've seen you for most of the day." I couldn't help the laugh that escaped me, shaking my head from side to side.

"Well, we didn't see enough of each other, obviously." He winked, starting the engine and pulling away.

"How did you feel there? Did they make you feel comfortable?" Dex asked, his voice was soft and gentle.

"I felt really comfortable." I nodded. "I was apprehensive, just because of what happened when I had to do my work placements." I sighed, my head tilting back slightly as I rested it on the chair.

My eyes widened as I watched Dex's grip tighten around the steering wheel. I had told Dex what happened when I had my work placement, I didn't feel comfortable keeping it from him.

"But anyway..." My voice was high pitched and cheery. "Moving on." I leant forward and turned the radio on. The car filling with *Song Bird – Eva Cassidy.*

I started singing softly, trying to push past Dex's foul mood. His fingers started to soften their death grip on the steering wheel.

"You have a beautiful voice," he whispered, not looking at me though, he was focusing on the trail of red lights in front of us.

"You must be deaf, my love, because I sound like a drowning cat." I laughed, but he didn't respond. The car fell silent. Sitting and watching, his jaw was tight and ticking, his hands rubbing the steering wheel, his eyes narrowing in front of him.

"Are you okay?" I asked, my hand gliding across the car and to his thigh, giving it a gentle squeeze.

"Just this song." His voice was low, blunt, cold.

"Want me to turn it off?" I asked, pulling my hand back. He shook his head from side to side.

"My mum always wanted this song at her funeral, so that's what we had. She said it was her song to me and she used to sing it when I was a baby." I saw the tears fill his eyes; he didn't blink. He was scared to let the tears fall.

"I'm sorry," I whispered.

"Don't be sorry, just you singing it, plus the song well

it triggered old memories that I had pushed far down." He turned his head slightly, giving me a heart-breaking smile as a tear rolled down his cheek. Reaching across, I rubbed my thumb over his cheek, absorbing the tear into my skin.

I was stunned, I didn't know what to say to comfort him. This was just proof we didn't... well, I didn't know him. At all.

My hand slipped back to his thigh, and that's where it stayed for the duration of the journey. A small bit of comfort that I knew he would appreciate it.

"Have you ever thought about your funeral song?" He surprised me by asking the question.

"Ummm, I have actually." I tucked my hair behind my ear. "*I was here – Beyonce.*"

"I haven't heard that one," he admitted, his fingers fumbling with the radio before he handed me his phone.

"Put it on." He nodded.

"Okay," I breathed, scrolling through his phone and finding the song then pressing play.

Dex's hand moved to my leg, squeezing it as he listened to the words.

"This song suits you." He snorted a laugh, his eyes leaving mine as we broke through the traffic.

"You think?"

"Yup. You're a force to be reckoned with, Sage James." He smiled, and fuck, his smile was beautiful.

I blushed.

"What about you Dex? What would your funeral song be?"

"Living in a box." He shrugged before bursting into laughter, the beautiful sound filling the car. It was lovely to hear him laughing, a young, carefree Dex.

"Stop it." I laughed with him.

"Nah, I'm joking... maybe burn baby burn?"

"Oh my fucking God, stop it." I was crying by this point; I couldn't deal with him. I swatted his arm. "You're a disgrace, Dex Rutherford." I scowled.

"A beautiful, sexy as fuck disgrace though, right?" He smirked.

"Absolutely."

He leaned across the middle of the car and pecked a kiss on my lips.

"Score." He winked.

Pulling up outside his house, I sighed in blissful happiness. I felt wrecked, I needed a nice bath and an early night.

Dex cut the engine, opening his door and stepping onto the pavement. I followed, waiting for him to open the door. Once in, I kicked my shoes off.

"I'm going to go and run a bath, is that okay?" I asked.

"Of course it is, you don't have to ask, Sage, this is your house too." He smiled, reaching for my hand and rubbing his thumb across the back.

"Okay." I lifted one of my shoulders up to meet my chin as I gave him a sweet smile.

He pulled me towards him, kissing me on my temple.

"Don't forget my dad's letter."

I stilled. Shit, his letter.

"I won't," I whispered, slipping my hand out of his as I walked up the stairs.

"Don't be long, I'll get started on dinner." He stood at the bottom of the stairs, watching me walk away, a huge grin on his face. Why did he always look so good?

Sighing blissfully, I turned my head and headed to my bathroom.

Sitting on my bed, I rummaged in my bag and pulled out the letter. Did I really want to read this? I suppose I had to. I had to get past this. If me and Dex were going to move on in our relationship, then I needed to get past the betrayal of Rhaegar. We would be seeing each other, as well as me and Shay, but I would deal with that little issue another day.

Inhaling deeply, I ran my finger under the envelope flap and opened the letter.

Sage,

Let me apologise first off, I am so sorry for what I have done to you. It was never my intention to hurt you the way I did.

Truth is, I was falling for you fast and hard. That worried me. What with everything that happened with Dex's mother, I found it very hard to trust and put my heart into someone else's hands. I know what Dex said must have rung alarm bells, but it isn't as it seems.

Dex's mother, Jackie, God rest her soul, was an addict. She was clean for years, but after Dex was born, she fell for her dealer. He treated her like shit, as did I. But he was manipulating her, keeping her high most of the time. She started failing as a mother, leaving Dex at school, not feeding or taking care of him like a mother should. That's when I came back on the scene. I raised Dex while his mother was in rehab, I needed her clean and well for Dex's sake. I was no angel with his mother, she was feisty, strong willed and so stubborn. She was a force to be reckoned with.

That's what I loved about her.

Did I lay a hand on her? Yes. It was more if she was high, and Dex was involved somehow. We used to argue, going back and forth until one of us snapped. She was no saint either.

I didn't want my son around that, I didn't want him seeing me act that way, but he did. It took us a long while to make our relationship better. Once his mother passed, he found me again.

SOMETHING WORTH STEALING

After seeing what happened to his mother, therefore he wanted to help your mum. Your mum has her own addiction, not like Jackie's, but rehab will help her, and I am so proud of Dex for doing what he has.

After I saw you and Dex together, the way you looked at each other, I knew I was being selfish keeping you to myself.

I wasn't right for you, Sage. Even though I wanted to be.

You and Dex were made for each other.

So, what did I do? I moved on without you. Shay makes me feel things I didn't know existed.

Everything happens for a reason.

Yes, I went about it the wrong way, and I am so sorry. I hope in time you can find it in your generous, beautiful heart to forgive me.

I'm setting you free, Kitten. I couldn't deny your happiness. That's all I ever wanted for you. I'm just sorry we didn't find it with each other.

But at least I can find peace in knowing that you will be happy with my son.

Our contract is terminated, you have been paid out, and don't argue me on this, Sage. Spend the money, buy a new home, treat your mother to the world and more.

You deserve it all.

I'll see you around, Sage, and remember, if you ever need anything, you know where to find me.

Love,
Rhaegar.

Well, fuck.

CHAPTER Twenty Six

Horny, frustrated girl here.

It had been two months.

Two fucking months since me and Dex became *official*.

And we still haven't had sex.

We have done everything else, but not sex.

What in the loving fuck?

I didn't get it.

Did he not find me attractive?

I knew it wasn't a small dick thing... I mean, I've seen his dick. Touched it and licked it. Sucked it just not fucked it.

I was horny and frustrated.

Sure, the oral was good, and so was being fingered, but it just didn't hit the same spot as being fucked would.

I sat twisting in my chair at work. Fuck, I was glad it was Thursday. I was out on the floor tomorrow and I couldn't wait to get my hands dirty. Dex kept his distance while I was at work, he lingered, but he didn't hover around me. He had planned dinner for tomorrow night with him cooking. I made a joke, saying I wanted him to be naked, but he didn't seem amused.

I sighed, everything was perfect between us, apart from the sex. So, tomorrow, once we have eaten, I am going to bring it up with him. Or just fuck his brains out.

My phone buzzed. It was Spring Hills, the rehab centre that my mum was in. Smiling, I clicked the green phone.

"Hello."

"Hi, Sage, darling." My mum's voice warmed me.

"Hi, Mum!" I said, a little over excitedly. I stood from the desk and closed the door so we could have a little privacy. The walls were thin in the self-made offices and the workshop floor echoed.

"How are you?" I asked as I walked back to my desk.

"I am wonderful, darling. Dex visited me, he left about ten minutes ago." I could hear from her tone she was smiling, her voice upbeat "Did he?" I leaned back, looking outside the front of the shutter to see the car pull back up.

Sneaky.

"Yup, was lovely to see him. When can you come and see me?" she asked, the shimmer of hope lacing her voice.

SOMETHING WORTH STEALING

"Sunday? How does that work?" I smiled as Dex walked towards my office, looking through the window and pointing at the door.

I nodded.

"Sunday is perfect, you can eat Sunday roast with me. Will you bring Dex?"

"Of course."

"Okay. I miss you, Sage, I can't wait to come back home." I heard the quiver in her voice that broke my heart. I hated that she was there and not home where she should be.

"I know, Mum, I can't wait for you to be home too..." I let my voice trail off for a moment, trying to push the burning lump that was lodged in my throat back down. "I've been thinking, Mum, how do you feel about me selling the house and looking for something a little closer to Dex and more suitable for us?" I needed to tread carefully with this conversation, her home was all she had and all she knew. It wasn't going to be easy to convince her.

"Oh, Sagey, I don't know... what about all my stuff?" I could hear the apprehension in her voice.

"We would bring all of our stuff with us." I saw Dex nodding, silently telling me to keep going.

"And just think, it's a fresh start for all of us. We will be close to Dex, so I am sure he will drop in a lot more. I will look for something with a nice garden so you can potter about outside."

She didn't reply, I could just hear her breathing down the phone.

"Mum, we haven't got to make any decisions now, okay? It was just an idea. That's all." Now I sounded defeated.

"How about we talk on Sunday?" My voice was hopeful.

After another few minutes of silence, she spoke. "Okay."

"Okay? Okay is good." I gave Dex the thumbs up.

"I'll see you Sunday, Sage, I love you."

"I love you more, Mum."

She cut the phone off.

Letting my shoulders sag, I dropped the phone on my desk then placed my head on my hands as I rested my elbows on the edge.

"It's okay, Sage." Dex's voice comforted me, his hands rubbing my tense shoulders.

"I know, I just feel shitty. I shouldn't have said that to her today, maybe I should have waited till Sunday?"

I lifted my head, sitting back in my chair, my eyes falling onto Dex.

"No, telling her was the right thing. That way, come Sunday, she would have thought about it and how much of a good idea it is. Whereas if you had sprung it on her Sunday, she would have freaked out even more." His voice was low as his lips sat next to my ear.

He was right.

"I know." I sighed. "I just don't like it when she withdraws herself, she seems to be doing so well and now I feel like I have put a small halt in that recovery."

"She is doing exceptionally well; she has eight weeks left and then she is home. I stopped at her therapist's office today to ask how she was doing, and he was gobsmacked at the progress. She has told him some pretty heavy stuff by the sounds of it, stuff that she hasn't spoken a word of." He stilled for a moment, his lips pressing to my cheek. "Trust me, baby," he whispered.

"I do." I nodded, turning my face and kissing him on the lips.

"Let's go home, shall we?" He stood tall, holding his hand out for me.

"I still have twenty minutes." I scowled.

"I spoke to your boss; he says you're good to go."

With a roll of my eyes, I stood up.

Did I forget to mention that my boss is my boyfriend?

Yup.

After my *'I need to do this for me, you need to give me some space'* chat, Dex reinterpreted that as, *'I need to buy the company, so I am always with her.'*

Did I kick off? Yes, I did.

Did it change anything? Absolutely not.

He was still a possessive, obsessive man.
And I loved it.
Fuck, I loved him.

Stepping under the shower, I washed the day off me. I was enjoying work, but I was ready for more now. I needed to show them what I could do. The guys got a little put out when Dex offered to buy Malcolm's Custom Fixes, I got it, but Bryce couldn't turn down his offer.

I mean, even if he wanted to, he couldn't. Take that as you will. Bryce was also not best pleased when Dex changed the name of his late father's garage to '*Sage's.*'

Dex would never have allowed it to not be changed.

I am surprised he went to visit my mum without me, leaving me alone for all of an hour.

Shock.

Smirking as I lathered the shampoo into my hair, I heard the bathroom door go. Looking over my shoulder, my eyes raked up the God-like naked body that was standing outside the glass shower door.

His muscles flexed under his skin as he ran his hands through his hair, messing it up and letting it fall loose.

My mouth slowly dropped open. The whole top half of his body was covered in tattoos. His hands, arms, neck, shoulders, chest, stomach, back…

My eyes continued down his body, his thick, toned thighs were also wrapped in his beautiful tattoos. Even his feet were covered.

He was a beautiful piece of art. Each tattoo had a meaning, a hidden story. He has told me a few, but I let him tell me. I never push and ask.

Dex stepped towards the shower, pulling the door back. He stepped under the cascading water, his hands around my face, pushing me against the wall. I felt his fingers entangling in my hair, tugging so my head tipped back, lips pressing against my neck and trailing down to my breast. He fell to his knees, his hands skimming down the side of my body, wrapping around my waist as he held himself up. His mouth locked around my nipple, sucking and puckering it, his tongue swirling around before he bit it gently. I moaned, my head tipping back against the wall. Pushing his tongue flat against my skin, he trailed it across to my other breast, one of his large hands grabbing my boob, squeezing as he licked and sucked. This time, a bolt of pleasure shot between my legs. "Dex, please, fuck me," I begged.

He groaned, biting my nipple before his lips moved to my skin, sucking hard, marking me.

"Not yet," he mouthed against my skin.

I whined, his hand slipping between my legs as he pushes two fingers inside of me, his ring finger teasing at my bum.

My hands flew to his hair, grabbing and tugging as his lips trailed across and around my hardened nipples, biting my skin occasionally.

He slipped his fingers out to the tip, swirling them in my arousal before pumping them into me.

I cried out, I loved feeling him inside of me. His thumb brushed against my clit, my skin tingling, shivers dancing up and down my spine as I felt my impending orgasm.

"Touch yourself," he ordered, falling back on his knees, breaking his lips away from me. My head fell forward as I watched him finger fuck me, slow, torturous pumps in and out of me.

My trembling hands skimmed down my belly before finding their place in-between my legs. My index and middle finger found my swollen clit, rubbing gently, matching the pace of his fingers.

"I want you to sit on the floor, legs open for me, baby, okay?" His voice was slow and low. I moaned through a nod.

Pulling his fingers from me, I let out a shaky breath as I slid down the wall, doing as he said. Opening my legs wide, I saw his face light up, grinning wide.

"Do you realise how perfect your pussy is?" he groaned, his fingers rubbing my clit fast before gliding them down between my folds and swirling them at my opening.

"Dex, please," I begged.

"What, little one?" His lips pressed to my neck.

"You know what…" I cried out as his fingers plunged inside of me, stretching me.

"All good things come to those who wait…" he whispered, licking the shell of my ear.

I looked between my legs, he had three fingers inside of me.

"Fuck," I breathed out, my pussy clamping around his fingers.

"Such a tight little cunt." He growled as he sat back, watching as he finger fucked me. "Rub your clit."

I could just about nod, the pleasure consuming me.

My two fingers swirled around on my clit, which only heightened my pleasure.

I could hear and feel how wet I was, and Dex's eyes darkened as he slipped his fingers out of me.

"Keep rubbing."

He moved up, turning the shower down.

"We don't want to wash any of this honey off of you now, do we?" He licked his lips, pressing his three fingers into his mouth, moaning in appreciation as he licked them clean.

Lining them up at my opening, he pushed the three of them back in, a slight sting and burn as my pussy stretched for him.

"Dex, I'm getting close." I breathed out, my eyes on

him.

Smirking, he slipped his fingers out that were dripping in my arousal and rubbed them around my arsehole, slipping the tip of two fingers inside of the place that only he had been.

I gasped; the feeling so unfamiliar but so right as he pushed them in a little deeper.

"I can't wait to fuck your arse," he moaned, licking his lips. His free hand wrapped around the back of my neck, pulling me forward so I could see.

"Look how responsive your body is, I can see your honey dripping from your pretty, plump cunt."

He was right.

I was so fucking turned on and wet.

He had his middle and ring finger in my arse, pumping in and out slowly as he brought me to new realms of pleasure.

"I think your pussy is feeling a little left out." He winked. Lining his index finger up at my pussy opening, he slipped it in with ease, all three fingers pumping into me slowly.

"Oh fuck, Dex, shit," I moaned out, my fingers rubbing faster over my clit now. He took my outburst as his go ahead to speed up his thrusts, and fuck did he speed them up.

I was soaked, his fingers slipping in and out of my holes with ease, the juices from my pussy dripping down, making his fingers slip in and out of my tight arse.

I clenched, my pussy throbbing as my legs trembled. A shiver exploded across my skin. "Keep going, baby, fuck," I cried out.

It was too much.

A shiver danced up and down my spine, bursting into a tingle as I came, loud and hard. My back arched off the wall, my head tipped back as his fingers continued fucking me.

"There's a good girl, little one." He licked his lips.

Slipping his fingers out of me, he pushed all three past his lips.

Fuck.

He slowly stood up, looking down at me with a devilish smirk on his face.

"Now, little one, get on your fucking knees and suck my dick." His hand flew to my hair, his fingers lacing themselves within it as he guided me to his thick cock.

Batting my lashes, my eyes looked up at him. Licking the tip of his cock, I heard the breath suck through his teeth.

I loved watching him fall apart because of me.

Pushing my lips around his head, I pushed them down to the base of his cock, taking him deep.

I was so much more used to him now, no more gagging for little old me.

I sucked him hard and fast, my hand wrapping

around his dick as I pumped him into my mouth over and over. My spare hand cupped his balls, massaging and tickling them with my nails.

"Fuck, Sage, yes, baby, oh, yes!" he cried out, his hips thrusting into my mouth fast, his cock hitting the back of my throat.

My eyes watered, the dribble slipping from my lips. I was a fucking mess, but I was enjoying it too much to give a fuck what I looked like.

"Little one, you look so fucking hot with my big cock in your mouth." He groaned, slowing his thrusts, pulling his cock out to the tip. I locked my lips around his head, placing kisses and licking the pre cum off that was beaded on him.

Smirking, I pushed my lips back down his girth, stopping at the base as I slowly moved my head side to side so he could feel just how deep I had taken him.

My eyes streamed.

My hand pumped him as I pulled my mouth from him. I watched him fall apart, my mouth parting.

His hand tugged my head back, his spare hand taking my hand off his cock. His greedy hand wrapped around himself tightly, wanking himself off as he brought himself to his high. Pressing his cock to my lips, he came, spurting it into my mouth as I swallowed every drop of him. I licked around his head, making sure I didn't miss any.

"Oh, Sage, you're phenomenal. I have never had my dick sucked that good." He groaned, pulling me up before slanting his mouth over mine.

I had fallen so fucking hard for this man.

I was scared the dream was going to be over at any minute.

We spent the evening chilling and watching *Pretty Woman*. He moaned about it, but once he got into it, he loved it.

"I feel like I am Richard Gere, and you're Julia Roberts." He smiled, placing a kiss on the top of my head.

"You mean Vivienne and Edward?" I pulled back out of his cuddle, furrowing my brow as I watched his facial expression.

"Whoever." He rolled his eyes. "But yes, them... I feel like I saved you." He sat there, feeling proud as punch.

"You did save me, but I also feel like I saved you." My smile was small.

"You did." He leaned into me, kissing me. "I'm never letting you go."

"Good, because I don't want to ever leave."

CHAPTER Twenty Seven

So, we meet again. The ex-sugar daddy and his pet.

I woke with excitement in my belly. Today was the day that I got to work on my own in *my* garage.

It still felt surreal saying that.

I had a garage.

I made sure Dex was not involved in the running of it. I paid my way, paid the bills and even injected a lump of money into the company to re-brand.

Slipping into high-waisted *mom* jeans and a racerback vest top, I pulled my hair into a high ponytail.

Dex appeared at the doorway, leaning against the door frame. Even though we slept together in his room now, I always got ready in this room. It was light and airy; the natural light was perfect for doing my make-up.

"You nearly ready?" He smiled at me, his eyes glistening as they trailed up and down my body.

"Yup." I nodded, slipping my feet into my chunky

doc martens. Strolling towards him, I placed my hand on his chest and pushed onto my toes as I kissed him softly on his lips.

His lips were so soft, just like the inside of a rose.

"Let's go, little one." He smirked against my lips, his fingers lacing through mine as he led me to the car.

I had fallen so hard for this man, and I don't even think he knew.

He had my heart, my soul and my body.

-

DEX

How the fuck did I land her?

Oh yeah, I obsessed, I stalked, and I stole.

It was always going to be me and her. Her and me.

Even if it took years, I would have gotten her in the end. Because she was made for me. She was it for me.

I had fallen head over fucking heels for her, there was no stumbling, no catching my step. No. I full on fell, smashing into the hard ground. I was obsessed with her. Everything about her made my heart sing, my skin tingle, and my dick hard.

Her jet-black hair, I loved nothing more than entangling my fingers through it, twirling and tugging on it.

Her shining green, emerald eyes. A little vixen. I

loved how she couldn't hide any of her emotions, thoughts or feelings because her beautiful eyes gave her away. Every single time.

Her lips, fuck, her lips. Plump and pink, all natural. She had a natural pout, and the way she locked them around my cock... I can't even. I internally groan, my cock twitching in my tight suit trousers.

Her curves, fuck, her curves. Bringing my fist to my lips, I open them, biting down on my knuckles. Her big tits, more than a handful, perfect for kneading and squeezing. Her waist tiny, her hips wide and curvaceous, then you get to her thighs. Thick. Toned. Perfection.

Pulling up outside her garage, I sat for a while, just watching her. I was good at that. Watching her. Perfected it over the years, and she wouldn't even know I was here.

Smirking, I watched her in admiration. She was wearing black overalls, bending over a car hood. Do you know the restraint I am feeling to stop myself from walking in there and just fucking her?

I mean, I am desperate to fuck her.

But not yet.

Biding my time.

It had to be right. I have dreamt of this moment for months, years even. As perverted as that sounds... fuck, that does sound perverted. Scrap that, I have been dreaming of it since I saw her all grown and shit.

SOMETHING WORTH STEALING

I watched with possessive eyes as Hugo approached her, leaning over the other side of the hood, his eyes roaming down her body.

I didn't even give him a chance. I flew out the car, storming into the garage, pushing Sage out of the way as I stood face to face with him. Hot air snorted out my nostrils as they flared in rage, my fists balling.

"I am getting a little tired of you keep eyeing my girl," I growled.

"I'm not fucking eyeing your girl." Hugo puffed his chest out, his eyes not leaving mine.

I swear to fucking Lucifer, I will end him.

"Well, from where I was watching, you fucking were. How many times do I have to remind you that she is mine? MINE!" My voice boomed around the workshop, and Hugo flinched.

"Dex..." Sage's arm reached out, her hand wrapping around my forearm. It took me a moment for my red rage haze to disappear. Turning my head to look down at her, her eyes bored into mine as she shook her head slowly from side to side.

I had fucked up.

Relaxing my closed fists, I inhaled deeply before turning on my feet and walking out of the workshop. Slamming the car door, I rested my elbow on the window of the car, my hand on my forehead as I rubbed it back and forth. I needed to cool it. Calm the fuck down.

But then again, the thought of not having her near me, with me, in love with me, fucking paralyzed me.

I couldn't cope or function without her.

It was bad enough that I had to go and sort shit with my sperm donor this morning... okay, that's a little harsh. He isn't a sperm donor. Just because I am in a shit mood, I can't take it out on him.

I still needed to tell Sage I had invited him and Shay to dinner tonight. That was going to go down like a shit sandwich. But we had to move on. We had to socialise with them. He was my father and business partner, it's not like I can cut him out of our lives. Wait... or could I? If she handed me the scissors, would I, could I cut him out?

No, I couldn't.

I shook my head at my thoughts.

My head snapped to the right when I heard a light tap on the window, letting out a breath of relief when I saw my baby standing there, a cute as fuck smile on her face.

Pushing the button, the window slipped down quickly.

"Can I help you?" I teased.

"Dex, stop." She pushed at my shoulder through the open window. "That was not cool." She bent down, resting both of her arms on the window, her head tilting to the side.

"It was pretty cool." I smirked.

She rolled her eyes before looking over her shoulder.

"Just an FYI, you look phenomenal in that boiler suit." I wiggled my eyebrows, her attention back on me as she blushed. "And your tits... fuck, don't even get me started. Might have to have a quick wank in the car."

Sage burst into a fit of giggles.

"You wouldn't." She rubbed her lips together, shaking her head from side to side.

"Oh, I would." I nodded enthusiastically.

"Perv."

"You love it." I winked. "And also, I think you should bring that suit home with you one night, I want to fuck you in it." His voice was raspy and low.

"Well, you'll be waiting a while, seeing as you won't make a move on me." She sighed then pouted her lips.

"Stop pouting, angel, it'll be worth it... just wait and see." I licked my lips.

"Mmhmm, I'll believe it when it happens, it'll be closed up with cobwebs by the time you make a move, or maybe, I might even be dead." She stood up, smacking her hands down on the seal of the window. "Anyway, you think about that. Some of us have work to do." She stepped back from the car, one corner of her lips turning up into a smile. "And leave Hugo alone. He is my friend, that's all..." She winked, turning on her heel and walking away from me. Her arse and hips sashaying as she did.

Damn woman. Being all sexy and shit.

My dick was hard and throbbing. Maybe I needed that wank sooner than I thought.

-

SAGE

I don't know why but I was grateful when work was over with for the day. Perks of it being my business now… I didn't have to work weekends anymore.

Slipping into the car next to Dex, his eyes trailed up and down my body, the fire and desire flitting across his brown eyes.

"Hey." I smiled, leaning across and kissing him on the lips, lingering a little longer than usual. His kisses were addicting.

"Hey." He smiled against my lips before I pulled away.

He started the car and pulled off.

"So, dinner tonight, slight change of plans," he said breezily.

I knew what was coming.

"Go on," I said nonchalantly.

"Dad and Shay are coming for dinner tonight." I saw as he side-eyed me, waiting to gauge my reaction.

"Lovely." My lips pressed into a tight smile.

It's going to be fine.

Rhaegs wasn't the problem.

Shay was.

Rhaegs apologised.

Shay didn't.

She hasn't even tried, and that's what has pissed me off.

"Sage, you okay?"

I nodded curtly.

"Okay..." His voice trailed off as he pushed the metal to the floor, taking us home.

Was I looking forward to making small talk with her? No.

Will I make small talk? Yes.

For Dex's sake, and Rhaegar's, of course.

Once me and Dex were both cleaned up after a hot and heavy make out session, I was buzzing. Not from excitement, no, it was from being horny.

Dex wrapped his fingers around my waist and pulled me to him, my hands pressing against his firm chest.

"You look lovely," he breathed, his lips hovering over mine.

I was wearing a tight, fitted in all the right places, silver mini dress. Most of my tattoos were on show, and I felt amazing.

"As do you," I whispered back to him. Dex was in

fitted black jeans and a tight white tee, gripping to his muscles. His own tattoos were on show.

We looked hot together. That couldn't be denied.

He went to kiss me, but I pulled away, pressing my fingers against his lips.

"I am going to say this once, and once only." My voice was still low, my lips close to his as my breath danced over his skin. "If you do not fuck me tonight, I will find someone who will…" I winked, pulling my finger from his lips and patting my flat hand to his chest. Turning on my heel, I stopped, a growing smirk spreading across my lips. Looking over my shoulder at him, his head lowered slightly, his eyes dark and brooding, his jaw tight and clenched.

"I'm not wearing any knickers." My tongue darted out, running across my top lip seductively, while one of my hands gripped the hem of my dress and lifted it, revealing one of my bum cheeks.

Giggling, I let go of my dress and walked out of the room like a damn queen.

Take that Dex Rutherford.

The table was set, and smiling at my work, I clapped my hands together. The dining room walls were white, the bottom half of the walls panelled. Coving was wrapped around the top of the walls, hugging the ceilings. The high ceilings had silver, crystal chandeliers hanging from them. The room was stunning. Large black picture frames sat on the top half of the wall, filled with abstract images. I had no clue what they were, and to me, they looked like a two-year-old had drawn them. But then again, who am I to judge? I'm no art critic, or artist for that matter.

I paced up and down, I felt anxious. I kept fiddling with the tablecloth, re-arranging the knives and forks. Fork and knife first? Knife and fork first? Shit.

Think back to Pretty Woman, think back to Pretty Woman.

Once I had the order right, I think, I placed two bottles of wine in the chiller. White and Rosé. Beers were stocked in the mini fridge.

"Stop worrying." Dex's voice broke my thoughts.

"I'm not." I smiled, my fingers wrapping around the top of the chair.

"Good, because they're here." He smiled back at me, holding his hand out for me to take. Stepping towards him, I laced my fingers through his. Pulling me close, he placed a kiss on my temple. "I love you," he whispered against my skin before pulling me towards the front door.

He loves me.
HE LOVES ME.
My heart.
I love him.
I LOVE him, shit, I needed to tell him.

His hand curled around the door handle, and I

placed my hand over his, stopping him for a moment.

"I love you, Dex." I felt the tears pool in my eyes. I did. I loved him more than he would ever know. So we had only been together two months, but what did that matter?

Once you know, you know, right?

"Fuck, do you know how good it is to hear that, little one?" He gripped onto my chin, tilting my head back slightly before kissing me. His kisses were everything.

"Now, let's get this dinner over with so I can show you just how much I fucking love you." He groaned, dropping my chin and opening the door.

"Welcome." Dex beamed, stepping aside and letting them walk through the door.

Game time baby.

CHAPTER Twenty Eight

He wants to show me how much he loves me?
Let's hope that's with a good dicking.

"Sage." Rhaegar stepped through the door, his hand snaking around my waist as he kissed me on the cheek. "It's so good to see you, happiness suits you." He winked. I heard the possessive growl that came from Dex's throat. I chose to ignore it. There didn't need to be any animosity tonight.

Shay was next through the door, wearing a tight black mini dress, her boobs basically spilling out the top of the loose neckline.

Don't be a bitch.

"Shay." I plastered the fakest smile on my face as I embraced her, her hands spreading up my back as they pressed between my shoulder blades. *Oh look, she is removing the knife she put there.*

"Sage." Her voice was laced in fakeness.

Good show.

Bravo.

Bitch.

We pulled apart, and I stepped aside of Dex and held my hand out to the dining room. Rhaegar held Shay's hand as they walked into the dining room.

Dex closed the door, wrapping his hand around my waist as he pulled me to him. His lips pressed to my cheek before they moved to the shell of my ear.

"I don't like her," he whispered, his hand still firmly holding me in place.

"Me either," I breathed. But that was a lie. I did like her. I was just fucking angry with her.

Placing my hand over his, I removed it from my stomach, leading him into the dining room with our guests. Dex pulled my seat out, I thanked him sweetly and sat down opposite Shay. Her long, scrawny fingers trailed along Rhaegar's shoulders repeatedly.

I was over Rhaegar. One hundred percent, but what was getting me was Shay. I felt like she was using him. Money? Most likely. She had her own sugar daddy, so what happened for her to want to move onto Rhaegar? I didn't get it. But the difference was, I didn't have to. As long as Rhaegar is happy, I'm happy.

"Thank you for inviting us, Dex, Sage." Rhaegar smiled at his son before his eyes landed on me. A waitress appeared, popping the cork on the white wine and pouring us all a glass. Shay covered the top of her glass and shook her head, moving her hand to her non-existent bump.

No. Fucking. Way.

Dex's eyes pinned to her stomach before they widened at his father.

He was thinking the same as me.

Nice little honey trap she set up there.

Idiot.

"Oh, wow…" I said, my brows sitting high on my face as my hand dropped under the table, squeezing Dex's thigh.

"I know." She smiled wide, her head turning to look at Rhaegar. He didn't move his eyes from Dex.

"Well, I suppose congratulations are in order," I chirped, reaching for my glass and holding it up.

"To Shay and Rhaegar, Dad at sixty, congratulations." I nodded before knocking the glass of wine back.

"He is fifty-seven actually." Shay's smart-arse comment just riled me up.

He is nearly fifty-eight, you dick.

I didn't wait for the waitress, I reached across and grabbed the bottle, shaking my head as the waitress came to pour me a glass.

"I've got it, thank you. Can you just grab the starters and a straw, please? I'll drink it straight from the bottle." Nodding like a maniac, my voice was high.

The waitress dropped her head and scuttled away through the double doors that led to the kitchen, slamming them closed behind her.

"Are you fucking mad?" Dex seethed at Rhaegs.

"It just happened," Rhaegs snapped.

"Excuse me?" Shay's head turned quickly, her eyes burning into Rhaegar. If looks could kill, he would be six feet under by now. Sucks to be him.

"You're nearly sixty, by the time the kid is in school you'll be mid-sixties, and fuck, by the time it leaves high school, you'll probably be dead." Dex slams his hand on the table. "What the fuck were you thinking?"

"I love her," Rhaegar responded weakly, his eyes falling from his son's for a moment.

"Bravo for you. I love Sage but I didn't knock her up after two months!"

I nodded, tilting my head to the side while shrugging one shoulder up.

Nope, because for that to happen, we would need to have sex.

Common knowledge.

Bringing the bottle to my lips, I took a big mouthful. Screw the straw.

"Dex, please."

"No, Dad. Don't fucking 'Dex please' me. I'm not happy for you, sorry." Dex sat back in the chair.

I blew out my breath, puffing my cheeks out.

SOMETHING WORTH STEALING

"At least it'll be nice for your son or daughter to grow up with your grandchild, Rhaegs, mine and Dex's child. Lovely little bond we will all have. Sounds a little incestuous when you work out the dynamics in your head... but how lovely." I smiled.

Rhaegs and Dex's head snapped to me.

"You're pregnant too?" Shay asked, her brows furrowing.

"Nope, not yet. But with the fucking I am getting tonight, it'll probably end that way." A burst of hysteria bubbled out of me.

Dex choked on his own breath at my outburst, Rhaegs continued sipping his wine.

The waitress arrived, placing our plates down in front of us. King prawns smothered in a chilli and garlic marinade. Fresh French stick was placed on the side of the plate.

"I don't like fish." Shay turned her nose up, pushing the plate away.

"Don't eat it then. Pretty simple." I smiled, happily tucking into my food.

We ate in silence; the tension was high.

It was bad.

Once the starters had been cleared away, I inhaled deeply. One of us had to be the bigger person, and by the looks of things, that would be me.

"Right, I think we need to have it out, don't we?" I placed my elbows on the table, my eyes darting between Rhaegs and Shay.

"I don't think we do." Shay crossed her arms defensively across her chest.

"No, we really do. Stop being a child." I rolled my eyes, shaking my head. Rhaegs turned to look at Shay.

"We really do," he agreed with me.

She sighed.

I turned to look at Dex, he said nothing. Just stared at his dad.

He was hurt, I got it. Maybe he was angry? Whatever he was feeling, we couldn't leave our relationship between us all like this.

"We're all adults, well… one of us acts like a child." I licked my lips, smirking towards Shay.

Her hard face exterior softened slightly as a laugh escaped out of her.

There she was.

"Look, what happened in the past is done. Was it wrong that you went about it the way you did? Yes, one hundred percent. But it's done. Let's just move on with our lives and be amicable, for the child's sake at least." I smiled warmly before I let out a deep sigh. I didn't want to lose my friendship with Rhaegar or Shay.

Rhaegar nodded. Shay smiled.

Dex just sat there, face like thunder.

He would come around, I hoped.

Once we had eaten our dinner, we moved to the lounge area.

"It's a lovely home you have here, Dex." Shay smiled.

"It's Sage's home too," Dex snapped.

"Of course." Shay held her hands up in submission.

"Dex..." I warned.

He didn't say anything, just sighed.

We lost ourselves in light chatter, Dex not really saying anything. After an hour, he excused himself and disappeared upstairs.

"I'm sorry," I said quietly, giving Rhaegar a small smile.

"It's fine, I get it..." Rhaegar dropped his voice to a whisper. "You've got to understand, Dex's upbringing wasn't great, he has a lot of issues." Rhaegs pressed his lips into a thin line.

I kept quiet; I didn't feel comfortable discussing Dex's upbringing.

"We're going to call it a night, go and see to Dex." Rhaegs stood tall, holding his hand for Shay to take, which she did gladly.

I stood with them, walking them to the front door.

"Thanks for coming, hopefully we can do this again soon and Dex won't be such an arse." I smiled fondly as me and Rhaegs embraced each other.

"I hope so." Rhaegar smiled as he let me go. I moved to Shay, hugging her tightly.

"Congratulations, both of you," I whispered, feeling tears prick my eyes for some reason.

"Thank you," Shay whispered back, looking just as glassy eyed as me.

"I'm sorry." I sniffed.

"No, you don't need to say sorry." She sighed, taking my hands in hers. "I'm the one that needs to be sorry, I shouldn't have done what I did to you. Truth is, Rhaegs saved me. Take that how you want, but without him stepping in, I most likely would have been dead." Her eyes welled again, and looking over her shoulder at Rhaegar, she let go of my hand and held it out for Rhaegar to take.

"Night, Sage, wish Dex goodnight for us," she said softly as she stepped away. I nodded silently, watching them walk hand in hand out the front door, Rhaegar pressing his lips to the top of her head.

Closing the door and locking up, I went through the bottom of the house making sure everything was turned off.

Now to go and find a sulking Dex.

CHAPTER Twenty Nine

D meet V. Nice to finally meet you.

Climbing the stairs, I walked into the bedroom to see Dex laying on the bed in just a pair of black shorts, TV remote in his hand as he watched trash on tele.

"You okay?" I asked, my fingers wrapping around the door frame.

He nodded, his head turning to look at me.

"Good." I smiled. "Now..." Slipping my fingers under the straps of my dress, I let them fall down my arms. "Have you thought about what I said?" I purred, pulling the straps off my hands.

Dex's eyes narrowed, spinning his legs round so he was sitting on the edge of the bed. My thumbs slipped into the side of my dress, pushing it down my thighs and letting it pool at my feet. Slipping my feet out of my shoes, I stood completely naked in front of him.

His tongue shot out, swiping along his bottom lip before his teeth sunk into his lip, pulling it behind his teeth.

"I have." His finger curled, calling me over.

I wanted to squeal in delight.

Sauntering over to him, I stepped between his legs. His hands were on my hips.

"Do you know why I wanted to wait?" he whispered, his lips pressing in the middle of my boobs.

"Why?" My hands moved to his head, linking my fingers around the back.

"Because..." His lips pressed harder to my skin now. "I wanted to make sure this was real between us, I wanted to get to know you, wanted to make sure your mum was okay, wanted to make sure that *you* were okay." I felt his lips break into a smile against my skin.

"I'm more than okay." I breathed, his kisses making my skin tingle. "Everything is more than okay, it's perfect," I whispered, lifting his head so he was looking at me.

"I need you." My voice was quiet as my hair fell around my face, shielding us from the outside world.

Dropping to my knees, his eyes followed me. Pressing my palms to his chest, I skimmed them down his body, stopping at the waistband of his shorts. Tugging them greedily, I pulled them down his legs, freeing his cock.

My mouth watered.

I was so ready for him.

Gripping onto my chin, he pulled me towards him, our lips crashing together as our tongues entwined.

"Let's take it slow, baby, I want to remember everything." His voice was hoarse.

His fingertips skimmed over my sensitive skin, kneading my boobs then rolling my nipples between his fingers.

"Dex," I whispered.

He continued his teasing. I couldn't. I needed him.

Pushing his hands off me, I lifted my legs one at a time and placed them over his thighs.

"Baby," he breathed.

"I need you," I moaned. His hands gripped my waist, my fingers wrapped around his thick cock, lining it up with my pussy. Letting go, my fingers gripped onto his shoulders as I lowered myself onto him, stilling as the head of his cock stretched me.

Fuck.

My breath caught at the unfamiliar sting.

"Take it slow." Dex groaned, his head tipping back as I lowered a little more of myself on him.

My breathing fastened as I continued sliding down him. His huge cock stretched me in the most delicious way.

"Oh, fuck," I moaned out, my head tipped back as I stilled, letting my pussy get used to the size of him.

"You okay?" Dex asked, his voice tight as he was

trying to control himself.

I nodded.

"You feel so good, your pussy is so tight," he choked out, his grip tightening on my waist. Dropping my hands from his shoulders, I rested them on his knees behind me. "Oh," I moaned loudly, just that small movement made him hit me a little deeper.

"Angel, I need you to move," Dex pleaded, his cock throbbing inside of me.

Pushing my hips forward slowly, I thrust over him. Fuck, he felt so good.

My eyes fluttered shut before opening them and gazing into his eyes. He met my thrusts, his dick hitting my G-spot again and again.

I wouldn't last long; I was too turned on.

"I am going to ruin you," he groaned before his mouth locked around my nipples. He sucked them hard, a sting pulsing through me.

"Your pussy feels amazing stretching around me." His voice was muffled as he spoke.

Moaning in agreement, my hips rotated, my pussy tightening around him.

"Sage, I am going to fuck you until you're sore." His head tipped back, and his fingers glided down my skin before they wrapped back around my waist. I loved watching him, his eyes falling between us as he pushed me back a little more, his eyes lighting up as he watched his cock slip in and out of me. He grunted, holding me still as he rocked his hips up into me fast and hard.

"Yes," I moaned. "Keep fucking me like that, Dex, oh God," I cried out.

I could feel my orgasm building, my skin tingling.

"You like being fucked hard, little one?" He smiled, his eyes finding mine before watching my pussy.

"Yes," I cried out, my hips grinding into him every time his cock pushed into me.

"I can feel your tight little cunt tightening around me. Come for me, I want to feel you come all over my cock." He panted, groaning as he dug his fingers into my skin, pinching and burning.

My pussy ached; I was sore but so fucking full.

"Come on, baby," he growled, one of his hands moving from my hip as he pushed his fingers into his mouth, licking them before slapping them on my clit then rubbing hard and fast. A burn coursed through me as I came, my orgasm exploding as I trembled, my head tipping back.

"Yes, little one. I can feel you." He continued his harsh pounds now. "Fuuuuuuuck," he drawled out.

"I'm going to come," he spat through gritted teeth, both hands back on my hips as he pumped his cum into me.

I didn't get a chance to do anything. He stood, spinning me round and dropping me on the bed. Pulling out, he dropped to his knees and pushed my legs wide.

"What a fucking view, your tight little cunt is leaking with my cum." His fingers trailed from the inside of my knee all the way down to my pussy. Covering his fingers in our arousal, he swirled his tips in it before pushing it all back into me. "I want your little cunt full of me. I want you to feel it running down your legs, I want your cunt so sore that all you can think about is me," he growled, his fingers still pumping inside of me hard and fast.

"You want to be fucked, Sage?" he asked, kneeling up so he was looking over me. I couldn't speak.

"Answer me. You want me to fuck your pussy?"

I moaned, his dirty mouth enough to make me come again.

"You love being fucked with my fingers, don't you? Such a greedy little girl." He lowered down, his lips pressing to the inside of my leg. "Shit, I can't wait to fuck your arse, with a dildo pushed deep into your pussy. I want every part of you, Sage." He panted through kisses. "Your tight little arse is going to love being filled deep with my cock, you will be begging for an arse fucking," he growled.

Pushing another two fingers inside of me, I could hear just how wet I was. My hands moved to my boobs, squeezing and grabbing my nipples.

"Four fingers inside of you, and room for more, little one." His voice was hushed. My pussy burned and ached, but not in a bad way. I wanted more, was that wrong of me?

My thoughts were soon diminished as he pushed a finger into my arse, causing an erotic moan to pass my lips.

"Rub your swollen clit, I want you coming again before I fuck you. I want to see how many orgasms I can get out of you." He smirked, his fingers pulsing in and out of me. I felt lightheaded. Leaning up on one elbow, I watched as he finger fucked me. I could see how much he stretched my pussy. His eyes fell from mine to the apex of my thighs, spitting on my clit. "Oh," I moaned, my legs trembling as he pumped his fingers hard and fast into me.

Pressing two fingers over my clit, I rubbed myself like he asked, I could feel my arousal running out of me.

"Dex," I cried out, watching his fingers push in and out of me.

"Dex!" I cried again.

I was in heaven, the pleasure that was consuming me was overwhelming.

"Don't stop," I moaned, my head tipping back as my whole body was blanketed in a shiver, sweat glistening on my skin.

I needed to watch, I needed to watch myself come.

I wanted him to see how he made me feel, what he made me feel.

"Faster," I begged. "That's it, fuck, yes." I moaned,

my toes curling, my legs trembling as I came. A tidal wave crashed through me, this orgasm more intense. My whole body trembled, a high-pitched ringing in my ears. His fingers swirled in my cum, rubbing it all over my pussy and my arse. I was spent, collapsing on the bed, exhausted.

"Oh, little one, I am nowhere near finished with you yet. You have unleashed the beast."

He growled, flipping me over and pulling my hips in the air. Spanking my arse cheek hard, he lined his swollen head at my opening, slipping straight in with no warning.

"This is going to be hard and fast; I want you crying my name, Sage, and don't you dare hold an orgasm from me," he said through gritted teeth, his hand in my hair, wrapping it around his fingers as he tugged it back, my back arching, a delicious pull on my roots.

"Tell me, little one, have you ever been fucked like this before?" he grunted through punishing thrusts into me, and the sound of our skin clapping together was enough to make me convulse on the spot.

"No," I cried out.

"Do you promise?" His cock speared in and out of me.

"Yes, I promise," I panted back, the feel of his cock filling me to the hilt was too much. Every sense in my body was heightened, my skin beginning to tingle again.

"Your tight little cunt was made for me, only me," he

growled, pulling his cock out to the tip, stilling for a second then slamming back into me.

"I'm close," I moaned, his grip tightening on my hair.

"Come for me," he ordered, his cock slipping in and out, his thumb slipping into my pussy before it pressed against my arse.

"You like it when I finger your arse, don't you?" he asked.

Moaning in agreement, his thumb pushed deep into me, his cock pumping in and out as I felt myself tightening around him. "Fuck!" I screamed. I felt my orgasm rip through me quickly, my skin erupting in goosebumps.

"Yes, baby," he growled, slipping his thumb out of my arse and slapping my arse cheek, a loud slap echoing around the room. Dex came, pumping inside of me before we both collapsed on the bed.

His fingertips trailed up and down my bare spine, tingles spreading across my skin. I lay on my front, my head resting on my arms that were folded underneath my cheek. Dex lay on his elbow, gazing down at me.

"Sage, that was..."

"Amazing." I finished his sentence.

"So amazing," he whispered.

Smiling at him, I lifted my head. His fingers stopped their trail as his hand cupped my cheek, his thumb brushing across my skin.

"I love you so much, Sage." His voice was low, his eyes looking deep into my soul.

"Not as much as I love you," I whispered.

"That's not possible." He leaned in, our lips inches away from one another's. "Today. Tomorrow. Always."

"Always," I replied, moving into him, kissing passionately.

My heart beat for only him.
Always him.

-

DEX

My fingers trailed up and down her bare skin, drawing small love hearts. The moonlight shone through our bedroom window, the light making her skin glisten. Her shallow breaths filled the room. I loved watching her, but my favourite time was when she was asleep. I lay and think back to when I used to follow her in her shadows, always at least ten steps behind her. She never knew. I snorted a laugh. My little one.

Her raven black hair was fanned out behind her, her head resting on my bare chest. I never wanted her out of my sight.

I'm obsessed.

Lifting my eyes for a moment, a stupid grin spread

across my face when I saw the black toy train that sat proudly on my bedside unit. It was the best gift I had ever been given.

She has made me grow so much, there are things that I hate about myself, but she makes me love every single part of me.

Sure, I'm a jealous, possessive prick, but that is out of pure fear that someone will take her from me. Even thinking about her being ripped from me sears a pain straight through my heart.

The nerves that crash over me again and again when she looks into my eyes, and I mean really looks. She is looking straight through the window to my soul. I am open for her and only her. She sees everything.

The good.

The bad.

And everything in-between.

I never knew you could love like this for another person, and yet, here I am. Head over fucking heels in love with a woman who has stolen not only my breath on numerous occasions, but also my ice-cold heart.

She has thawed every piece of ice and wrapped it in her warm and loving hands.

How did I get so lucky? I ask myself this every day when I look at her. And the answer is, persistence.

I would have kept going until the time came for me to be stripped of this life. But then thinking about it, even then I don't think I would have stopped. I would have haunted her, stayed by her side until she crossed over to meet me again.

She was my obsession. The best fucking kind. A drug that I needed a hit of, over and over again. Just one high, it didn't matter how much she gave me, one taste was enough to have me buzzing for hours.

Was I a cunt for taking her while she was with my dad?

Of course I was.

Did I care?

Absolutely fucking not.

She was mine from day dot, there was no keeping away from her. Her scent was an aphrodisiac that pulled me in. I couldn't stay away even if I wanted to.

It was written in the stars.

We were written in the stars.

I swear it to this day, she is my end game.

Today. Tomorrow. Always.

-

SAGE

We pulled up outside the rehab centre. I felt a little apprehensive and I didn't know why, it felt like so much had happened since I last saw my mum, and I suppose in a way it had. Me and Dex were official, work was booming, and Rhaegar and Shay were having a fucking baby.

That one thing I struggled to get my head round.

"You okay, baby?" Dex asked, scooping my hand in his and bringing it to his lips.

"I am." I smiled a wide, toothy grin.

"Good." He smirked. "And how is my princess pussy?"

"A little sore..." I blushed.

"I'll make sure to give her some TLC tonight." He leant over the middle of the car, my hand still in his as he placed a kiss on the tip of my nose.

"Let's go." He breathed, dropping my hand and opening the door. I missed the contact from him immediately.

He was at my side of the car, opening the door. Within seconds, his hand was in mine where it belonged. Everything with him just felt so right.

Strolling through the glass double doors, I felt a little tremble ripple through me. Dex's hand tightened around mine as we stopped at the receptionist's desk. He gave my mum's name as the young lady kept her eyes pinned to my man.

"Shouldn't you be looking at your computer and not my husband?" I snarled.

Jealousy was *definitely* my colour. Okay, Dex wasn't my husband *but* I wanted to see her squirm.

I watched as she blushed, her long fake nails tapping away on the keyboard.

"She is in the garden room, through the double doors and second door on the left," the young girl stammered, handing me and Dex a visitor lanyard.

"Thank you." I snatched them, tugging Dex down the hallway. He had a stupid grin on his face.

"Oh, my little Sage, acting all jealous." He laughed.

"Well, she tried taking what's mine." I scowled, looking over my shoulder at the girl whose head was dipped low behind the desk.

"Darling, no one will take me. I am yours." He pulled me to his side, wrapping his arm around my shoulders as we walked towards where my mum was.

Walking into the large, bright and airy garden room, my eyes found my mum instantly. My eyes pricked with happy tears. Pulling away from Dex, I rushed over to my mum, running through the chairs that were in my way. She stood from the chair she was sitting on. Our arms wrapped around each other, holding one another tight, neither of us wanting to let go.

"I've missed you so much." I sobbed into her blouse, inhaling her scent as deep as I could.

"I've missed you so much more, darling." She let go of me, her hands cupping my face as she beamed at me. Her eyes watered before she broke our gaze and locked eyes with Dex.

"Dex," she breathed, walking to him and hugging him tightly.

"Hey, Lisa." His hand rubbed up and down her back.

She let go of him, rushing to her seat and patting the two empty spaces on her table.

I turned to Dex, giving him a smile before walking over to where my mum was.

"So, tell me all, what's the latest?" she asked, her eyes darting between me and Dex.

I inhaled deeply. Where to start?

After an hour of telling my mum everything that happened, she was shocked, pleased and proud.

She kept going back to Shay, saying she couldn't believe that she was going to be a mum and what happened between her and Rhaegar. We also spoke about how I am trying to mend burned bridges between the four of us and start a fresh with our relationships. My mum worried and told me and Dex to just look out for ourselves and not to concern ourselves in anyone else's drama.

I loved her.

"Mum." I started a new conversation, placing my cup of juice down on the table.

"Yes, darling?" she asked, stopping her conversation with Dex for a moment.

"The house..." I winced as soon as I said it, I knew she was going to start getting anxious, but I needed her to trust me.

"Sell it." She nodded firmly, her fingers tightening around the small 'D' shaped teacup handle.

"But, Mum..." I shook my head slightly, pulling my shoulders back slightly. Had I just heard her right?

"You heard right." She placed her teacup down, her hands linking around her knee that was sitting crossed over the other.

"Well..."

"Surprised?" Dex's voice next to me made me turn my head.

"Yeah." I laughed. "Just a little."

"The house is already on the market," my mum continued. "When Dex came here a few days ago, we spoke about it in great detail, and I needed to make the decision without you here. I had to let go of all memories and attachment to that house." She coughed, clearing her throat. "I, we, us" she smiled at Dex, "need a fresh start, and part of my healing process is letting go of things in the past that cause me hurt, upset and trauma. The house, without even realising it myself, was a trigger." She sighed, her eyes batting down to her hands, her fingers rubbing over the knuckles on her other hand. I couldn't help but notice the small sores. Was this a new thing? I lifted my eyes to meet hers.

SOMETHING WORTH STEALING

"So much happened in that house, that even though it was my safe place, it was also my own personal hell. I would relive what happened inside those four walls. Whatever room I went into triggered some memory. Whether it be the beatings, the rape or even just raising you on my own. I would spend most of my nights crying myself to sleep when I lost my temper with you. I mean, how could I lose my temper with you? You were just a baby, but I took my anger, upset and frustration out on you..." My mum's tears began to flow. "And I am so sorry I did that to you. I know I didn't physically hurt you but emotionally? Surely you must have some memories?" She sniffed, palming her tears away. Dex reached inside his suit pocket and pulled out a soft handkerchief.

She thanked him, then dabbed her eyes.

"I didn't, Mum." I gasped. "I promise you." My voice was stern. Scooting forward to the edge of the sofa, I took my mum's hands in mine. "The only memories I have with you are happy ones. The laughs, the cuddles, the kisses and the unconditional love that you gave me, day in and day out despite your struggles." Now tears were running down my cheeks. "Please don't feel guilty for something I don't remember," I pleaded.

She let go of my hands, wiping her eyes dry.

"I'm sorry." Her trembling hand moved towards her teacup.

"Please don't apologise," I begged, my voice

cracking. Fuck, she broke my heart.

She nodded, bringing her cup to her lips, taking a mouthful. The conversation died soon after my mum's confessions. I didn't want to rush her, I wanted to wait till she was ready. Once her tea was finished, she placed the cup back on the table.

She gave me a gentle nod and a tight-lipped smile.

"You okay?" I asked. I couldn't help but worry. It was only natural.

"I will be, and each day I am getting better. I'm sorry for my admissions." She placed her head in her hands.

"Mum, please don't apologise. I'm glad you told me." I smiled at her, pulling her hands from her face.

"You are?"

"I am." I rubbed my thumbs across the back of her bony hands.

"I love you so much, Sage, I wouldn't have coped if I didn't have you."

"Well, it's a good job I was sent to you then, wasn't it?" A laugh bubbled out of me, trying to make a small bit of light heartedness out of this. "I'm not going anywhere." I shook my head, my eyes glistening. I felt Dex's arm wrap around me, his other hand squeezing my thigh.

"Neither of us are." Dex's voice was low and laced with assertiveness.

My mum's eyes volleyed back and forth between the both of us.

SOMETHING WORTH STEALING

"We promise," we both said in unison.

"We all need to move forward, as a family." I smiled, sitting back into the cushioned sofa.

"Agreed." Dex nodded, smirking at my mum before looking back at me over his shoulder.

"Let's go for a little walk, shall we?" he asked, standing and holding his hand out for me. I would always take it.

He helped my mum up as we walked out of a set of doors and into the acres and acres of gardens that surrounded the centre.

"Wow, how beautiful." I hummed as we approached a flower garden, turning and taking everything in, my eyes widening with all the pretty things that were dotted round. Flowered arches, water fountains, small ponds, and my favourite... an old swing that sat under a large blossom tree.

I couldn't help myself, I skipped over to it, wrapping my fingers around the string as I squeezed my bum onto the plank of wood.

I felt like a kid again, well, how a kid should feel. My mum never took me to a park, so I never got to go on the swings a lot. I always promised myself that I would make time when I was older to go to the park and sit on a swing. But life always got in the way.

Pushing off the floor, I kicked my legs gently in and out, making the swing lift higher.

I beamed as Dex strolled towards me, hands fisted in his pockets.

"Having fun, little one?"

I blushed.

"I am." I giggled, the cherry blossom falling down around me. I felt so free, calm and happy.

"Good." Dex smiled at me, his head cocking as he watched me.

"Think it's the right time now?" He looked over his shoulder, speaking to my mum as she approached and stopped next to him.

"Absolutely."

I stopped swinging my legs, putting them down to stop myself when I saw Dex step towards me and drop to one knee.

No fucking way.

He pulled a black velvet box out of his pocket and opened it.

"Sage..." His beautiful brown eyes glistened.

"Is it not too soon? We haven't been together that long? What about traditions?" Questions started spilling out of my lips. *It was the nerves.*

"Baby, fuck traditions. When have we once been traditional?" He snorted a laugh. He was right. Why was I even questioning him? Before I could tell him to carry on, he continued.

"Be my wife, I can't live a day without you. I need

you. Today. Tomorrow..."

"Always," I whispered, my hands flying over my mouth as I began to cry happy tears.

"I think that's a yes," my mum exclaimed, cheering, her own happy tears streaming down her face.

"Yes! It's a yes!" I squealed. Jumping off the swing, I moved towards him, leaping into his arms as my arms wrapped around his neck. He stood as soon as my body crashed into his, my legs wrapping around his waist as I kissed him over and over again.

"A million times yes." I sobbed.

"I get it, you want to marry me." He let out the most beautiful laugh.

I saw my mum's hand rest on Dex's shoulder and giving him a sweet smile. I dropped from his waist, one of my arms still around his neck as my eyes saw the ring.

Holding my trembling hand out, Dex slipped the red, pear-shaped diamond that sat cushioned with diamonds ring onto my finger. I stared at how it glistened and shined. My eyes lifted to Dex, his big, brown eyes sucking me in.

"I love you," I cried, pressing my lips to his.

"Not as much as I love you, little one." I felt his hands snake around my waist, pulling me closer to him as we lost ourselves in each other.

Sorry, Mum.

Here was to the start of our forever.

CHAPTER Thirty

Six Months Later

I suppose you are wondering what we are up to since we got engaged.

Well...

- We're still not married. Of course, we both want to, but work has been so busy which is amazing, and I haven't had a moment to think about weddings. Dex on the other hand has had his head buried in wedding magazines since I said yes.
- My garage has expanded over three garages, and our latest one is in the heart of London. It's my customs garage, it's everything I ever dreamed of and more.
- Hugo partnered with me and deals with the mechanics side while I deal more with customisations. Dex still has moments with him, but he knows that Hugo is my friend, and Dex, whether he will admit or not, has become quite fond of his

friend.
- Yes, we all made up. Dex and Shay can still have moments, but baby steps and all that.
- Talking of babies, Dex has become an older brother, as weird as that sounds. I still find it hard to get my head around.
- My mum is living three houses down from me and Dex which is amazing, and she is doing better than ever. She still has episodes, but she feels better knowing she can walk two minutes down the street, and she is with us.
- Wes... Wes is amazing. He has a new boyfriend; you might remember him? Roman. He was the guy I called a sleaze at the club. Yeah, you remember. It's him. They're so happy together, and we get together once a month. Wes flirts with Dex and it's hilarious.
- Babies for me and Dex? Not just yet... if Dex had his way, I would be bare foot and pregnant in the kitchen right about now.

But of course, you want to know if we go on to live happily ever after with mini-Sage's and Dex's running around?

You'll have to wait and see.

Epilogue

Tapping my foot impatiently, I waited for the kettle to boil. I needed a coffee. It was gone seven and I was here late, working on a Saturday. Don't get me wrong, I don't mind working the odd weekend, but not when it's a date night that Dex planned.

"Finally," I groaned as I lifted the kettle off its stand and poured the boiling water over the coffee granules, the smell instantly filling my nose and waking me up. Stirring the milk in, I dropped the spoon on the sink, the echo filling the garage.

My new garage was a lot smaller than the old one. This one was for purely customs, so we didn't need as much floor space as such. I liked to only take one job on at a time. Hugo came over with me along with a new guy called Shaun.

He was young but claimed to have experience.

If what I am dealing with out there is experience, then he is going to be jobless by the morning.

"I mean, look at the fucking state of that." I shook my

head as I walked towards the car, moaning out loud to myself. The customer wanted his ford mustang capri painted in cherry red.

This was cherry red.

But it was streaky as fuck on the hood and one door panel.

I wasn't sure where this guy learned to spray, but it wasn't acceptable.

It wasn't a five-minute job either. The bonnet and door panel were going to have to come off, be rubbed down then re-primed. Once they were primed, I would paint them, and seeing as the old colour is black, it'll need at least two or three coats. Then the fun bit… waiting for them to bake.

It isn't going to be done tonight, this could take all weekend. All because this guy decided to spray up and down instead of side to side.

Fucked off was an understatement.

I sat on a stool, staring at the car as I sipped my coffee. I didn't want anyone to be able to tell this had been repainted. To a trained eye, you could spot a newly sprayed panel from a mile away. It doesn't matter if the paint matches, you can still see the difference.

I was annoyed.

I was muttering away to myself, my eyes scanning up and down the car.

"Fucking moron," I cursed, tipping my head back.

Yes, I was annoyed about the car. But I was more annoyed that I was missing date night with Dex. Tonight, it had been six months since we officially got together, and I'm here sorting out some fucktards mess up.

My hands wrapped around the hot cup of coffee; the cold air had a nip to it now as autumn started to show signs of her arrival.

Sitting in silence for a moment more, I enjoyed my drink before cracking on. I would like to be out of here by midnight at least, but let's see how well I can get this job done.

Placing my cup on the floor, I pulled my overalls up from my waist and pushed my arms through. I would be sweating in a bit, but I was freezing right now. Strolling towards the car, I popped the hood. I always like to have a moment to look at the beauty that sat under it.

Before I knew what I was doing, I was checking the oil and the filter.

"Seriously Sage?" I groaned to myself. "We have more important things to do like get this fucking car rubbed down and primed so you can go and get your brains fucked out by your hot as sin fiancé." Even I could hear the desperation in my voice.

"And if any of you twats watch this back on the CCTV, turn it off," I shouted out, a stupid grin on my face as I turned towards the camera and stuck my two fingers up. Shaking my head, I dropped the hood of the car down.

SOMETHING WORTH STEALING

Stepping aside, I walked over to the shelving racks that were situated at the side of the garage. I grabbed my mask and sprayer before walking back to the car. Placing the sprayer down by my feet, I held my mask in my hand as I bent over the car, running my hand across the bumpy and uneven paint job. I furrowed my brow in annoyance.

Footsteps echoed around the workshop; the smell of food wafted through. My skin prickled in goosebumps, a smile spreading on my face.

"Did I hear you say you wanted your brains fucked out?" His voice louder now, his large hand snaking around my waist as he buried his lips in my hair.

"I wasn't talking about you." I giggled as I spun round, my legs pressing against the grill of the car.

"Oh really?" His eyebrows sat high, his eyes devouring me as they fell to my heaving chest.

"Mmhhmm," I hummed, my fingers trailing up his buttons.

"Well, I suppose this hot as sin fiancé of yours won't be giving you a good fuck now..." He licked his lips slowly, one of his hands still gripping a brown paper bag, the other hand skimming up my body before gripping my chin.

"Don't play games, little one." His voice was hushed.

I smirked, my eyes volleying back and forth from his.

"I don't play games." I licked my lips. I like to goad him, he liked me goading him. It was our love language, well, one of them.

Dropping my chin, he stepped back from me, turning and placing the brown paper bag on the countertop to the side of where we were.

I was already panting, and we hadn't done anything. I knew what was coming.

Dex had that look in his eye, the hunger ran deep through them as he looked over his shoulder at me, his lips curling at the side. Shrugging his jacket off, he folded it neatly and placed it over the food bag.

"I've got so much work to do," I whispered as he undid his belt from his trousers, closing the gap between us.

"I know you have," he whispered back, his belt hitting the floor.

"I'll be here till at least midnight, plus, I'll be in tomorrow." My eyes stayed pinned to him.

"That's a shame." He groaned, his fingers now fumbling with his shirt buttons.

"It really is." I sighed, leaning against the hood of the car as I watched him begin to undress.

"All because someone couldn't do their job right." I heard Dex tut as he shook his head softly side to side before letting his shirt hit the floor.

"I know," I breathed, marvelling at his body. I would never tire of how he looked, of how beautiful he was.

"How about I show you how to do the job right…" His

voice trailed off, his hands were on me. His fingers gripped the zip of my overalls and tugged it down in a teasing manner.

I hummed in agreement. "I think you need to." My lips parted; my skin tingled.

His hands glided up my body as he pushed the navy overalls off my shoulders, exposing my bare shoulders.

"You have too many layers on," he groaned.

"I do apologise, would you like me to stay naked under these overalls going forward?" I challenged him which resulted in a primal growl.

"Didn't think so." I giggled.

His lips pressed to my bare skin on my shoulders, trailing across to my collar bone. His hungry hands skimmed down my sides before gripping the hem of my vest. I pulled my arms out of my overalls eagerly, waiting for him to take my vest off.

"Eager are we, little one?" he teased, pulling his lips from my burning skin.

I nodded.

Tugging the vest over my head, he discarded it. His lips were on my neck, sucking and licking as his hands kneaded my boobs through my bra.

"I can never get enough of you." His lips moved against my skin.

"Good," I panted.

His skilful fingers danced their way behind my back

and unclasped my bra in one swift movement before dangling it then letting it fall to the floor.

His mouth locked over my nipple, his other hand groping and massaging as he rolled my nipple between his fingers.

"Dex," I cried out, I was so horny. I didn't want to come like this.

"Patience, little one." He smirked against my hardened nipple before flicking his tongue over it.

"I don't have patience, please fuck me." My hands were in his hair as I tugged his head up, my mouth crashing to his as our tongues began to dance together.

"As you wish." He pulled away, pushing his trousers down to his ankles before his large hands pulled my overalls and leggings down in one swift movement.

Wrapping his fingers around my thong, he pulled it to the side, revealing me. Pushing me back, I was laying on the bonnet of the car, my legs spread and ready for him.

"So ready." He licked his lips, his hand wrapping around his thick cock as he lined himself up at my soaked opening. Rocking his hips forward, he pushed himself into me hard, filling me to the hilt.

"Oh fuck," I moaned, one of my hands trying to grip to the side of the bonnet, the other skimming across to my clit.

"This is going to be fast and hard, then once you're

finished with work, I am going to make love to you," he whispered, his body laying over mine. One of his hands glided to the base of my throat, his fingers wrapping around tightly.

I grinned at him.

I loved when he grabbed my throat while fucking me.

His free hand pinched my thigh as he lifted his body off me, his eyes falling in-between us as his cock slipped in and out of me fast.

"Fuck yeah," he groaned, his head tipping back as the pleasure coursed through him.

It was too much. I felt so naughty for doing this, but I was so turned on.

"Your little cunt is so tight," he groaned, his grip tightening around my thigh. "It's always mine."

"Always yours," I panted, my hands moving to my boobs as I squeezed them, rolling my nipples between my fingers.

"Such a greedy girl." He smirked, his eyes on mine.

"Only for you," I whispered.

"That's right," he agreed, removing his grip from my thigh and throat. Pulling himself out of me, he helped me up onto my trembling legs. I didn't have a chance to ask him what he was doing, he spun me round quickly and pushed me down on the bonnet, my chest flush and my legs spread. His hands skimmed around my waist, holding me in position before his thick cock filled me again.

"That feels so good," I moaned out, pressing my body up and holding myself up on my arms. My head turned to look over my shoulder at him, I know he liked it when I looked at him.

"Fuck, keep your eyes on me, I want you to watch me," he groaned, his head falling forward as he watched his cock slip in and out of my wet pussy. His thrusts slowed, and pulling his cock out to the tip, he let go of my hip and swirled his fingers in my arousal, making sure they were covered.

I knew what was coming.

Pushing his cock back into me hard, I cried out, my pussy tightening. My stomach coiled, a shiver blanketing me as my orgasm started to build.

I felt his two fingers tease at my bum, pressing softly as he dipped them in, all while his cock slipped in and out of me with ease.

"Oh," I moaned, my back arching a little more as he continued to push his fingers in deeper.

"You love being filled in every hole, don't you, my dirty girl?" He spat out.

"I do," I agreed with him, my moans echoing.

"So greedy." His pounds were harder now, his fingers pulling out to the tip before sinking back inside me.

I loved feeling so full of him, my orgasm teetering on

the edge of mountain, ready to crash down like an avalanche.

"Fuck me harder," I cried out. Fuck, I would love to be able to scrunch the bedsheets, but no, my hands are slipping down the bonnet.

I heard Dex groan through gritted teeth, his perfect dick hitting my G-spot again and again while his fingers fucked my arse.

"Shit, I'm going to come," I screamed. "Dex, keep going, please," I begged.

I felt a third finger tease at my bum which caused my orgasm to explode through me, my whole body trembled as I came hard, my screams filling the garage as Dex found his own release. My arms gave out as I let myself collapse on the bonnet of the car, Dex sprawled over my back.

"I love you, Sage," he whispered, his lips pressing to the shell of my ear.

"Not as much as I love you," I whispered back.

I felt the smile against my skin before he pushed himself up. I rolled over, watching him as he dropped to his knees, his fingers rubbing and swirling in our cum, his tongue lapping it up.

"I don't want to waste a drop." He winked before standing and placing a kiss on my lips. "Now go get cleaned up, I have dinner." He smirked as he pulled away. I watched for a moment as he began doing up the buttons on his shirt.

"Stop watching, the food is getting cold." He winked. Coming out of my trance, I nodded quickly and grabbed my clothes off the floor and ran for the toilet.

"Oh, and baby?" he called out, making me stop in my tracks.

"Take a copy of the CCTV so I can watch me fuck you again and again." His voice hummed through my ears, making my blood course through my veins. "Then wipe it, I don't want any of the guys in here seeing what's mine."

I blushed, shaking my head before heading into the toilet.

It wasn't normal for how much I loved that man. He was it for me. My end game.

Today.

Tomorrow.

Always.

THE END

Acknowledgements

Firstly, to my husband Daniel. Without you, none of this would have been possible. You support me in my dream, and push me when I feel like giving up. I couldn't do this without you by my side. I love you.

My amigos, thank you for being my ear when I have my moments of doubt, thank you for being my BETA readers. I am so glad I met you.

Lindsey, thank you for editing my book. I am so grateful to have met you.

Leanne, thank you for not only being an amazing, supportive friend but for also making my books go from boring word documents to an amazing finished product. I am so lucky I got to meet you two years ago.

My bookstagram community, my last thanks goes to you. I will never be able to thank you enough for the amount of love and support you show me. Thank you.

If you would like to follow me on social media to keep up with my upcoming releases and teasers the links are below:

Instagram: http://bit.ly/38nen4b
Facebook: http://bit.ly/38qujyi
Reader group: https://bit.ly/3dkaxfa
Goodreads: http://bit.ly/2hmuxpz
Amazon: https://amzn.to/2hojupf
Bookbub: http://bit.ly/2ssvisd

If you loved my book, please leave a review.

Printed in Great Britain
by Amazon